D0868319

MAINELY MONEY

MAINELY MONEY

A Goff Langdon Mainely Mystery

MATT COST

Encircle Publications
Farmington, Maine, U.S.A.

Mainely Money © 2021 Matt Cost

Paperback ISBN 13: 978-1-64599-099-4
Hardcover ISBN 13: 978-1-64599-166-3
E-book ISBN 13: 978-1-64599-100-7
Kindle ISBN 13: 978-1-64599-101-4

All rights reserved. In accordance with the U.S. Copyright Act of 1976, no part of this publication may be reproduced, distributed, or transmitted in any form or by any means, or stored in a database or retrieval system, without prior written permission of the publisher, Encircle Publications, Farmington, ME.

This book is a work of fiction. All names, characters, places and events are products of the author's imagination or are used fictitiously, and any resemblance to actual persons, living or dead, or to actual places or businesses, is entirely coincidental.

Editor, Encircle Publications: Cynthia Brackett-Vincent
Book design, cover design and digital illustration by Deirdre Wait
Cover images of Langdon, dog, and Brunswick by Ryan Poag

Published by:

Encircle Publications
PO Box 187
Farmington, ME 04938

info@encirclepub.com
http://encirclepub.com

Printed in U.S.A.

Acknowledgments

If you are reading this, I thank you, for without readers, writers would be obsolete.

I am grateful to my mother, Penelope McAlevey, and father, Charles Cost, who have always been my first readers and critics.

Much appreciation to the various friends and relatives who have also read my work and given helpful advice.

I would like to offer a big hand to my wife, Deborah Harper Cost, and to my children, Brittany, Pearson, Miranda, and Ryan, who have always had my back.

I'd also like to tip my hat to my editor, Michael Sanders, who has worked with me on several novels now, and always makes my writing the best that it can be.

Thank you to Encircle Publications and to the amazing duo of Cynthia Bracket-Vincent and Eddie Vincent for giving me this opportunity to be published. Also, kudos to Deirdre Wait for the fantastic cover art.

And of course, thank you to the Coffee Dog, his namesake bookstore, and the inspiration he provided.

Dedication

*To those that support the writing community
in good times and bad*

The Night Before

She should've taken an Uber. It was that darkest time of night, just a few hours before dawn with no moon to light the way, and the distance between streetlamps seemed endless. And she was drunk.

It was her senior year at the University of Southern Maine, and she was just back from summer vacation, three months of interning for a nonprofit organization in her hometown of Concord, New Hampshire. There had been few friends home for the summer, and her parents had been strict with a curfew, even though she had turned twenty-one months earlier. Not that there was much to do in Concord, not like Portland, where the Old Port rocked every night of the week.

Her roommate had plans with a boyfriend. She was disappointed to not have her roommate all to herself on her first night back, but she understood and was actually jealous. She wished she had a boyfriend. Her parents talked of a time when people used to date. Go to dinner and a movie. That was no longer the reality, as dating had been replaced by hooking up, a simple swipe right or left on Tinder. She'd tried this just once, meeting some asshole for a drink. The guy had slammed down two beers and asked if she wanted to go back to his place before she'd even half-finished her Moscow Mule.

Thursday night in the Old Port was probably the best night of the week to go out. People were ready to get a jump-start on the weekend, but it wasn't quite so crowded that you couldn't find a seat at a bar if you wanted. She had been jonesing to dance, and there were several clubs that would be hopping later on, so she'd agreed to meet up with some friends. She had taken a bath, dried her hair, carefully put on make-up, dabbed just a hint of perfume on her wrists and collarbone. Over the summer she had bought new and sexy panties and a lace bra that made her blush, but it was possible that tonight would be the night that she met The One. Sandra was not a prude. As a matter of fact, she daydreamed about being in love and what it would be like to lose her virginity. But not to just anybody, mind you.

She had slipped into her favorite yellow summer dress that made her black hair shine and her skin positively glow. She carried a sweater in case it got chilly later as this was the time of year when the nights turned from summer's warmth to fall's cold without warning. With a bounce to her step, she had walked the mile from her apartment on Park Street to Gritty McDuff's in the heart of Portland's bar section. It had been pleasant at that hour.

After the bars had closed, she went to a party—a friend of a friend's—where she dropped too many shots upon too many beers already consumed. When she had finally decided to head home, Uber had said it would be a forty-five minute wait. At that time, there were only seven people left at the party, one a heavy-set young man who'd been trying to strike up a conversation with her since she'd arrived. When he wasn't looking, Sandra had grabbed her sweater and trundled down the stairs and onto the street. It would only take her twenty minutes to walk home. Why wait?

Now, with the streets emptied, every doorway held a silent menace. And then the white van had sidled up next to her on a dark side street. She had thought of all the jokes about creeper vans, and this one certainly fit the bill, but it was no longer a joke. Why hadn't she waited for an Uber?

She'd cut down a one-way street and the vehicle had accelerated and driven away, but she couldn't help thinking that she'd be seeing it again. She probably should have called the police, but what would she say? She had seen a white van drive by?

She was on Grant Street, just behind her apartment, when she saw the two men coming in the opposite direction. A few more steps and she could turn right onto Mellen and be safely home in another hundred yards. Or she could retreat and go farther away. She broke into a run, turning to the right as the two men quickened their strides. She realized too late that the white van was parked just around the corner, and a third man stood blocking her way. The sliding door was opened. The two men came up behind her. She yelled just once, her voice a strangled plea for help, and then Sandra found herself on the cold metal floor of the white van, a boot pressed to her neck.

Chapter 1

Goff Langdon pulled his Jeep Wrangler into the all-day parking lot behind his bookstore on Brunswick's Maine Street. His red hair, shot through with a dignified gray especially apparent at the sideburns, was tousled atop his head from the wind. He'd always loved riding with the Jeep's top down when he could, particularly enjoying the refreshing coolness in the air, despite the fact that it was still late August. This was Maine, after all. He pulled his phone from the pocket of his shorts and reread the text from his wife.

> Got a live one waiting for you in the office. Probably cheated on his wife and got caught but he reeks of money.

When Langdon opened the Jeep's door, a brown bolt of fur crashed over him and tumbled to the ground, hoping to surprise a squirrel or a bird. But, as was so often the case, the big lug of a dog had no luck that morning. He instead inspected the bushes, and cocked a leg to reclaim his ownership of this parking lot from any other dogs that may have passed through in his absence.

As Langdon pushed opened the door to his store, his eyes read with pride the inscription, THE COFFEE DOG BOOKSTORE, and then in smaller letters down below, GOFF LANGDON, PRIVATE DETECTIVE. His wacky Aunt Zelda had left him the money to open the bookstore some twenty-five years earlier, the legacy allowing him to purchase the building outright. Even so, he'd quickly discovered that, in the book trade, it was difficult to make ends meet, and so he'd added the side business of private investigation. The two went hand-in-hand, as the shop carried primarily mysteries, and it was from Easy Rawlings, Dave Robicheaux, and Harry Bosch that he'd learned the business of being a gumshoe. Not that he bragged about that.

Of course, in small-town Brunswick, the jobs mostly involved carrying a camera and not a gat, and shooting pictures of cheating spouses rather than villains. That is, it had been until he'd been hired to investigate a mysterious death at a nuclear power plant twenty years earlier and ended up getting shot in the head. While he'd not been overly fond of having a bullet glance off his skull, the ensuing media coverage had been great for both businesses. It was, in fact, the best advertising he'd ever gotten, and he often wondered why he'd not tried it sooner, but maybe without the three weeks in a coma in a Boston hospital.

"Afternoon, boss," Jonathan Starling greeted him. Though he looked as if he were at least 100 years old and had fought in every war of the 20th century, in reality, he'd been in high school when Vietnam returned the surviving but largely broken soldiers to American soil. Each wrinkle of his face had been put there honestly by a liquor bottle, though he'd been dry for twenty years now, as far as Langdon knew. "Glad you could make it in."

Langdon smiled. "Supposed to be my day off, but Chabal texted to say she wasn't able to get any work done—and carry your load—so here I am."

Starling tossed the piece of donut he'd been saving to the lab, realizing the canine was mere seconds away from leaping up on the counter for the treat he knew was his. "Shoot. I got a law degree, do all the work, hardly get paid, and have to share my breakfast. Now you want me to put up with scurrilous attacks impugning my work ethic from some slacker detective and his foul-mouthed wife?"

"Speaking of my foul-mouthed wife, where she be at?"

"I'm willing to bet my dentures she's back in your office gabbing with some fellow who's a member of the bar, and not the drinking one."

"You recognize him?"

"Nah, must not be a reader, or maybe not from around here." Starling may have squinted, but it was hard to tell where his eyes even lay within the craggy landscape of his face.

"Okay," Langdon replied as he headed towards the office in the back of the store. "Keep up the good work providing your normal high-level of genial customer support."

An unintelligible, but most certainly obscene, curse followed Langdon into his nondescript office in the back room. The small space had no windows and limited lighting. Along the right side wall was an old leather couch where Langdon had taken many a nap, and even slept the night through a few times. His worn and beaten mahogany desk was perched in back, mostly clear of debris except for a few papers and a small lamp. On the right was another desk with his computer and printer, while the left had two tall gray filing cabinets.

There were two Clarkson wingback armchairs of rich brown leather similar to the couch, but much less worn, to one side of his desk. Settled into them was his wife, partner, accomplice, best friend—and a man he faintly recognized, but couldn't quite place. Chabal was the first to rise. She was petite, more than a foot shorter than Langdon, with blonde hair that cascaded to her shoulders in caramel-hued waves. Her cheeks bulged slightly as if she were a squirrel with a nut in each, an adorable feature that offset her thin features and rendered her pretty rather than beautiful.

"Langdon, glad you could get out of bed and make it in," Chabal teased, her green eyes gleaming impishly.

"Would've been here sooner if we banned cars with Massachusetts plates from entering the state," he growled in return.

"This is Michael Glover." Chabal touched her hand lightly to the man next to her.

"Good to meet you." The man extended his hand to shake. His reach was constricted by what was clearly a bespoke green tweed jacket, perhaps purchased when he had been a thinner, younger Glover.

"Goff Langdon," Langdon replied, gamely holding on as the man energetically pumped his hand up and down. He noted the shiny Louis Vuitton shoes and the designer jeans and realized the man was trying to strike a casual pose in an extravagant manner.

"Nice to meet you, Mr. Glover," Chabal said, excusing herself.

Langdon disengaged his hand with effort and moved around to his own desk chair, a cheap black vinyl roller from Staples. "What can I do for you, Mr. Glover?"

The man stooped to sit, revealing the top of his head, and the fact that he was not yet ready to give in to the impending baldness. The sides were thick enough with dark hair that Langdon suspected was dyed, with a mat resembling a horsetail flopped from his forehead back and over to the rear.

"I've heard good things about you, Mr. Langdon."

"You must not be speaking with my friends," Langdon replied, sitting as well.

Glover barked a sharp laugh, his jowls quivering with exertion. "You cut quite a figure in Brunswick, apparently," he said.

"And where are you from?"

"I've lived here for three years," Glover said, wiping his brow with a handkerchief. "I bought a house out on Mere Point."

"What brought you to our little corner of the coast?" Langdon was a bit impatient, doubting this man was a year-round resident, as Mere Point was largely populated with wealthy summer people from away, many of the same people clogging the road today, no doubt.

"Retirement."

Langdon did not feel like playing twenty questions and getting nowhere, so instead leaned back in his chair and folded his hands with his thumbs under his chin and surveyed the corpulent man in front of him, trying to look past the expensive clothes, bushy eyebrows, cowlick, and amiable smile to take the measure of the man. Most likely the man's trophy wife was cheating on him, and he wanted proof to enforce a prenuptial agreement, or at least lessen the financial impact that a divorce would have on his bank account.

After a lengthy silence, the man cleared his throat. "I've also been told that you are a discreet man?" He raised one thick eyebrow, his tone loading the question with portent.

Nobody ever wanted his or her sex life dragged through the muck for everybody to see. It didn't matter if the man had tasted the forbidden fruit or had been cuckolded, it was his business, and he didn't want his family, especially if there were kids, to know. "I am a professional," Langdon replied, adding what he judged a sincere nod of the head. Of course, this discretion did not extend to his wife or his friends, for he'd shared many a juicy morsel of his clients' lives with them over drinks. He almost always succeeded in avoiding names. Except when he forgot.

"I've a very delicate proposition of employment," Glover said carefully, the tip of his tongue running over the inside half of his bottom-lip.

"I assume that's why you're here."

"I'm here for a friend."

Langdon eyed him and sighed. "This isn't junior high, Glover. Tell me what you want—for 'your friend.'"

The man laughed again. "No. Really. I'm here doing a favor for… somebody… who can't be seen in public coming into your kind of business without the media digging into it and spreading their speculations all over the nightly news."

"That leaves us at a bit of an impasse, now, doesn't it?"

"As a matter of fact, that is why I am here, and not down in Portland visiting Kendall and Associates. If I were to go there, some intern would spill the beans and reporters would be all over us."

"So what do you suggest?"

Glover pulled an envelope from his briefcase and removed a sheaf of papers from it. He unfolded them and leaned forward to place them on the desk, smoothing the creases flat with the palms of his hands. "This is a confidentiality agreement. If you'd be willing to sign it, there is $500 in this envelope, and all you have to do is come to my house at three this afternoon and listen to my friend. The money is yours even if you decide not to take the case."

Who might the obviously wealthy friend be? Langdon wondered, his interest piqued. Five hundred dollars to meet with somebody was nothing to scoff at. Without bothering to read the seven-page document he rifled to the end and found the line where his signature was required.

"My address is on a card in the envelope with the cash," Glover said, rising to his feet and leaning forward to shake Langdon's hand again. "Three o'clock sharp."

Langdon walked him to the door of the bookstore, and watched him go out the front of the building onto Maine Street before turning back to Chabal and Starling who were pretending to ignore him, both dying to know what had transpired. Louis Armstrong's dulcet tones glided to and fro in the background, and Langdon took a moment to appreciate all that he had. The bookstore had become a well-loved fixture over the past twenty-five years in Brunswick, introducing the residents to the lives and times of Hercule Poirot, Sam Spade, and Spenser, while the younger generation got to meet the Hardy Boys, Nancy Drew, and Encyclopedia Brown.

Local artists adorned the walls with their latest creations, and once a month the Coffee Dog Bookstore hosted an art opening complete with wine and hors d'oeuvres. A long counter made from hard maple ran across the back of the store. Langdon's eyes lifted to that which truly kept him on a path of happiness in this tumultuous world of difficult politics, changing climate, lies, cheating, and overall distrust. Even after seventeen years of marriage, her gleaming green eyes and wide smile still made his heart thump in his chest.

"Spit it out, Langdon," Chabal said. Most of his friends called him simply by his last name, and she'd been a friend years before they'd realized there was more.

"I'm sorry, but client confidentiality doesn't allow me to reveal the nature of our business," Langdon replied.

"Fuck that," Starling spat out, and then hurriedly looked around to see if any of the three customers browsing the shelves had heard him.

"You know full well that we are part of your crack team of investigators, and that privacy shit doesn't apply to us," Chabal bantered with a toss of her head. "Not unless you want me to stop revealing myself to you?"

Langdon was going to retort on her description of 'crack' team of investigators, but a customer came to the counter with three Carl Hiaasen books. Once Starling had rung up the sale, Langdon decided to move the conversation forward. "First of all, I don't know much more than you do. I've been invited to his house this afternoon to meet a friend of his, and had to sign a seven page document promising to not reveal this person's name or any details of the get-together."

Starling whistled. "The guy with thousand dollar shoes was just an errand boy?"

"Looks that way," Langdon replied. "I guess I'll find out more at three."

~ ~ ~ ~ ~

Langdon caught up on paperwork in the office until it was time to keep his afternoon appointment out on Mere Point, the tip of the peninsula just a few miles south of town. He passed by Nate's Marina (a place that served up a pretty fantastic lobster roll in the summer), and then came to the end of the public way. Approximately thirty mailboxes were clustered next to a turnaround for those who didn't belong, a sign proclaiming residents and visitors only, and silently promising punishment for offenders. Langdon had never been invited to any of these homes, but, like every Brunswicker from the other side of the tracks, he'd driven the loop to try and spy upon the houses—some surprisingly modest seaside cottages, others sprawling 19th century mansions—that remained mostly hidden from view by long driveways and wooded areas. Of course, he'd worried about secret cameras or pedestrians who would immediately know that the awkward red-haired behemoth driving the banged-up Jeep didn't belong, but he'd made the trek without incident, other than being possessed by that vague sense of shame in feeling like an intruder.

Langdon turned into the drive next to the granite slab with the house number engraved into it, winding down the driveway to a compound of various shapes clustered together like a preschooler's learning activity game. The central rectangular building was the original Cape, Langdon surmised, but around this were cylindrical structures similar to lighthouses, and smaller square sheds. In keeping with the Maine coastal theme, weathered gray shingles covered the residence. The wraparound driveway held five other vehicles, none of them particularly fancy, but rather, quite nondescript.

Michael Glover, his forehead glistening, answered the door before Langdon was able to ring the bell. He'd tried to leave dog behind, but without the top on the Jeep, man's best friend had only to jump out the back. Indeed, when the door opened, dog went hurtling into the house. Langdon caught just the momentary vexation that flashed across Glover's face as the canine brushed past him on his way to investigate the manor. This was quickly replaced with a broad smile as the man grabbed his hand and pulled him inside, quickly closing the door behind. Langdon was momentarily fearful the man was going to hug him, but instead, allowed himself to be led into the interior of the home.

They went past a modern staircase working its way upward in a series of right angles with strings of blue shells cascading down around it and they emerged into a comfortably traditional living room. Langdon noted the arched ceiling, the piano prominently displayed, and two sofas and an armchair surrounding a brick fireplace. In the armchair was dog, proudly sitting on the lap of United States Senator Margaret Mercer.

Chapter 2

"Senator Mercer, this is Goff Langdon," Glover said, thrusting him forward.

"Hello, Mr. Langdon," Senator Mercer said without rising. "Is this bundle of joy yours?"

"He sure is," Langdon replied with a troubled expression of dismay. What had dog done now? "I'm awful sorry that he jumped up on you."

"He is delightful," Senator Mercer said. "I love dogs. What's his name?"

"Dog," Langdon replied.

"His name is dog?"

"Yep." Langdon glanced around the room. There was a man standing in the corner the size of a small house, his hands clasped behind his back. Did U.S. Senators have Secret Service, Langdon wondered? Or, perhaps just a bodyguard. Another man with a blue blazer, who looked like he should have a pipe in his mouth, stood by the empty fireplace. "Small d, as a matter of fact."

"Small d?" Senator Mercer pursed her lips. "You mean no capital?"

"You got it." Langdon wasn't sure why he'd brought this up. "At first it was small d, capital G at the end, but that got too complicated for the vet and what not, so now it's just all lower case."

"Very interesting, Mr. Langdon."

"You know, dog is my copilot."

Senator Mercer chuckled. She stood, jostling dog to the floor and held out her hand. She was tall and thin, her neck long, eyes gray, with short dark hair waved from left to right upon her head. She wore a knee-length gray dress with a navy-blue blazer, and a necklace of connected silver squares. "Thank you for coming."

"We met a few years back at a chamber thing," Langdon replied, releasing her hand. "I own a bookstore downtown, and used to be a regular at all of those Chamber of Commerce events. Somehow, I haven't been able to stomach them as of late."

"Of course, I remember you now," she replied, as all good politicians would. "Excuse my manners. This gentleman by the fireplace is my husband, Maxwell."

Langdon stepped forward to shake the man's hand. "You look familiar, Mr… Maxwell."

The man waved his hand, and Langdon could imagine the pipe leaving lazy tendrils of smoke in the air. "Please, Maxwell is fine. I've been into your store to purchase books many times. I do enjoy a good crime caper every once in a while." He had a gray mustache thick as a horse brush on his lip, matching the silver hair with a slight curl upon his head. His nose was prominent and sharp, while his eyes were keen and probing.

"Ahh, that must be it."

"Please sit, Mr. Langdon," Senator Mercer suggested, waving him to the couch. "Thank you, Michael, for setting this up. Perhaps you could get Dwayne a cup of coffee?"

Glover and the bodyguard took their cue and eased out of the room as Langdon settled into the plush cushions from which he feared he might never rise. As the Mercers sat, Langdon realized dog had left. He must've decided there was a better opportunity to mooch food by following the two men to the kitchen rather than staying in the living room and trying to survive on ear scratches and tummy rubs alone.

"Let me get straight to the point," Senator Mercer said, her voice going from casual to business with a snap of the fingers. "I'm being blackmailed, and I want you to find out who the extortionist is."

"Would you care to explain the circumstances in more detail?" Langdon remained stoic, but inside he was cheering madly. This had the makings of a real case.

"We'll get to that in a moment, Mr. Langdon."

"Why me?" Langdon spread his hands to the sides.

"Your question is, why don't I use the Secret Service or the FBI to root out the culprit?"

"Yes."

Senator Mercer hesitated, as her eyes flickered to her husband and back to Langdon. "It's a very delicate situation."

"Blackmail usually is," Langdon commented dryly.

"I would like to keep the... I'd prefer that the entire incident be kept quiet."

Langdon nodded. "You don't want anyone in the government knowing the details."

"I particularly don't want the media getting hold of any of this," Senator Mercer corrected him slightly.

"Which brings us back to the question of 'any of what?'" Langdon asked as gently as his deep voice allowed.

"Will you take the case, Mr. Langdon?"

"I don't know what the case is, Senator Mercer."

"You are a happily married man?" She rose and walked to the bay windows facing the water.

Langdon idly wondered if they were called bay windows because they were actually meant to face a bay, in this case, Maquoit. In regards to the question, he was silent.

"Were you happy with your first wife?" she continued.

"Mostly," he assented.

"Yet, you had an affair while you were married, an affair with the woman who would become your second wife?"

Langdon felt the blood rush to his face. It was not often that his clients turned the tables on him. "Are you hiring me to investigate myself?" he retorted sharply.

"Marriage is a difficult institution at times, Mr. Langdon," Senator Mercer replied, her hands clasped behind her back as she watched the fog roll in over the bay.

"I was separated from my wife before I… started up with Chabal," Langdon defended himself before he could stop the words.

Senator Mercer turned from the window, and gone was the cordial woman who had rubbed and patted dog. "So, Amanda had no problem with your infidelities?"

Langdon rose to his feet. "I'll be leaving now."

"How would you have felt, Mr. Langdon, if pictures of you and your lover were splashed across every newspaper and television screen in the country?"

Langdon paused as he reached the door.

"I'm being blackmailed with intimate pictures of myself with someone who is not my husband," Senator Mercer said to his back.

Langdon turned around. "Did you have to attack me to tell me this?"

"I just needed to level the playing field so that you see me as a person, no better or worse than anybody else. I know how this works, whether you're a policeman, a lawyer, or a private detective—you look down upon those you defend and investigate. You place yourself on the moral high ground."

"That's not true," Langdon said.

"Of course it is. Your primary business as a detective is finding the dirt on cheating spouses. Don't tell me it doesn't make you feel superior as you uncover the muck on other people. But the truth is, we're all human, and that sometimes means we find pleasure outside the boundaries of society's expectations."

Langdon stole a glance at Maxwell Mercer who'd kept silent throughout the entire exchange. His face seemed untroubled by the conversation. If there was any sign of distress, it was his steady consumption of red pistachios from a bowl on the mantle, the shells tossed with some force into the fireplace.

"My husband is fully aware of this affair," Senator Mercer said in a steely voice.

Langdon returned to the sofa and sat down. "Who is it that you're having an affair with? One would think that you'd have to look no further than that to find your blackmailer."

"You have signed a confidentiality contract, Mr. Langdon, but I want to know that you are accepting the case before we go any further."

"What is it that you're asking me to do?"

"I want you to identify the blackmailer for me, and then find them."

Langdon rubbed his forehead with first the back of his hand, and then his palm. "And then what?"

"And then nothing."

There was a threat implicit in those three words that chilled the room as much as if a cold fog had rolled in. "Ninety an hour plus expenses," Langdon replied. "Per diem expenses 200 bucks max." He figured she could afford it.

"You're hired, Mr. Langdon."

"Now tell me who you've been having an affair with?" Langdon pulled out his pocket notebook and grabbed a pen from where it clung to the collar of his shirt. It was obvious that the blackmailer was most likely the person the senator was having an affair with, so Langdon wondered briefly why he'd been called in for this simple task.

"I don't know."

Langdon paused with pen poised above paper. "Excuse me?"

"It was a one night stand," Senator Mercer said in barely audible words.

"And you didn't get his name?" Langdon asked in an incredulous tone.

"Of course I did, but it appears it was a false name. I've had people check it out, but they came up blank."

"What is the name, Senator Mercer?"

"Kamrin Jorgenson."

Langdon jotted down the name, a thought crossing his mind at the first name. "And may I see the pictures?" His face flushed, for he had taken many such pictures and realized that they were likely of the most compromising nature.

Senator Mercer walked to the mantel and removed a large yellow clasped envelope. Before turning to face him again, she spoke. "There is a double standard in the world in which we live, Mr. Langdon, and that includes the political arena. Nobody cares that men like Clinton and Trump cheated on their spouses, only that they lied about it. Hell, being playboys probably garnered them votes. But the media and the public would crucify me if this ever got out. My political career would be over. My neighbors would shun me. My family would look oddly at me."

"I will keep your secret, Senator Mercer," Langdon promised.

She turned around with resolve and marched over to him, extending the envelope in front of her as if it burned. "I've removed some of the more revealing photos of myself, but these should suffice for your investigation."

Langdon was going to wait until later to examine them but realized he might have questions, and thus gamely pulled the eight-by-twelves free. Senator Mercer walked back over to the bay window and stood pointedly with her back to him. Maxwell seemed intent on brushing something from his corduroys, perhaps a tuft or two of dog's fur. The first photo was a semi-clothed Senator Mercer embracing another person in a dimly lit room that might have been a hotel. The second picture showed clearly that both of them were female. Langdon looked at the senator, but it was Maxwell who spoke.

"Marge and I have been married for over thirty years now, Mr. Langdon. Some would demean it as a practical business merger, but it is really a very deep intellectual love. The societal standard of sexual attraction within a marriage does not apply to us. On occasion, our more basic instincts require us to find sexual fulfillment outside of our marriage. While I prefer to find my release with young women, Marge is attracted to a more mature woman." If that first fog had been merely cold, what followed Maxwell's pronouncement could only be characterized as glacial.

~ ~ ~ ~ ~

Once back in the Jeep, Langdon realized he'd missed lunch. He texted Chabal to see if she could join him for a bite and tell her that he'd be stopping through the shop ten minutes later. Half an hour later, Langdon unfolded his long frame from the Jeep and cursed the traffic that had made him late. Every Friday, there was a crowded farmers market on the rectangular grassy area of upper Maine Street known as the Mall, and it was this market and its associated commotion that had delayed his arrival.

It wasn't that he was opposed to local vegetables. He liked the occasional corn on the cob, and had even been known to eat a salad if it had some type of meat on it. Why every driver felt the need to park within three feet of the collected vendors, only to then walk around for half-an-hour deliberating on the merits of one squash over another, that was a mystery to him.

Motorists would troll their way along, looking for the telltale sign of taillights, indicating somebody leaving, and put their flashers on until that person carefully and slowly backed out into the street. Parking down the street and walking a few 100 feet was unimaginable.

It wouldn't be so bad once Labor Day weekend came and went, banishing the summer people back to their lives in Massachusetts, Connecticut, and New York. Again, it wasn't as if Langdon despised these sunbirds who each year fled the dog days for the cooling crispness of the Maine coast. Without them, his bookstore would probably be a dollar store by now, for the green these part-time dwellers brought to the local economy made July and August as profitable as the Christmas season, or the holidays, or whatever it was called now.

He gave a whistle for dog, the chocolate lab already busy mooching lunch items from the firemen next door. They knew dog by sight, name, and for his famous appetite for scraps, as did most of the people in town. Once, Langdon had shrugged his shoulders and left dog to his firemen friends, only to later hear the sirens as the trucks sped off, forcing him to track down the fire where he found his dog prancing around in great excitement.

Farmers markets and summer dwellers were not the only complications in Langdon's life. He was an environmentalist as well as a red meat eater. He was a football fan and played golf, although he wasn't very good at the latter. He, like most Mainers, voted for Independents, sometimes Democrats, but never Republicans. He'd been known to carry a gun, but believed gun laws should be tightened. He offset his excessive drinking with daily workouts, ate abundantly sometimes, and forgot to even nibble at other times.

The bookstore was devoid of customers, and Chabal had her purse in hand when he walked in the door. "No, I haven't eaten," she said, replying to his text. "You were supposed to bring me a sandwich earlier and obviously forgot."

Langdon knew he'd been forgetting something. "Star, do you think you can handle the store if I take my wife to lunch? I'll have her back in less than an hour."

"Again, the low guy on the totem pole does all the work, hardly makes a dollar, and has to work through lunch on an empty stomach."

"We'll bring you fried shrimp," Chabal said, grabbing her purse and heading for the door, knowing full well his weakness for this particular crustacean. "And you can go home when I get back. I'll close up the shop."

"I was thinking hot dogs on the mall?" Langdon said, trying gamely to keep a straight face. He was referring to Danny's, a red and white painted trailer converted into a hot dog stand.

"Think what you want, but I'm getting a salad at the Wretched Lobster," Chabal replied, walking out the door.

"Bring your dog with you," Starling said as Langdon followed her out the door minus dog.

The Wretched Lobster was just a block down the street. In spite of its name, the establishment was quite posh. The first-floor restaurant had lace tablecloths and was the kind of place where the music was muted soft rock, but Langdon and Chabal took the stairs descending to the basement bar. The bar itself was made of Brazilian cherry polished to a fine sheen with plush padded stools and shelves crowded with every liquor imaginable. Postcards, sent from patrons on vacation around the world, were pinned, taped, and tacked to every inch of available wall space. Lanterns with brass bases bolstered recessed lighting flickered along the bar, as well as on the seven or eight high tables scattered across the room. A dartboard took up one corner, while two pool tables sat on display, silent and inviting at this time of day.

They settled into a high table, continuing their conversation about Jack—at thirty-two years of age, Chabal's eldest child and the only one currently living at home with them. He'd worked for a company doing computer programming for the past several years but just recently had quit to begin his own business tailored more to his interests in gaming and video. This, of course, had meant moving home to save money, his only current income from working the espresso machine at the Lenin Stop Coffee Shop and occasionally helping out at the bookstore during busy times. Chabal had two younger children, also from her previous marriage, but they lived in Boston and Charleston, South Carolina, while Langdon had one daughter, Missouri, who was about to begin graduate school in New York City.

"Would you care for something to drink?"

Langdon looked up to see his friend and the owner of the Wretched Lobster approaching with two menus. Richam had fled some Caribbean island with his wife and children twenty plus years ago, beginning as a bartender right in this basement, working his way up the ladder, until four years ago when he'd bought the place. Even now, at sixty years old, he was trim and fit his suit just right, black glasses framing his serious face, a thin tie offsetting a bright yellow shirt.

"Shot of whiskey," Chabal responded.

"I'll have to see some ID." Richam waved a server over. Richam's mother had intended for him to be a Richard, but a mistake by a secretary at the hospital where he was born had never been rectified.

"Is that what you're trying to see down the front of my dress?"

Richam snorted. "It was looking down your dress that made me realize you must be underage."

The waitress, a thirty-something single mother with the moniker of Babs, arrived, certainly preventing what was sure to be a lewd rejoinder from Chabal. "What are the Langdons drinking today?"

"Ice tea," Chabal said meekly. "I still have to go back to work and then I'm meeting your wife later for drinks," she said to Richam.

"I'll have a Baxter Stowaway," Langdon said.

Once Babs had moved off, Richam turned serious. "Did you see the news? The Old Port Killer struck again. Another USM coed was found early this morning out on the Eastern Prom."

"Raped?" Langdon asked.

"Probably. She was naked. Pretty grisly scene, it sounded like."

"Same MO as the first two?" Langdon asked.

"Sounds like it. Raped and killed one place and then dumped out in public like a piece of trash. She'd been out in the Old Port drinking with friends. They slashed her throat with a knife."

"I can't imagine how her parents feel," Chabal said weakly. Her daughter, Darcy, had graduated from USM in Portland seven years earlier, so this sick animal preying on young college girls from that campus hit a little too close to home.

"The police have any leads?" Langdon wondered aloud.

"Not that they're sharing with the press."

"It's that damn creeping urbanization," Langdon complained. "Maine used to be a place where you might have a fistfight at closing time, but nobody shot or knifed anybody else. And predators certainly didn't prey upon young girls."

"That is, unless you count a grouchy hubby full of hooch on a Friday night, knocking the missus around, "Chabal retorted.

"Those were the days," Langdon replied with a dreamy look, and was promptly smacked in the side of the head for his efforts.

"We should do dinner sometime," Richam said. "Jewell is struggling with being an empty nester and getting that anxious look on her face that scares me. I think I need to get her out of the house."

"Any time," Langdon agreed. "We're pretty footloose and fancy free these days."

At that moment a brown blur shot into the bar, searching first for scraps, and then coming over and proudly jumping up with his paws on Langdon's lap. It was not the first time that dog had slipped out of the bookstore and tracked Langdon down after a customer had left the door open.

Of course, if he'd taken the Jeep somewhere, dog would still be wandering the streets of Brunswick, which had also happened more than once. Luckily, he was well known in town, and all Langdon had to do was wait for a phone call with a location to pick him up. He usually found dog at a restaurant, as the chances of obtaining food were greater there than at, say, the bank.

"I'm going to get drinks with Jewell after I close up the shop," Chabal said.

"Bring home a pizza, if you don't mind." Langdon replied. "I think I'm going home to see what I can dig up on Senator Margaret Mercer."

"It can't be easy being a gay woman in Washington, surely a man's world, if ever there was one," Chabal said.

Chapter 3

Still Friday

Chabal had hoped to sit outside at Goldilocks' Tavern, but storm clouds were brewing as she left the bookstore a little after six. She crossed the street on the newly raised crosswalk meant to slow traffic down, but which in reality just provided jumps for the local rednecks in their hotrods, a group that included her husband, Langdon. Some people thought that yellow lights were an invitation to speed up, and that she could almost understand, but why anyone would want to hurtle headlong over the raised pedestrian ways crisscrossing the only Maine Street in the country she found somewhat perplexing.

The four-lane street had proven dangerous to any that wanted to get to the other side. After a string of accidents, some fatal, the town tried various methods to reduce casualties. Flags had been placed in containers on either side at each crossing, so citizens could hoist these banners high overhead, alerting motorists as far as the Green Bridge on the north end and Bowdoin College on the south end to slow down and let them live to see another day.

Unfortunately, these flags had lasted exactly three days before they all went missing, most likely following the experiment of the green bikes, dozens of which had been distributed around town for people to ride when they needed to, leaving them in designated racks for the next person. It became a great game to throw the green bikes from the Green Bridge into the Androscoggin River below.

At least, these incidents of mild vandalism were, for the most part, the worst shenanigans the people of Brunswick got up to. Of course, like most towns, Brunswick had four or five families whose names perpetually popped up in the evening paper's police log for fighting, minor burglary, drug use, and, the bane of every rural Maine community, OUIs. A couple of times a year, scoundrels from Boston would come up and begin dealing harder drugs from motel rooms on the outskirts of town, but this was usually busted up fairly quickly. Those from away were usually obvious, and one of the four or five perpetual offenders would get arrested, raving about unicorns or flying elephants. This would tip the police off to open their eyes and check the parking lots for fancy cars with Massachusetts plates, and hotels that had more visitors than usual.

Most of the locals were good about stopping for pedestrians, but Chabal was cautious to make sure all four lanes had ceased movement before she journeyed across. She also stopped for yellow lights, was polite to salespeople, and corrected waiters when they forgot to charge her for something.

Goldilocks had fenced in part of the wide sidewalk with an array of wrought iron tables and chairs sprouting umbrellas. These outdoor pieces were chained at night so they didn't end up in the river. With the air rich with moisture, Chabal went inside, scanning the bar area for Jewell, who didn't appear to have arrived yet. The tables were filled, but two stools beckoned from the bar and she climbed up on one, her legs hovering well above the kicker.

"Chabal," the bartender said with a smile, "What can I get you?"

"Hi, Cheri. I'll do a vanilla madras."

"Is that man of yours joining you?"

"Not tonight—girl time. Jewell should be here soon."

Cheri nodded, set the vodka drink in a short glass in front of her, and moved down to a guy who'd finished his drink and was frantically beckoning for more before sobriety had a chance to sneak up on him. Cheri was the daughter of the namesake of the bar, having taken it over when he'd been murdered some twenty years earlier, and moving it to its current location about eight years ago.

"What is a vanilla madras?" The man next to her asked, turning on his stool to face Chabal.

"Orange juice with cranberry then you add vanilla vodka," Chabal replied.

"Bob Johnson," he said. "Just dropped my son off at Bowdoin for his freshman year orientation."

"You must be very proud of him." Now in her fifties, it wasn't that often she was hit on. Then again, she almost never found herself alone in a drinking establishment.

"I'm spending the night up the street at the Stowe Hotel."

"You're not worried about the bedbug problem?" she asked sweetly.

"Bedbug problem?"

"Sorry I'm late," Jewell interrupted, steaming into the seat next to her. "295 is wall to wall." She was dressed in a blue denim button-up shirt tucked into a split-red skirt that matched her bright lipstick. Her Afro encased her head like a frizzy helmet, with barely discernible silver hoop earrings hugging her jawline.

"Damn, girl, you be looking like a bad-ass from a Tarantino film," Chabal said. "What heads were you severing with swordplay today?"

"None yet, but soon. Maybe that joker next to you, if he don't stick his eyes back in his face and rotate his neck in a different direction," she growled, and then both women giggled as the man named Bob flushed and hurriedly turned his head away.

They exchanged the mandatory update on the kids, all of whom they worried nonstop about, but all seemed to be avoiding incarceration or starvation thus far. By the second drink they were venting their frustration over the quirks of their husbands. Jewell talking about how Richam had started smoking weed after work, thinking Jewell didn't know because she was asleep when he got home, but his clothes stank of it. It was not until the third, and hopefully final drink of the day, that they migrated from the day-today banter to the real girl-time conversation that was too infrequent in their lives.

"You heard the OPK struck again in Portland last night?" Jewell asked.

"Yeah, Richam was talking about it when we had lunch earlier. He didn't know many details. Do they know anything more about who's doing this?"

"The cops came over today and were sniffing around our office asking questions, and Don had to tell them to leave until they got a warrant. It sounded an awful lot like they think an immigrant is responsible for the murders." Jewell worked for the Christian Helpers for Entering Refugees and Immigrants Services and Hospitality in Portland.

"They say anything as to why they were at CHERISH?"

"Nah. Tight-lipped the whole way, and treated us like we were harboring criminals, instead of giving human beings a helping hand."

"Richam said the girl was found up on the Eastern Prom?"

"She was dumped on the East End Beach, just off that parking lot there. But she had been out drinking in the Old Port. A few people came forward and said she walked home from a party. Probably that's when the bastard got her."

"What is wrong with people?"

"There's a lot of nastiness in the world," Jewell said. "I see it every day with how people treat the immigrants I work with. Not a day goes by I don't hear a racist comment or threat."

"I could never do what you do," Chabal admitted. "I break down in tears when somebody comes in and says the book I recommended to them was awful."

"You certainly develop a thick skin being a black immigrant, but I came in the easy way. My man had a job lined up and a house for us to live in. Most of the people I deal with have nothing but the clothes on their backs when they get here. Don't know English. Don't have much for skills, unless you count the will to work hard as a skill. And of course, they're not allowed to work for six months until they get their refugee status sorted out. Sort of a recipe for abuse."

With the third drink almost gone, Chabal ordered a pizza, loaded, and a shrimp Caesar salad to bring home to share with Langdon and her son, Jack. Jewell was meeting Richam for dinner, and then they were going to a play at the Maine Music Theater. As they got ready to leave, Jewell and Chabal made vague plans to get together soon, but even though the kids were grown, life was still a busy proposition.

~ ~ ~ ~ ~

Dog's barking woke Langdon up in the middle of the night. When dog was a puppy, Langdon and Chabal had briefly given in to letting the canine sleep with them, but he was a restless soul, and often stepped on them moving around, and was soon banished to the living room. He was not averse to loudly announcing the presence of squirrels in the yard, or deer passing through the Town Commons out back, but usually exited through the dog door in the mudroom for such antics.

They'd turned in earlier than normal that evening. Langdon and Chabal had eaten pizza and salad in front of the television, texted Jack that there were leftovers, and retired to the bedroom, where they made sleepy love before drifting off.

"What's that mutt's problem?" Langdon mumbled.

"What?" Chabal feigned sleep, even though it'd been she who woke Langdon, elbowing him, as he was busy sleeping his way through the woofing.

Langdon swung his legs sideways and pulled a pair of shorts on, then a T-shirt. The dark window suggested it must be the middle of the night, and the alarm clocked confirmed it by reading 2:30. "He's probably dreaming of chasing rabbits." Langdon carefully closed the door behind him in case this was a ruse by the dog to sneak into their bedroom for the night.

Two men were in the living room, one rubbing dog's head, and the other eating a slice of pizza. They both wore seersucker suits, puckered, navy on navy—almost like a uniform. They could have been grown up poster children for Boy Scouts, or even Mormons, so immaculate was their dress and appearance. The man on the left sported a blue tie to match his eyes, his features dark with thick brows, and a hairline that came to a point in the middle of his forehead. The fellow making friends with dog had a dark red tie, was pale, with a wide forehead, a broad smile, and thin, silver glasses.

"Are you friends of Jack?" Langdon looked around. "Where is he?"

"Nice dog you have here," Red Tie said. "Lab?"

"Yeah, chocolate," Langdon replied. Although Jack sometimes brought friends home on a weekend night, it was unusual for them to be this well dressed. They were about the same age, but didn't fit the artsy casualness of his stepson. Maybe they were some sort of business partners in the new venture he was trying to get off the ground? But why were they here at 2:30 a.m.?

"You get the pizza from Goldilocks?" Blue Tie asked.

Langdon stood in the wide opening to the living room, unsure whether to go back to bed, enter and sit down, or call the police. "Yeah, sure," he said, rubbing his eyes to clear the tendrils of sleep away. "I'm Goff Langdon, Jack's stepfather."

"What do you do, Mr. Langdon?" Red Tie asked, settling back in the armchair and crossing his legs. He pulled a handful of red pistachios from his pocket and set them in his lap as he picked them open and popped them into his mouth.

"I own a bookstore downtown." Langdon moved to his desk in the corner of the room and sat on the rolling chair. "Who are you?"

"A bookstore? Fascinating," Blue Tie interjected. "That must be the Coffee Dog Bookstore?" There were two bookstores in town.

"That's the one."

"And you're a private detective as well?"

"On occasion."

"Are you working any interesting cases?"

"Not so much."

Red Tie pushed his glasses more firmly on as he sat forward. He had a blocky head that made Langdon think of Matt Damon. "Rumor has it you met with Senator Mercer today." It was not a question.

"Who told you that?"

"We were down at Goldilocks earlier and heard your wife, what is her name, Chabal? What kind of name is that, anyways? She was talking to some black woman with a faint accent, Caribbean perhaps?"

"Who are you?" Langdon asked, his sleepiness having turned to unease, and now approaching anger.

"We were just leaving," Blue Tie said, standing up as he rubbed dog's head one final time. "No dog tag? What if he gets lost?"

Langdon stood flummoxed. Should he demand they stay? Or should he kick them out? But they were already leaving.

At the door, Red Tie paused. "I'm sorry Chabal didn't get up to say hello. I'd have loved to get a closer look at her in that white T-shirt she sleeps in." And then he pulled the door shut behind him, and the two men walked down the driveway into the darkness.

Jack came trotting down the stairs as if he'd been awake during dog's barking and when the two men had entered "Who are you talking to down here?" he asked.

Chapter 4

Saturday

Once Jack returned upstairs, Langdon went into the closet of the bedroom and removed his pistol from the lock box, easing back around the bed so as not to awaken Chabal, who had gone back to sleep as evidenced by her soft snoring. Back in the kitchen, he pressed the thumb piece forward and cracked the cylinder open to the left, careful to keep his finger far from the trigger. With shaking fingers he slid five cartridges into the slots and closed it back up. Not much of a private detective, he thought wryly, but the truth was that guns made him nervous as hell. It was a Smith & Wesson .38 with a crimson trace laser, recommended to him by his friend, Bart, who was a policeman in town.

With the revolver on the kitchen island in front of him, Langdon pulled up a stool and waited for daylight. He'd just had his dog and his wife threatened, and he had no idea why. He was a pretty affable kind of guy. He'd played football, proving he was not adverse to hitting and being hit, but past that, he had never seen the reason for violence. He had lost most of the fights he'd ever been in, mainly because he didn't see much sense in beating another human being, even if the other guy had provoked the attack by being a smart-ass.

On a few occasions in life when his ire was raised, a bit of the ancient Viking blood would boil up in his veins. Two clean-cut young men with polite manners had invaded the sanctity of his home. Not gangbangers up from Boston or opioid users strung out and looking for a fix. What was the motive for their visit? That took no real mental struggle to figure out. It wasn't an unhappy bookstore customer, and it certainly wasn't Craig Morgan who Langdon had recently taken pictures of with a woman who wasn't his wife. As a matter of fact, he was fairly certain that Craig had already been dealt with, as he'd seen him on the street a few days prior, and noticed him sporting a shiner.

So, the motivation for the visit was clear: it was obviously related to the blackmail case he'd just picked up. Far murkier was who was threatening him and why? Was Chabal truly in danger? Dog? No, this had been just a gentle warning, and he was willing to bet dollars to donuts that the two respectable fellows recently in his house were little more than messenger boys, but for whom?

Langdon waited for the sky to begin lightening in the east, indicating it was almost six, before he texted Bart to call him. He knew his bad-tempered friend would be annoyed to be bothered at this hour—or at any hour—but was also certain he'd call, because he wouldn't want Langdon thinking he was still sleeping. Within a minute his phone rang.

"Morning, Bart." Langdon also knew not to say "good" morning.

"Langdon," growled his surly crony.

"Was wondering if I might buy you some breakfast this morning?"

"Ate already."

"I need to talk about something."

"I gotta work."

"I had some early morning visitors," Langdon relented. "They threatened Chabal."

"I could eat again."

"Rosie's in fifteen minutes?"

"Yep."

As Langdon closed the call, Chabal walked into the kitchen in her sweatpants and white T-shirt. "Who threatened me?" She noticed the gun on the counter.

"Better get some coffee," Langdon replied.

~ ~ ~ ~ ~

Twenty-five minutes later, Langdon pulled into the parking lot of Rosie's Diner. He'd told Chabal about the nighttime phantoms, and she'd retrieved her own weapon, a 9mm Beretta APX Compact with 13 plus 1 capacity. Langdon noticed her hands didn't shake when she slid the full magazine into the clip, but then again, she'd grown up with four brothers who she'd hunted with many a fall.

Bart was sitting in his patrol car, and Langdon idly wondered if he'd driven here from the police station, just a block down. Rosie's was not one of those smug shiny diners, but rather was crammed into a structure that may have once been a double-wide trailer, with a few additions jutting out here and there. What had once been bright red siding was now faded, but despite appearances, the food was excellent, and the people were local and real.

Lieutenant Jeremiah Bartholomew—a name which anyone who knew him shortened to just "Bart," had grown up dirt poor in the County, which was how the northern most region of Maine was locally referenced. He'd actually been born in Brunswick, but soon after birth, his mother had brought him up to Aroostook County following a man, a relationship that had lasted less time than the trip north.

For some reason, perhaps because she didn't have enough money to move, they'd stayed, and their only income other than welfare came during the potato harvest that lasted most of the month of September into early October. Aroostook County schools used to start in early August, so they could close during the harvest to allow students to work the fields in this crucial period when every hand and every hour was turned to unearthing and storing the black gold that much of the population depended on. Bart was one of the few to escape the crushing poverty of this rural area of Maine, going to the academy when he was eighteen, and then returning to Brunswick.

"Where the hell ya been?" Bart asked as he emerged from the cruiser like an inflatable Santa Claus. He was seven inches over six-feet and would have made Mama Claus proud with his rotund paunch.

"Sorry, had to show Chabal how to load her piece," Langdon said, wondering if it was Philip Marlowe that referred to a pistol in this fashion.

Bart snorted, his pudgy face convulsing. His balding head, culled carefully for what hair remained, came to a jagged point in the center of his forehead, giving him a demonic appearance. "Sorry. That's rich. Don't forget I've been to the firing range with both of you."

There were twelve round stools with padded red tops along the counter of the diner. There was no chance that Bart would fit into one of the eight small booths, and after only a second of realization, a man moved down, freeing up three stools. Langdon settled into the one on the left, wondering if his officer buddy didn't perhaps need three spaces.

"You boys drinking coffee this morning?" Rosie didn't bother waiting for a response as she grabbed their mugs off the back wall and sloshed some of the thick mud into the chipped pottery. Not much over five-feet and just about as wide, her gleaming face was a mixture of oven heat and zest for life. Langdon had known her for twenty-five years, and she'd appeared to be sixty-five years old for that entire time.

"So you gonna' tell me what's going on?" Bart asked.

"Not too much to tell. I woke up in the middle of the night and found two Boy Scouts in my living room petting dog."

"Boy Scouts?"

"Short-hair, perfectly dressed, well-mannered," Langdon replied. "They sure fooled dog."

"Where is that by-product of too much laundry lint?"

"I left him home to keep an eye on Chabal."

This time Bart laughed outright. "You seem to overestimate both you and your dog's abilities."

Langdon nodded that perhaps this was an accurate statement. "I thought they might be friends of Jack's, but they were too well dressed and polite, and acting mighty awkward."

Rosie came to take their order, two eggs, bacon, home fries, and toast for Langdon. Bart had the lumberjack special that included everything in the diner.

"You want me to put out a BOLO?"

"Be on the look-out for what? Stealing a piece of pizza?"

"They broke into your house and threatened your wife."

"And my dog," Langdon added. "But not really. They just suggested they'd like to get a better look at Chabal, describing the shirt she was wearing in bed at that very moment."

"I can imagine," Bart said. "Can't hardly blame them for that, now, can we?"

Langdon ignored the backhanded compliment to his wife. "Perhaps you can just informally share some details about it and have a squad car swing by my house a couple times of day to check on things?"

"So, ya gonna' tell me why they paid you a visit?"

"It must have to do with the case I just picked up."

"Which is?"

Langdon sighed. Less than a day had passed and he was going to shatter the confidentiality agreement. "I was hired by Senator Mercer to investigate who might be blackmailing her with photographs of her having an affair with another woman." That should do it.

Bart whistled. "I always wondered about her. Not that it's any of my business, but isn't she married to a man?"

Langdon nodded. "They are in love in an intellectual way and not physically, or some sort of rich people bullshit like that."

"And her husband knows about her affairs?"

"They both indulge in the occasional tryst," Langdon replied. "I believe Maxwell, the husband, said that he likes his women younger, while Margaret prefers them more mature."

"Quite the household." Bart observed dryly. "It seems the logical place to start would be the other woman in the photos?"

"She doesn't know her."

"Doesn't know her? Was it a hook-up after last call in some dive?"

"She was at a function at the Bernard Hotel, a fundraiser for the United Way. She hit it off with a woman who suggested they continue their discussion in her room upstairs. The senator left and came back later on her own and snuck up the back way."

"But she got her name?"

"Kamrin Jorgenson. There are actually two people by that name in the world, but neither is within twenty years of the age of this woman."

"So it was a set up from the beginning."

"Maybe. Maybe not."

"And why maybe not?"

"You never gave a fake name when picking up a woman before?"

Bart glared at him. "No."

"Me neither." Langdon admitted. "But I know people do it. I know people who have done it."

"Yeah," Bart agreed. "That bun-haired lawyer probably doesn't even know his real name any more."

Both men took a moment to think about the philandering ways of their friend, Jimmy 4 by Four, a corporate lawyer turned hippie who was seemingly practicing as much womanizing as he was the law.

Langdon shook his head and continued, "I'm leaning towards a set up, but want to remain objective. If you seduce a United States Senator, you might give a false name to keep your real identity a secret from the newspapers. Or the woman is married, or in a relationship?"

"Let's work from another angle, then," Bart said. "Who'd want to blackmail Mercer?"

Langdon laughed. "I made the same mistake and asked her that very question. The senator is on the Intelligence Committee, which is currently investigating the President for collusion with Russia; the Appropriations Committee, which is responsible for budgeting 770 billion dollars to the Department of Defense; and is a swing vote on health, education, and just about anything else you can think of."

"Yeah, it's a little more difficult than having recently fired a disgruntled employee," Bart agreed.

"That, too. She just replaced her press secretary due to differences of opinion."

Rosie leaned her thick forearms on the counter. "Susan comes in here when she's not in D.C. I could ask her a few questions if you want?"

Langdon shook his head, not in negation, but in consternation. "We're having a private discussion here, Rosie."

"Nothing private about this diner," Rosie replied. "You know that, Goff Langdon."

"True that," an old codger named Ray said from the booth behind them. "Talking to myself in here is what led to my divorce. Speaking of, what's Mercer's husband think of his wife being a lesbo?"

"Who's Susan?" Bart spread his catcher's-mitt-sized hands to each side.

"The senator's former press secretary," Langdon said wearily. He thought he should probably admonish Ray for the slur, but didn't want to get sidetracked.

"Yes or no?" Rosie asked.

"Sure, but try to be discreet. She should be in town more now that she's been let go."

"Like a church mouse," Rosie said, making a motion as if zipping her lips.

"How about some pie?" Bart asked, stuffing the last piece of bread into his mouth.

"Ha," Ray chortled from behind them.

"To go, please and thank you, Rosie," Langdon said, pulling out his money clip. He knew without words that the tab was on him.

"Where're we going?" Bart asked, crushing half the pie into his mouth as they moved toward the door, dripping blueberries down his brown corduroy jacket, matching the syrup that was already smeared on his red striped tie.

"For a ride so we can talk in private," Langdon replied.

~ ~ ~ ~ ~

An hour later, Langdon unlocked the bookstore and flipped on the lights. Once he had the coffee brewing and the cash register filled, he placed seven special order for books with Ingram. He noted that one woman had requested several older Patricia Cornwell books featuring the heroine Dr. Kay Scarpetta. This was not the first request for these older titles, and he decided to bolster the shelf selection with the entire backlist instead of just the best sellers the store currently had.

At five minutes before 9:00 he went and unlocked the door. There was already a customer waiting there, promising a busy Saturday. He was on his own until noontime, and was barely able to keep up with the stream of people looking for mysteries to enliven their routine lives. The line was three deep when Jonathan Starling arrived for work.

Five minutes later, the store was empty and they were overstaffed. "I was flat out until you got here," Langdon said. "I think people must be peering in the window and seeing your ugly mug and choosing to keep going."

"I think you probably just forgot how to work. Get a customer or two and you get overwhelmed," Star replied.

"Not that we have a dress code, but did you ever think of combing your hair?" It was true that Starling's hair sprouted from his head in various clumps.

"I'm just following your lead, boss."

"What do you know about Senator Margaret Mercer?"

"She pretends to be a moderate, but when push came to shove she trashed Obamacare. If you didn't give me health insurance with this job, I'd be stuck up a tree right now."

Langdon nodded. "She seems to have caved under pressure from the President. You know anything about her personal life?"

"Seen her around town a few times. Never spoke to her. She lives over in Bath, doesn't she?"

Langdon placed the manila envelope on the counter in front of Starling. "She hired me to find the woman in these pictures."

Starling took out the five glossy photos. Where Bart had made crude comments when he thumbed through the pictures, Starling's face didn't show any surprise at the revealing nature of the prints, but he did intently stare at each of them with a faraway look clouding his eyes.

"Remember my old law partner, boss?"

"Governor Truman? Sure. We put him in jail twenty years ago."

"Not Harper," Starling said. "Jordan."

"Of course." Jordan Fitzpatrick had gone rogue and sabotaged a nuclear power plant to get it shut down, and then disappeared into thin air when the police caught on to her. "What about her?"

"I'm pretty sure this is her," Starling tapped the top image that best captured the woman's face with Senator Mercer.

Langdon walked over and stared at the slightly fuzzy photo of the woman with the senator. "Holy shit! She used nude photos to blackmail the chief of police way back then, didn't she?"

"That's why he killed himself," Starling concurred.

Two men came through the door, and Langdon tucked the photos under the counter. It was Maxwell Mercer and Michael Glover.

"Good afternoon, gentlemen," Langdon said. He blushed slightly, realizing he'd just been looking at nude photos of this man's wife.

"Mr. Langdon," Maxwell replied, and Glover merely nodded. "We were just having lunch across the street, and Mike commented that he'd not read a mystery novel in years, so we thought we'd pop in."

"We have mysteries," Langdon said wryly. "Anything I can help you find?"

Maxwell laughed. "Other than the mystery woman, you mean?"

Langdon steered the two men deeper into the store as the phone rang and Starling answered it. "What sort of books do you like, Mr. Glover?"

"Please call me Mike. I like a fast pace, I suppose."

"Maybe something by David Baldacci."

While Glover was perusing Baldacci titles, Langdon turned to Maxwell. "Do you know anything about two men who appeared in my house in the middle of the night last night?"

"What? Why would I know anything about that?"

Langdon had wanted to see what reaction his abruptness would provoke. He deemed the surprise to be real, but it had struck him that the two men could very well have been Secret Service in the employment of the senator. If they were, Maxwell genuinely didn't know about it.

"You mean they broke in?"

"They were in my living room eating my food and patting my dog when I woke up. I assume it has to be related in some way to my meeting with your wife yesterday."

"What did they say?"

"They brought up my meeting with the two of you."

Maxwell shook his head tiredly. "The perks of being married to a senator seem to be dwindling away. We used to be able to have a semblance of privacy. Nowadays, it seems that as soon as we step out the door, our pictures pop up on Facebook or Instagram or some type of social media. Now we're being blackmailed. You're being threatened. I've had about enough."

"What choice do you have?"

"To be honest with you, I've been after Marge to not run for reelection in 2020."

"And what are her thoughts on that?"

"She could make a million a year as a lobbyist. It'd still be a life in politics, better money, less work, and nobody cares about who you are. Can you name a single lobbyist?"

Glover came over carrying a book. "What about *Absolute Power*?"

"As bad as this sounds, I've never actually read it, but I did see the movie with Clint Eastwood," Langdon said with a chuckle.

"I think I'll give it a try. Didn't you say you were going to pick up a book as well?" Glover directed the question at Maxwell.

"Ah, yes, indeed I did. Do you have *The Murder of Roger Ackroyd*?"

"I believe so," Langdon replied, scanning the books just to their left. "Right here." He pulled the slim paperback from the shelf. "I'm not a huge Agatha Christie fan, but I did read this one."

"I've read them all twice," Maxwell said. "I was thinking of this one the other day, but couldn't find it in my study."

"You were thinking about it? Because it involves blackmail?"

Maxwell laughed, his thick mustache bouncing stiffly up and down. The humor didn't quite reach his eyes. "Good point, Mr. Langdon. That must be why Marge hired you, but no, it wasn't the blackmail. I was trying to remember how Poirot knew it was the doctor who killed Ackroyd. I guess I could've just looked it up, or asked my local mystery bookstore owner. But thought I'd give it a read over."

"One of her better mysteries, I think. It's fascinating how one investigation turns up so many other characters' unrelated secrets, but after a bit, I get bored with the English stuffiness," Langdon said. "I won't ruin it for you." He made to walk away, then turned. "Do you think people in real life carry so many secrets with them?"

~ ~ ~ ~ ~

It was near to closing time when Jewell came into the store. She swept in with a purpose, her long legs covering the distance to the counter in just a few strides despite the ankle-strap stilettos on her feet. "Your wife said I'd find you here."

"Here I am," Langdon confessed. "I can't put anything past that woman."

"Can we talk in your office?"

"Sure," Langdon came around from behind the counter. "Star," he called to where the man was repairing the carnage of the day's earlier browsers. "I'm going out back, so the store is yours."

"You could have just called." Langdon ventured as they walked down the aisle. He wondered what could have brought her looking for him. It was true that he and Chabal were good friends with the Denevieuxes, but he rarely found himself speaking with Jewell without Richam or Chabal present. He idly wondered why that was.

"Do you have your phone?" she asked.

Langdon patted his pockets. When had he last seen his phone?

"When you find it, you will also find a voicemail and seven text messages I sent you." Jewell set the green leather shoulder bag on the floor, a bag that perfectly matched her blouse in color, as well as her toe and fingernails.

"I certainly hope my wife doesn't have my phone. She'll be thinking we're having an affair," Langdon cracked. In reality he'd be more afraid of Jewell than Chabal if he were to engage in any sort of physical interaction, especially now when her anger appeared to be piqued.

"Did your wife tell you last night that the Portland Police were zeroing in on an immigrant as their main suspect for the OPK?" The media had coined the phrase in regards to the victims all having been out in Portland's Old Port neighborhood when they were abducted, raped, and killed.

"I don't think so. You sent her home pretty lit, as I remember. We gobbled down a few slices of the pizza and tumbled into bed."

"Well, the cops were nosing around yesterday, and they came back today with a whole mess of ICE agents. It seems they arrested a boy I worked with 'cuz they think he's the one who butchered and raped those poor girls."

"Did he do it?"

"Hell, no, he didn't do it, Goff Langdon. That's why I'm here."

"And you're here because you want me to do… what exactly?"

"I want to hire you to prove his innocence."

Chapter 5

Still Saturday

The meeting place was a rustic farmhouse in Bowdoinham. Kamrin Jorgenson had taken a right at the light onto Elm Street in Topsham, which had turned into Middlesex Road, and now proclaimed itself to be Route 24. She'd only been back in Maine a few weeks, and had forgotten how much she enjoyed the scenery.

Maine had long been known as the Pine Tree State, but it was the hardwoods swaying gracefully in the breeze like hot-air balloons interspersed with slender birches that always made her heart flutter a little quicker. Some of the leaves had already begun to change color, and she looked forward to the height of foliage season. Colorado, Washington State, and South Dakota, where she'd spent the last years, had been beautiful in their own way, but this was truly where she felt at home, even if it'd been over twenty years since she'd lived here.

Kamrin had been born in Connecticut, her family moving to Maine when she was four, perhaps to escape the pressure of a grandfather that had been incredibly successful in business and wanted the same for his son. Kamrin's father fled a life in an office for the woods of Maine.

Her parents were part of the back-to-the-land movement in the early 1970s, selling everything and buying acreage in Athens, Maine. With few carpentry skills, they had built a post-and-beam house in the woods. The closest neighbor was three miles down the road. Kamrin had gone to the public schools, elementary school in Athens, and then to junior high school in Madison, a bus trip of almost an hour. When her parents realized that these back-wood public schools were not challenging Kamrin, they pulled her out and home-schooled her.

Life in Athens provided little for a child who might want to fit into normal society out in the big, bad, world some day. Other than the Fourth of July parade, an event Kamrin eagerly anticipated each year, social events among her parents' set more usually included being taken to nude swimming holes, with a rough-and-tumble daily life that included doing her business in outhouses and buckets, as well as being privy to non-stop drug use. Her parents' circle gobbled acid and magic mushrooms on a regular basis, and she had first smoked pot when she was only twelve.

It wasn't until she joined her peers at Wesleyan in Middletown, Connecticut, that she realized her parents had given her more than an embarrassing childhood and the ability to smoke copious amounts of weed. The intellectual conversations she had grown up with were far superior to anything she engaged in at college. Many of the back-to-the-landers were extremely educated, talented, and freethinking people. One consistent theme, other than denigrating 'The Man,' was the earth, and the bounty it provided mankind, and how to stop the abuse to which it was being subjected. This had led her to found the Flower First environmental group, and as its leader, becoming one of the radicals on campus in a world that had a dearth of radicals.

After Wesleyan, Kamrin moved half an hour south down Interstate 91 to Yale Law School. This had been easier to achieve than one might think, with her grandfather on the board, but she had excelled in her academics and her LSAT scores were sky-high, so perhaps she deserved it. She had decided that having a law degree was the way in which she could best protect the earth. Members of her Flower First group went off to various endeavors in life, but a core group stayed in touch, and she began an offshoot in

New Haven. After graduation, she had moved home to Maine, the frontier of the battle to save the earth, and her home. It was here she joined the law firm of Truman and Starling, adding her surname of Fitzpatrick to the sign out front. In the years since, she'd had a few different names as circumstances dictated.

The road dipped to the right briefly, and she was able to see Merrymeeting Bay. It was the point where the Cathance, Androscoggin, and Kennebec Rivers joined for their final push to the sea. Kamrin pulled over and shielded her eyes from the glare of the sun, and then got out and walked over to the water. Up to the right was where the Kennebec River flowed into the Bay, and if she were to follow the river upstream, she would come to the town of Madison, where she'd attended school until it no longer suited her. It was also the last place she'd last used her real name, with a job as a partner at that law firm. While at first, she'd merely pushed hard at the boundaries of legality in fighting the forestry corporations and lumbermen and paper companies, over time she'd started to ignore that line in the sand, taking those first fateful steps to being a criminal.

~ ~ ~ ~ ~

That had been long ago, and much had happened since. She had been a beautiful woman with a razor-keen intellect and a passion for Mother Nature—and for sex. These were dangerous qualities, and had indeed, led her on a precarious path. She was still a fine-looking woman, she acknowledged, judging from the attentions she received from younger as well as older men and women. There were a few wrinkles around her eyes, but time spent outdoors would do that, and while critical of the creases, she'd earned every one of them. If anything, her acumen had increased, and her dedication had not wavered. She climbed back into the car and continued on to her clandestine meeting.

The mailbox was clearly labeled with the number 54. Kamrin

eased her car into the mouth of the driveway and assessed the meeting spot. It wasn't that she didn't trust the two men she was rendezvousing with, but that over the years she had come to discover that faith was reserved for those with no other options. The driveway was several hundred yards long, cutting a straight path through fields that had once grown crops but were now just endless fields of grass needing to be mowed. At the end was a farmhouse complete with barns and sheds, although not even a chicken or a dog adorned the scene. There was one vehicle pulled in front of the colonial with shingles and a front porch, two additions giving length to either side. As Kamrin drove up to the house, she noted the SUV was a GMC Yukon Denali, and she archived the license plate in her memory.

Six weeks earlier, the two men she was meeting had shown up on the doorstep of the trailer she shared with a man named Bob in rural South Dakota. The one who she'd nicknamed Glasses, seeing as she knew the names they gave were false, claimed they were from a rather diffuse and shadowy environmental organization called the Earth Liberation Front, a group that she'd claimed membership to, but one that had no central structure, just cells operating independently. These two men hinted that they were part of a secretive, well-funded core network that operated on a global stage instead of just the local arena.

Glasses had told her she was needed in an effort far larger than sabotaging the construction of the Keystone Pipeline. The other man, Eyebrows, had said little, but merely stared at her as Glasses spoke.

"We understand that you grew up and lived for years in Maine?" Glasses had asked.

How did he know that? That had been twenty years and several names ago, but Kamrin had merely nodded. She had not stayed out of jail all these years by running her mouth.

"And that you worked in the MidCoast area?"

"Yes."

"We are running an operation to force our government to rejoin the Paris Climate Accord. I know, I know." He said, looking away and nodding. "It may sound a little grandiose, but," he paused, and a creepy smile flitted across his face, "let's say we have our own ways of moving the levers of power in the real world. Would you be interested in helping?"

Kamrin had seriously doubted that these two fellows were environmentalists. They smelled more like ex-military. But she had listened to their pitch because she was sick of her current lover and missed Maine deeply. Kamrin thought back to her response, a resounding 'Hell yes.' It had been easy to leave Bob, who was beginning to annoy her anyway, a paunchy white man with dreadlocks who smoked weed all day and spoke of sticking it to The Man like that was still cool.

The request from Glasses and Eyebrows was like a ray of sunshine breaking through the clouds. She had not realized how miserable her existence had become until something better presented itself, as is often the case. Bob had made up for a lack of dexterity in the bedroom by supplying her with endless quantities of weed, and this haze had enveloped her body, mind, senses, and spirit.

"How do you feel about seducing a woman?" Glasses had asked.

Her body felt pleasure as most did, and she'd been with women before, though how long before she didn't care to admit. And if that pleasure could go hand in hand with protecting the environment?

"The target is a closet lesbian, who also happens to be a moderate Republican Senator. She wields the potential to stop many of the President's more disastrous environmental roll-backs, and perhaps even the clout to push him back into the Paris Agreement," Glasses said with a sneer.

It was then that Kamrin realized the target was Senator Margaret Mercer. This was certainly on a larger scale than the grim efforts to delay the construction of a pipeline from Canada to Steele City, Nebraska.

"How do you know she'll be attracted to me?" Kamrin had asked.

"Seems you fit her type to a T. We can't be sure, but it's worth a shot."

"And then we blackmail her?" She had done this very thing before. While the last time it had been effective in the short run, the end result had not been so brilliant.

The Keystone Pipeline protests had largely fizzled out as old news now that the current administration was fully backing running pipelines through Native lands and under major waterways, heedless of the spills and other consequences. Construction had not yet begun, so the business of pouring sand in gas tanks and shooting out the huge truck tires had not yet commenced.

Kamrin shook her head, banishing the past, and returning to the here and now. Perhaps she would be back to carry on that fight, she thought. The drive from Brunswick to Bowdoinham had stirred too many memories, however, and she doubted that she'd be able to leave Maine again. No, this is where she would live the rest of her days, and it was here she would be buried. Whoever Glasses and Eyebrows really were, she was happy they'd persuaded her to return.

With these thoughts swirling around her like black flies in the spring, Kamrin pushed open the small, low front door of the farmhouse, it as much as anything suggesting the antiquity of the home. Glasses and Eyebrows were waiting for her at the kitchen table. Spread out in front of them were pictures of her naked with the senator. She knew it was meant to make her uncomfortable and put them in a position of superiority, but she had no problem with the body she'd been blessed with.

"Do you think those pictures make me look fat?" she asked.

"Not at all," Eyebrows replied with a leer.

"What's the play?"

"Time to send a blackmail note. We've written it and we'll deliver it," Glasses said.

"And what do I do?"

Glasses and Eyebrows exchanged glances, the slightest flickering of the eyes, but Kamrin caught it and was not sure she liked the meaning.

"Stay out of sight."

The statement was simple, more like an order, but Kamrin was able to fill in the blanks. She'd done her part, and she began to wonder what her role might be going forward, if any.

"We've rented this place for you. The fridge is stocked. There is cable and internet. You need to keep your head low."

"Did she put the Secret Service on me?"

"No. She hired some local hack private detective to search for you. She couldn't risk bringing the Secret Service in and exposing her... proclivities."

"Who is this detective?"

"Guy by the name of Goff Langdon."

Kamrin didn't even blink, but inside her chest grew so tight it was hard to breathe. She knew Langdon. She had drunk with Langdon. They had played a cat-and-mouse game years earlier, back when she had a different name. As her mind raced with this new information, she suddenly realized her position was extremely precarious. She had done what was needed for these two men who claimed to be from ELF, and now she'd been sidelined, her role simply to stay out of sight. But what if they knew—or figured out—her previous connection to Langdon? Kamrin wondered how high the stakes of the game she was playing were. She was pretty sure she was the pawn in this particular chess game, and everyone knew how easy it was to sacrifice a pawn. There was coldness about these two men that suggested she did not want to find out how well or poorly they played.

"I'll need to get my stuff and check out of the Greenlander Motel," she said, once she was sure her voice would be steady.

"Do it tomorrow," Glasses said. "Who's going to be looking for you on a Sunday?"

Kamrin seriously doubted these two men were interested in the environment, and she was even more skeptical of any compunction on their part in killing one Kamrin Jorgenson. True, they'd given her $20,000, and brought her back to Maine.... Maybe she could still twist this blackmail scheme for the good of Mother Earth.

Chapter 6

Still Saturday

Langdon sat next to Jewell, while Jimmy 4 by Four sat behind his large walnut desk. 4 by Four's office was in Fort Andross, an old mill that was perched on the Androscoggin River, overlooking the Green Bridge that separated Brunswick from Topsham. If he'd been there an hour earlier, he might have seen a familiar figure from the past driving over that same bridge on her way to a rendezvous in Bowdoinham. The water was low and lazy down below, not like in the spring when it raged over the dam and against the rocks.

The office was spacious with high ceilings and large windows. For a time, 4 by Four had worked alone, but recently had given in and hired a secretary. He'd told Langdon over drinks one night that it was his goal to not seduce her, a confession clouded by his passing comment that it was a daily effort. Langdon didn't think that the man had had a relationship that had lasted more than a few months in the twenty-plus years he'd known him.

4 by Four had been born in the Bronx, and a driving ambition got him into Rutgers University where he finished seventh in his class before being accepted into Yale Law. He worked two or three jobs to pay his bills, but still the debt mounted up, and Jimmy plowed forward like an express train, only stopping at the most important destinations. Upon graduation, he was courted by several firms and ended up accepting the offer of Wachtler, Bilgewasser, and

Tompkins, one of the more prestigious law firms in New York City. He worked fifteen hours a day, seven days a week, and billed for all of them. He was a legal genius driven by his desire for wealth and power, but he smoked four packs of cigarettes a day, drank twelve cups of coffee, and lived in a high-rise he never saw in the light of day.

One morning, Jim Angstrom, as he was known then, woke up and said 'enough.' By 11:30 a.m. he was driving north in his BMW. At 2:00 p.m., somewhere between Hartford and Boston, he traded the car straight up for a Volkswagen bus that sat in the farthest corner of the lot. The dealer thought he was taking a real chance with what he assumed was a stolen car, but his greed got the better of him. The bus maxed out at fifty-six miles an hour, which was just fine with him. He broke down on 295 North, the Volkswagen just able to limp off the exit into Bowdoinham, Maine, and he'd never left. It wasn't the deep woods he'd been shooting for, his goal having been Dexter, but he was able to rent a house without plumbing, have a garden where he could grow plenty of pot, entertain a revolving door of girlfriends, all with plenty of time to just contemplate life.

Slowly he'd re-emerged from his cocoon, took and passed the Maine Bar Exam, and began practicing in Brunswick, but no longer was he a slave to the work. He was good at two things in life. The first was law, and the second was the seduction of women.

One corner of the room held a small bar with a shelf of fine liquors, and an old glass-door Coke cooler holding an array of beers. Langdon opted for scotch while Jimmy had tequila with a lime, and Jewell stuck to her water.

Over the past twenty years, 4 by Four had transformed from the heedless dress of a hippie back into the attire he'd worn years earlier as a corporate lawyer. His long hair was piled into a bun that appeared casual, but Langdon was well aware of the careful construction of this topknot hairstyle. His thick and carefully manicured beard perched on his face as if false, and his left ear had a meticulously polished gold stud. His tailored blazer hugged his wiry frame with a Burberry silk pocket square that matched the Archival Collection silk tie from Brooks Brothers. The white collar of his striped shirt was crisp, as was the crease in the jeans he wore. All that remained of the hippy that had been was his name and his fondness for weed.

"I haven't seen you in too long," 4 by Four was saying to Jewell. "What's it been? Three months since we were all over at Langdon's for a barbecue?"

"Summer in Brunswick sure gets busy," Jewell agreed. "What have you been up to?"

"I'm actually looking to open a restaurant."

"What?" Langdon jerked his head around.

"I've got a buddy who has his grow license, and we've been tossing the idea around of opening up a joint. We're thinking of calling it 'Edible Apps'."

"You mean appetizers with pot in them?" Langdon asked.

"Nobody calls it pot anymore. If you smoke it, it's weed. If you eat it, it's an edible. But we have dabbled with having a pot pie on the menu."

"I have to say that's pretty smart," Jewell said. "Will the munchies kick in before they order the main course?"

"Probably not, but think of all the people who normally skip dessert because they're full. Our final course will be a game-changer."

"You still need a card to buy marijuana, don't you?" Langdon asked.

"Yeah, but everybody has one. Or anybody who has ever had an ache or pain. But we're banking on full legalization within the next couple of years. By the spring there will be cannabis stores opening all over the state, and we'll be on the ground floor ready to run with our idea." 4 by four stood and walked to the window, his cowboy boots clicking the floor like high heels. He liked the extra two inches of height the heels gave him as well as the intricate stitched pattern of the rich leather.

"I thought you were thinking of running for state rep?" Langdon asked.

"That's a very real possibility," 4 by Four answered.

"You don't see any conflict between owning a marijuana restaurant and state politics?"

"Times are changing. It's time you got with the agenda."

"Maybe you're right," Langdon admitted.

"You have any time in your schedule for some legal work?" Jewell broke the pause that had left them swirling with the thoughts of the rapid changes happening in life.

"What do you got?"

"Did you hear they tagged some guy for being the Old Port Killer?"

"I just got a notification on my phone, but there was no real detail. I'm glad they got the sick fuck."

"They arrested the wrong guy," Jewell said.

"How do you know?" 4 by Four walked back over and sat down, all of a sudden realizing that his two friends were here to have him defend a serial rapist and murderer.

"I know him. He wouldn't have done what they said."

"What's his name?"

"Tugiramhoro Mduwimana. We call him Tug for short."

4 by Four refrained from saying it sure sounded like a terrorist name. There was a day that he would've said this to Jewell, just to get her goat. But as he had just said, times were changing, and he somehow knew this would make her more than annoyed. It might even put him further down her list than his philandering ways had already plummeted him to.

"He's from Burundi," Langdon added.

"That's in Africa?"

"It's a tiny country just east of the Congo."

"I take it you know him through your job at CHERISH?" 4 by Four directed the question at Jewell.

"He came to the United States back in 2015 after a failed coup. He was a journalist, and President Nkurunziza considered him an enemy of the state. Luckily, he had a visa and escaped to the United States right before being arrested. He has a cousin who lived in Portland, so he worked his way up the coast and requested asylum," Jewell said, repeating the story she'd just told Langdon a few hours earlier. "His English was limited, but his French quite good, so I was assigned his case, and helped him with all the paperwork. He's had a green card for two years now and hopes to become a citizen in 2020."

4 by Four leaned forward and tapped his Cross pen on the desk. "And why do the police think he's guilty of rape and murder?"

Jewell sighed. "There was an anonymous tip. The police went to the house where he was staying. It belongs to a very nice old lady who rents rooms cheaply to immigrants until they can find places of their own. They found a girl's USM ID badge, those swipe card things, and a knife with a trace of blood that they're running DNA tests on now, but the blade is consistent with the weapon used to kill all three girls. Or that's what my source in the police department tells me."

"Anonymous tip? That sounds suspicious. And convenient. Did they have a warrant?"

"I don't know." Jewell shrugged her shoulders. "All of this just happened. But I figured he needed some help."

"That where you come in?" 4 by Four looked at Langdon.

"Jewell wants me to poke around a bit and see what I can turn up. If she's right, and the dude didn't do the crime, then there's something funny afoot."

4 by Four nodded. "Like, where did the ID and knife come from? They must have been planted, either by the killer or someone who knows the killer, anyway."

"Tugiramhoro is a decent young man. There's no way he killed those girls," Jewell said.

"What do you want from me?" 4 by Four knew, but wanted it said plainly.

"You could begin by checking into things. Like, did they have a warrant? And if it comes to it, defend him in court."

"So you would like to retain my services?"

"Unofficially, yes."

"That means I'm not getting paid."

"Tugiramhoro works as a valet in a hotel down in Portland. He has a degree from the University in Burundi, speaks three languages, was a top journalist, and the only job he's been able to get here is carrying bags."

"Doesn't CHERISH have lawyers on the payroll?"

"Three of them, but they're overloaded as it is. Plus, they do mostly immigration paperwork. I don't think any of them have ever seen the inside of a courtroom."

"Defending murderers is not exactly my stock in trade," 4 by Four said dryly. "You could get one of those publicity-seeking television lawyers who'd just love the attention that a murder trial of an immigrant is going to bring."

"Be a pretty good feather in the cap of somebody wanting to run for state representative," Langdon said.

"I don't know about that. We get much off the coast or outside of Lewiston/Auburn and people aren't so sure about people from away coming and taking all the good jobs," 4 by Four replied.

"First of all, those people aren't coming to the cities to find work and the immigrants aren't going into the country to take their jobs," Jewell said angrily.

"Right or wrong, they still vote, is all I'm saying," 4 by Four said.

"You know Brunswick is largely democratic and very pro-immigrant."

"Yeah, I suppose you're right." 4 by Four tapped the desk, as he stared out the window. "So, this is pro bono?"

"I could talk with the board down at CHERISH and see if we can come up with something to compensate you." Jewell sat forward, knowing that she had him now.

"Don't worry about it," 4 by Four said magnanimously.

"So, you'll do it?"

"You're friends with Cary Stockton, aren't you?"

"Yeah, sure," Jewell replied with a quizzical look.

"I heard her husband moved out a few months back?"

Jewell nodded. Now she knew where this was going.

"Maybe you could have her and me both over to dinner some night at your house?"

"I'll see what I can do."

"Excellent. I will get the three of us in to see Tugir… the young man in question. Probably be Monday morning at the earliest. It'd be helpful if you email me everything you know about him, like how to pronounce his name."

~ ~ ~ ~ ~

Langdon walked the short distance back to the bookstore with Jewell and bid her farewell, as he wanted to duck in and grab something from his office. The building was still open because the gift shop across the way kept later hours than he did, but life needed some sort of balance, didn't it? Speaking of balance, he realized that he should sign up Jack for some store hours, as Langdon was most likely going to be busy with the two cases he'd recently acquired.

As he walked, he thought, wasn't life funny like that? He hadn't had a case in months, and even then, it was nothing of substance, and now he had two blockbuster cases on his docket. Suddenly he was immersed neck deep in blackmail, serial murders, immigration, and frame-ups. "What's next?" he asked under his breath as he went through the front door of the building.

Standing in the hallway peering through the doorway to his shop was the most stunning woman he'd ever seen.

"I'm sorry, we closed at six," Langdon said, wondering if the front side of this lady with coiled waves of blonde hair was as alluring as the backside.

She squealed and whirled around in surprise.

Langdon gulped and stepped back. He felt as if he was cheating on his wife, but his eyes wouldn't mind their own business. "I didn't mean to startle you," he blurted out.

She laughed. "I guess I felt sort of guilty peeking in the windows like that," she said. She flashed a brilliant smile that was a bit crooked, sarcastic, and wholly sexy. "Is this your place?"

Langdon was doing his best to look into her blue eyes, but the white halter-top that exposed her belly and far too much of her chest was like a magnet and his eyes bits of steel. "Yes. Yes it is."

"You're Goff Langdon?"

"That's me. If you want to grab a book quickly, I can ring you up before I head home," he said, stepping past her to unlock the door, the faint scent of perfume tickling his nose as his fingers fumbled to work the key.

"Actually, it's you I'm looking for, although I do need a new book to read as well."

"What can I do for you?" he asked, finally succeeding in working the lock and swinging the door open.

"I lost my sister."

"You lost your sister?"

"Your website says, amongst other things, that you locate missing persons?"

"Ah, yes, of course, Miss…" Langdon looked down to see if she had a wedding ring on but was distracted by the light-blue denim shorts, wondering if they were actually painted on, like they supposedly did with those Sports Illustrated swimsuit models.

"Delilah Friday." She stepped forward and shook his hand with a firm and no-nonsense grip. "And no, there is no Mr. Friday."

"Do you mind if I lock us in?" Langdon asked, closing the door behind her and flicking on the lights. "We can talk in my office, but I don't want any customers coming in thinking we're open."

"That's fine. I guess if I'm not safe with a private detective, than I'm not safe with anyone." She reached over and squeezed his arm.

She kept her hand on him as they walked back to his office.

"Chair or couch?" Langdon asked, motioning her into the office. She chose comfort over style and he joined her on the old battered couch. "Tell me about your sister, Miss Friday."

She crossed a perfectly browned calf over her leg and leaned back. "What do you want to know?"

"Let's start with a name."

"Amy Springer."

"So, she is married?"

"Yes."

"And the husband? He doesn't know where she is?"

"I believe he is the issue."

"How so?"

"I've become increasingly concerned that he was abusing her. They live in Falmouth, and I live in Virginia, so it's hard to tell. I haven't seen her in a year, but we text every week, or we used to. I have to admit I was caught up in my own life, but then a week ago I received this letter." She handed Langdon a crumpled envelope.

It was addressed to Delilah Friday with a Virginia address. The postmark was Brunswick, Maine. There was no return address. He pulled out the yellow-lined piece of paper.

Delilah,
    I just wanted to let you know that I'm okay. Paul and I have been having trouble over the past year, and he has gone so far as to hit me. He claims that if I ever left him that he would kill me. For this reason I am going to disappear for a little while. Once everything blows over, I will contact you, but until then, know that I am safe.
                                Love and hugs,
                                Amy

"It sounds as if she is safe and doesn't want to be found." Langdon stood and walked over to sit at his desk. He found it hard to think straight when with the scent of her perfume in his nostrils. "And who still sends letters?"

"I hope that is true, Mr. Langdon, but what if he's done something to her? What if he forced her to write the letter and has her locked in the basement? Or worse, what if he murdered her?"

Langdon nodded, thinking the latter was a bit dramatic. "Have you talked to him?"

"I called him right after I got the note, and he said she ran off with some guy, using a name for her I choose not to repeat."

Langdon had a bookstore to run. In the past two days he'd been hired to investigate the blackmail of a United States Senator, and the murder of three young women with the accused being his client. He had a wife. His daughter was coming home for a visit next week. He had a dog. He knew he should not take on another case. He just didn't have the time.

"I don't know what else to do, Mr. Langdon. You have to help me."

~ ~ ~ ~ ~

He would've taken the case even if she weren't gorgeous, Langdon told himself as he drove home. Downtown Brunswick was nestled between the Androscoggin River down by Fort Andross to the north, and Bowdoin College at the top of the hill, a distance of just about half-a-mile, to the south. That morning, he'd seen incoming freshman traveling in packs around the campus, but now they must have gone off into the wilds for orientation events, and the college was desolate in the dusk.

He had yet to begin his search for the blackmailer, but somehow had managed to pick up two more cases. Come to think of it, if you didn't count the senator sleeping with a woman not her husband, these were the first three cases of the year that didn't involve some sort of adultery. Oh, yeah, of course, there had been the helicopter parent who wanted tabs kept on her precious son, a Bowdoin kid who'd taken a bigger interest in weed, alcohol, and girls than in his studies. He'd felt bad ratting the kid out, but mom was going to find out anyway when he failed. All the same, Langdon had held back some of the more damning evidence, as not even a helicopter mom wants to see her son passed out in a bathtub with puke on his face.

Though three cases were over his limit by two, he hadn't even started investigating and the first clue had fallen from the sky. It had been a piece of luck, Star recognizing the woman in the picture as his former law partner. Langdon had known the woman as well, but would never have matched the angular lady from the past to the more mature woman in the photo. Luck like that doesn't come along very often. Now, all he had to do was find her. Chabal had promised to do some photo editing and get a head shot, minus the senator, of Abigail Austin-Peters, Jordan Fitzpatrick, or, perhaps it was best to use the name she was currently using, Kamrin Jorgenson.

He could hoof it around all the local hotels and motels tomorrow asking if anybody had seen the woman. He'd concoct some story about her having been left an inheritance or some sort of thing. People were more liable to finger a person if they thought they were helping them out instead of getting them in trouble. He guessed that spoke to the basic goodness of humanity.

If he could get Jack to work the bookstore, then he'd take Chabal with him. People talked to Chabal. There was something trustworthy about her. Of course, that trust was a double-edged sword because it was also not in his wife to lie, cheat, or steal—all necessary to be an effective private dick. Nah, he'd bring her if he could. She was better company than most other human beings, he'd found.

But, he asked himself, what was going to happen if he did find Kamrin Jorgenson? The directions had been very specific that he was not to approach her, but rather simply notify Maxwell Mercer rather than the senator. It had been suggested he would make a better point person, simply because his schedule was much less demanding. The senator was in Washington Monday through Thursday of every week, coming home for long weekends, but these were usually filled with events as well. And it certainly wouldn't do to have anyone catch on that the senator was in communication with a private dick. The media would just love that.

Langdon pulled into his driveway, hitting the remote for the garage, and eased the Jeep into his space. He hadn't yet decided if he was going to mention to Chabal that his latest client was possibly the most beautiful woman he'd ever seen. Might get awkward. Maybe it was just best not to mention anything other than she'd hired him to find her sister. He sighed. Then, certainly, Chabal would be angry if she met the woman and Langdon had *not* mentioned her loveliness. Maybe he should just say she was a good-looking woman? Or was that worse?

It wasn't like he was going to have an affair with the lady. First of all, he loved his wife, was very happy with Chabal. He would never jeopardize that, even if this new client showed an interest other than a harmless flirtation. Also, she had to be at least fifteen years younger than him, and even if he were in his prime, she was way out of his league. Plus, he knew that he'd developed a bit of a paunch over the past few years and his face was a bit puffier than it used to be, despite the fact he still went to the gym most days, played basketball a couple of times a week, and walked the woods with dog almost daily.

He almost wished he hadn't gone back to the bookstore for his briefcase. Almost.

Chapter 7

Sunday

Langdon woke Sunday morning and eased his body carefully from bed. Dog was waiting for him to serve breakfast. It never ceased to amaze Langdon that the canine could get so excited about a small cup of dried food with a splash of salmon oil. Every day, twice a day— the same thing; it would drive him nuts.

They grabbed the Sunday paper from the box and read about the horrible state of the nation for a bit, before skipping to the sports pages and checking the Red Sox score. While baseball was intriguing when the Sox were doing well, it was almost football season, and Langdon skimmed through looking for the latest on Brady and Gronk.

Chabal wandered out, grabbed a cup of joe, and turned the television on so that she could, in turn, curse at the state of affairs in the Oval Office. She wore sweatpants and had put on a long-sleeve striped sweatshirt that zippered in the front, covering her white tee underneath. Langdon was reminded of the not-so-subtle threat made just a night ago against his wife, and he again felt the anger in the pit of his stomach.

He'd gotten in the night before and eaten some leftover pasta, checked if Jack could open the store, and then he and Chabal had tumbled into bed like the fifty-year-olds they were. It was not yet 10:00 on a Saturday night, but once there, they'd indeed given in to the twenty-year-olds' urges that still ran strong within them.

Langdon put some bacon on the skillet and cut up some potatoes and onions to put in the pan. Soon, the magic combo of aromas brought Jack down the stairs, better than any alarm clock, ensuring that he was up in time to go sell books. Langdon dropped a couple of English muffins in the toaster and fried up six eggs, and the three of them sat down for breakfast.

"You all set with the store?" Langdon asked Jack. "I should have your mother in by 2:00 at the latest to help you out."

"No problem," Jack replied. "What are you guys doing?"

"Working a case," Langdon said.

Chabal laughed. "Real private detective stuff. We're going to visit all the hotels and motels from Freeport to Bath looking for a woman."

"Usually I find the woman first and then go to the motel," Langdon cracked, and then cringed, remembering that he hadn't yet mentioned his latest client to Chabal.

"And by 'usually,' you mean *in your dreams?*" Chabal retorted.

"What's her name? I could skim the internet in my free time to see if I can find out anything about her." Jack was used to their crass banter, but he was interested in helping out with more than the bookstore. He'd always wanted to be part of the private detective business, having grown up hearing the stories of the more important cases Langdon had worked.

Langdon had skimmed the internet looking for information on Senator Mercer, but he hadn't thought to search for Kamrin Jorgenson, or any of her aliases.

"I believe her name was originally Jordan Fitzpatrick. She was in a law firm with Star back in the day, trying to save the environment. When she couldn't get it done legally, she started down a darker path of preserving the earth. Twenty years ago, she was using the name of Abigail Austin-Peters and working for a nuclear power plant. When her plot to sabotage the plant was foiled," Chabal snickered at his use of the word foiled, "she disappeared into thin air. She recently reappeared under the name of Kamrin Jorgenson in a case I'm working on."

"Wow," Jack said. "Text me those names, and I'll see what I can find. She was the woman in the DownEast Power case? I'm all over it. Beautiful Sunday in the summer? The bookstore should be pretty slow."

~ ~ ~ ~ ~

They took the back way to Freeport, winding along Maquoit Bay and passing at intervals the long driveways they imagined led to wealthy mansions on the water, tall pines intentionally blocking their view. The Bernard Hotel—where the illicit affair that lead to blackmail had occurred—was in Freeport, so it seemed that would be the likely place to start. Langdon was fairly certain the woman wouldn't still be there, but it was as good as any place to begin.

"So, you're telling me this woman blackmailing the senator with dirty pictures is the same one who shut down DownEast Power, blackmailed the chief so that he killed himself, broke Jimmy's jaw after fucking him, and then disappeared into thin air?" Chabal was summarizing aloud what they'd come up with so far.

"Star is certain that it's her, and he should know. Once Star has seen a customer, he never forgets them. I can't imagine he wouldn't recognize a former law partner—not to mention passionate lover—even if it is some twenty years later."

"And you think she's still around?"

"She's gotta be somewhere."

"She could be anywhere in the world, for all we know."

"Somebody slid the envelope with the pictures under the senator's doorway in Bath just a few days ago. That would suggest that, as of then, she was still around."

"Or somebody she's working with," Chabal observed.

"That could be, but I got a sense she's still around. The woman I remember from DownEast Power days wouldn't let other people play her hand."

"Okay, we'll trust your private dick instincts." She chuckled, pointedly eyeing his crotch. "What did the blackmail note say? I don't think you ever told me that."

"There was no note. Just the pictures."

Chabal cursed and then laughed. "How can we be working a blackmail case if there is no blackmail?"

"You think somebody just dropped off those pictures as a friendly gesture? Hey, I had a camera in your hotel room and took some pictures of you having sex with somebody who doesn't appear to be your husband—somebody who doesn't even have the same anatomy as your husband—and I thought you might like copies for yourself. Put them on the mantle or use it as a Christmas card?"

"I'm just saying that, minus a blackmail note, it's a little strange. You don't have to be a dink."

Langdon pulled into the back parking lot of the Bernard Hotel. "What is it you're trying to say when you call me a dink?" He offered a few possible definitions as Chabal punched him in the arm.

"How do you know she's the blackmailer? Maybe she just hooked up and, unbeknownst to herself, somebody was filming it?"

"I had thought of that until Star identified her. A, she's a known criminal, and B, she's used pictures for blackmail before."

"Okay. How do you want to handle this?"

"How about I go to the front desk and you go to the bar, each with a picture of KJ."

"KJ?"

"Kamrin Jorgenson is the most recent name she's used, so I guess that's what we should go with," Langdon said, somewhat sheepishly.

Chabal shook her head and Langdon thought she may have uttered "what a dink" under her breath.

~ ~ ~ ~ ~

Twenty minutes later they met in the car with nothing to show for their efforts. The manager had refused to be helpful, and when Langdon had pushed him because it involved a crime at the hotel, he'd suggested they call the police. Unfortunately, this was unacceptable due to the sensitivity of the case. Langdon had been under the false assumption that, just like on television, the manager would want to keep the whole affair very hush-hush, and thus would be incredibly helpful. He then had the equally wrong notion that just like on television, his offer of a double sawbuck would loosen the man's tongue, but that had led to a threat to call the police.

The bartender had thought he'd seen her earlier in the previous week, but after that was no help. Chabal had the bright idea to call the hotel and ask to speak to Kamrin Jorgenson, and was told that nobody by that name was staying there. She also checked on Jordan Fitzpatrick and Abigail Austin-Peters, the two known aliases of the woman—or perhaps one of them was actually her real name?

The next three places were motels, and Langdon went with his original plan that they were looking for their sister because their mother had died and her share of the estate was $20,000. This seemed to receive a better response, and most of the desk workers agreed to keep a picture of KJ with Langdon's card attached in case they spotted her. In this way they worked their way back up the Route 1 corridor where the majority of lodging opportunities had been built over the years to capitalize on the tourists heading north up the coast to Bar Harbor.

They stopped at the 7-11 in Brunswick to see if Danny T. was working. He was. Danny T. was about five inches over five feet and a minimum of 300 pounds. His hair was greasy and his clothes dirty, but Langdon was well aware that nobody had the pulse on the town of Brunswick like the former fisherman, blackballed from the Gulf of Maine waterfront for having made the choice to cut through a net full of herring to save a buddy's arm. The young man had spent the last thirty years clerking at various establishments until his slovenly appearance and utter lack of personal hygiene got him fired. Luckily, unemployment was very low these days, and the bits of that morning's bacon and eggs on his shirt had been overlooked by the manager, as well as his slovenly appearance.

"Yankees/Red Sox tonight," Danny T. said without a hello when he saw Langdon. "I got a fin says Sox mop them up."

Langdon looked around, but the only person in the store was back at the drink cooler looking for cheap beer. "You're on." He didn't want to be caught betting on the hated Yankees, but the bet was Danny T.'s unspoken quid pro quo, payment for the information the little guy had immediately realized Langdon was seeking. Five dollars was cheap, far cheaper than the shame of being caught betting against the Sox.

"Where you been?" Danny T. demanded. "I ain't seen ya over at Rosie's in a couple of weeks."

"I'm usually there before eight," Langdon replied. This was the normal pitter-patter of their conversation. It was like comfort food for a hangover.

"I'm on the twelve to seven shift here, so I'm not usually there until after ten," Danny T. said, repeating a conversation whose narrow ground they'd trodden five times in the past year. "You looking for that lesbo blackmailing the senator?"

Langdon was shocked momentarily but then realized his conversation with Bart had probably been the grist of the gossip mill at the diner since yesterday morning. Then there was Danny T.'s slander. It was one thing for Ray to spit out insults, but this man was a friend, sort of, even if he was redneck and uneducated. "Lesbo isn't really an acceptable term," he observed mildly, turning to look at Chabal who was shaking her head and frowning.

Danny T. glared at them both, but his friendship with Langdon was a highlight of his life, and he quickly backed down. "I didn't mean nothing by it. Hell, it's none of my business who sleeps with who. You looking for the... lady... who is blackmailing the senator?"

Langdon smiled, for Danny T. did make it his business to know who was sleeping with whom, but he accepted the apology. "I am." He placed the picture of KJ flat down on the counter. "You seen her?"

"She ain't been in here." 7-11 was the hub of downtown Brunswick, located right on the corner where Pleasant Street spilled into Maine Street. "But I mightta got something for you. One of the boys out front said he was cleaning rooms out to the Greenlander Motel, you know the place out past Cook's Corner across from the bowling alley, and a nice-looking older woman gave him a twenty for his troubles. He said she's driving a rental with Masshole plates and has been there all week."

"One of the guys out front right now?" Langdon demanded.

"Yeah, I just smoked a butt with him." Danny T. waddled around the corner to the door. "Larry, there on the end, he's the one."

"Thanks, Danny T. I'll give you four-to-one odds on the game tonight." Langdon led Chabal out the door to the front of the store where three rough looking codgers were smoking cigarettes right next to a three-foot-tall sign that read "No Smoking Within 25 feet of Store Entrance." One of them tucked a brown bag behind his leg as they approached.

"Hello, honey," a crusty man with wrinkled leather for skin said to Chabal, his eyes crawling up and down the blue floral wrap summer dress she wore.

"Hi, bub. What's that you're hiding?" she asked.

"You Larry?" Langdon asked the man on the end. He knew Chabal could more than take care of herself.

"Who's asking?" the man asked, licking his parched lips.

"Andrew Jackson," Langdon replied, taking a crumpled bill from his pocket.

"I might be," the codger replied. "Depends what Andrew Jackson wants." They both knew this was a lie, as twenty dollars would buy a fifth of Allen's Coffee Brandy, the high-octane tipple of choice in this part of the world, and a pack of smokes.

"You seen this lady?" Langdon asked, holding out the picture of KJ. Larry took the eight-by-ten and peered intently at it. "Maybe."

Langdon handed him the bill. He pulled his money clip out and retrieved a crisper twenty from its magnetic grasp. "You give me the right answer where, and this one is yours as well." He knew Larry would tell him anything he wanted to hear for the money, and wanted to ensure the man's story matched that of Danny T's.

It did.

~ ~ ~ ~ ~

Twelve minutes later, Langdon and Chabal pulled into the entrance of The Greenlander Motel. The main office was nestled next to the busy Bath Road, and was centered in the drive that curled around in a full circle, all ground units with parking in front of each. Langdon trolled the loop looking for Massachusetts plates. Two of the thirteen cars had the red, white, and blue Spirit of America car tags, but neither gave the impression of being a rental car, not at least from this century.

He went to pull out, not really able to stake out the units without sticking out like a sore thumb, when Chabal grabbed his arm and said, "Wait, I've got an idea."

"What?" he asked.

"Wait here," she replied, jumping out of the car. She went into the front office, and Langdon truly hoped she wasn't flashing the picture of KJ around, which was a sure-fire way of scaring the woman off.

Ten minutes later she jumped back into the passenger seat. "Pull over there," she said, pointing at a corner unit. "I got us a room."

"You what?"

"I booked a room. Seventy-nine bucks. Got the receipt, so you can write it off as a deduction."

Langdon began to argue, thought better of it, realized it was a pretty good idea, and pulled over to the indicated room. It was an excellent choice with a view of the entrance, the exit, and about eighty percent of the rooms in the complex.

~ ~ ~ ~ ~

"So, what should we do?" Chabal had sprawled out on the bed. The room was run-down, but clean, with a medium fridge and a two-burner stove.

"We wait, and watch," Langdon replied. He'd pulled a chair over to the window, off to an angle, watching the entrance. "If she doesn't come in by sundown, I'll take the picture over to the front desk and ask if she's still here. If you want to take the Jeep, you can leave me here."

Chabal sighed. "I've got a better idea." She stood up and lifted her sundress over her head. Somehow, her bra was already off. She stood there in blue panties and sandals and nothing else.

"Cut it out," Langdon said, his eyes riveted to her body. "We have to keep an eye out."

"Oh, come on." Chabal sashayed to the corner of the bed closest to him. "Cops always fall asleep during stakeouts in the movies. How is this any different?" She picked up the matching blue bra from the floor, threw it at his head, clapping her hands when she got a full ringer.

"That's usually when somebody gets murdered," Langdon retorted in a whisper.

Chabal sidled next to Langdon who was in the corner, her hands on the plate glass window, bent over at a forty-five degree angle, eyebrows lifted in suggestion. "This way I can get what I want, and we can keep an eye out for the bad people."

Langdon wrapped one arm around her and slung her onto the bed. "Get out of the window, already," he said, kissing her neck.

~ ~ ~ ~ ~

Twenty minutes later Chabal's phone buzzed, disturbing their post-coital languor. It was Jack, calling from the bookstore to say that it was starting to get pretty busy, he had to pee, and he was hungry. Chabal promised to be right there, pulled her undergarments from the floor, and slid her dress back on. The sandals had never come off. She checked her hair in the bathroom mirror and was out the door. That left Langdon without a vehicle, but it wasn't like he was supposed to do anything if he found KJ, other than to call Maxwell Mercer, that is.

Langdon went back to his spot in the chair watching the parking lot. Patience was a skill that he'd learned over the years, never suspecting back when he was ten and first wanted to be a private detective that this was the most important trait in his chosen line of work. He was an avid fan of the Hardy Boys, most likely because of the relationship Frank and Joe had with their detective father, unlike Langdon's own deadbeat dad. He decided on his tenth birthday that he either wanted to be a detective, or an author like Franklin Dixon. A few years later, when he realized with disappointment that Dixon was just a pen name for an assortment of writers, his career choice seemed fated, and a private detective was born.

He was his own first client, assigning himself the case of finding his missing father, who'd walked out on them when Langdon was just seven years old. The day after he graduated high school, he'd packed his thirteen-year-old twin brothers into his Chevy Nova and took a road trip to Buffalo, the last known address of John Langdon, according to his mother. She had refused to talk about him, except for once when Langdon was sixteen, which was how he knew to start the search in Buffalo.

They hadn't found their father, and the idea of becoming a private detective languished until his loony Aunt Zelda died a few years later and left him a chunk of money, enough to open a bookstore and hang out a private detective shingle. The rest, as they say, was history. Someday, he still planned on tracking down his father, but it no longer seemed all that important.

After a bit, Langdon pulled on his own Madras shorts, and carefully buttoned up his white shirt with its more formal collar. It wasn't often that he coordinated his colors, but he'd chosen this plain shirt for occasions when his job demanded he blend into the background, just another tourist or maybe a shop owner out on his lunch break. He slid into his Bean sandals, ran his fingers through his scraggly hair, and popped on purple-tinted sunglasses. Making sure he had the room key, he took a stroll around the motel parking lot to make certain he hadn't missed the arrival of KJ. He was just returning to the room when she pulled in and drove to one of the rear units. The driver was a woman no longer young, and the car had Mass. plates, some midrange Ford that shouted "rental." He paused by the door, as if fiddling with the key, a real key, not one of those plastic cards.

As she climbed out of the car, he glimpsed her face, bringing back a rush of memories. He'd been investigating a murder at a nuclear power plant where she was the public relations director, and he'd met with her several times. She was intelligent, good-looking, and brash in a good way. Only later he'd realized she was running a scam to get the plant shut down. This deception had included blackmail, violence, and had led to several deaths. Yet, Langdon thought with a shake of his head, he had to admit that he still had a fondness for the woman, even after all of that. He respected the driving determination to protect the environment that seemingly motivated her every action. She was also, he remembered, very good at manipulating men to further her ambitions. Jonathan Starling had been one of her first victims, taking her on as a law—and bed—partner before she discarded him like a used tissue when he dragged his feet in resistance to her more radical and violent methods. Instead, she'd started sleeping with his partner and drove that man to become the Governor of Maine. When political power had not been strong enough to close DownEast Power, the nuclear power plant, she'd played the other men involved, including the town's chief of police, like pawns in a chess game. Jimmy 4 by Four had been the last to succumb to her sexual appetite and manipulation, drawing the lawyer into her web just when Langdon had begun to close in on her illegal activities.

Now the woman was blackmailing a United States Senator. Langdon stepped into his room and called Maxwell Mercer. The man answered on the third ring. Langdon told him that the blackmailer was at the Greenlander Motel, and gave the man directions, even though he'd probably driven by it a thousand times. Room 19. Then he sat back to wait and see what would happen. Would the senator's bodyguards show up? Would Maxwell himself come and try to broker a deal? They couldn't very well arrest the woman, since the point was to cover-up the extra-marital affair and the fact that Senator Mercer was gay to boot. While that last part shouldn't matter, with the bulk of her supporters being faithful and conservative churchgoers, Langdon had an inkling that it would matter tremendously.

Surely, they wouldn't go so far as to kill Kamrin? He asked himself the question only half wondering if that was just plain crazy. Langdon had little idea how big politics worked, but he'd seen enough movies and he'd read enough books to know that even an informed citizen didn't hear about half the things mercenaries and such got up to for the good of the Republic. One death was miniscule in the greater effort to make the world a better place, or so the argument went. *Shut up!* Langdon told himself. He was letting his imagination run wild. The real disappointment was that he'd solved the case in less than three days. He was counting on the $90 an hour to help bolster the finances. At least now he could concentrate on his other two cases. Delilah was paying for his services, even if it was far less than the senator was paying, but it was better than the pro bono work investigating the Old Port Killer.

KJ interrupted his financial calculations by abruptly coming out of her room, walking around the corner of the building and disappearing behind it. Langdon hurriedly exited his own room and followed her, coming around the corner only to see her running full-tilt through the scrub brush that dotted the landscape. How the hell had she made him? With a grunt of exasperation, he began to chase her. What would he do if he caught her? He was about fifty yards behind her, not certain if he even wanted to catch her at all. She looked over her shoulder and spotted him and began running faster. Langdon cursed and forced his aging body into a more determined effort.

They crossed a small, desolate, dead-end road, and almost immediately passed through the thicker brush on the edge of Route 1. KJ ran fearlessly across the northbound lane and into the trees on the median separating north from south. Langdon whacked his face on a pine branch, stumbled going up the incline to the road, and was almost flattened by a pick-up. With horns blaring behind him, he weaved his way across the two lanes of traffic, pausing as he made the safety of the median to gather his wits. There was a car parked in the breakdown lane of the southbound Route 1, and KJ was climbing into it. Langdon floundered his way across the fifty-foot strip of land, just in time to catch the license plate, 389JK.

Chapter 8

Langdon chose an armchair in a quiet corner of the Lenin Stop Coffee Shop to wait for Maxwell Mercer. The front of the store was filled with comfortable armchairs and sofas, and the middle with tables, while the walls to each side had counters just wide enough for a laptop, stools fitting neatly under them. At this time of day, the customer base was mostly a scattering of Bowdoin College students and not much more, so here Langdon and Maxwell could have some privacy. It had been a tough call to make, after losing KJ, to tell Maxwell Mercer that she had fled. It didn't help that his face was scratched from his headlong pursuit through the branches, adding a physical sting to an already battered ego.

He'd been forced to call a taxi, as Chabal had taken the Jeep earlier, and the cab took twenty minutes to arrive. Langdon had spent the time stewing, but then he'd gone over and convinced the manager to open KJ's room. There was nothing in it, and Langdon remembered a pack on her back. This did not help, to realize that she'd outrun him carrying her personal belongings along for the ride. Too bad he hadn't brought dog, because the canine would most certainly have raced ahead and tripped her up, thinking it was all a big game.

He ordered a large coffee, black, and was annoyed when it took too long to cool down enough to drink. He'd already scalded his lips and tongue three times by the time Maxwell came in. The man was smiling, and it struck Langdon that he'd never seen the man without a grin plastered to his face. His chin came to a point below his bright-white teeth, enclosed within a fold of neck, even though the man was not overweight. Langdon didn't think that finding the woman blackmailing the man's wife and then having her escape was a particularly good time to be smiling. Maxwell ordered himself a scone and a latte, waiting at the counter for the hot whipped coffee to be made before coming over to sit across from Langdon.

"Maxwell," Langdon said nodding his head once. "Are you sure it's okay to be seen together?"

"Nobody knows the husband of a senator, especially in Maine where people don't go in that much for the celebrity thing." He had on square silver glasses today, the metal blending in with his eyebrows. Langdon wasn't sure if the man had worn them the other day, so well did they meld with his features.

"Her car is still there in the parking lot if you want to search it," Langdon said, giving the man the license plate number. "Or better yet, keep an eye on it to see if she comes back for it. Do you want me to do that?"

"That won't be necessary."

"What were you going to do with her if she hadn't run?" This was the burning question in Langdon's mind.

"Buy her off," Maxwell said, more bluntly than Langdon would've expected.

"Is that a typical response?"

Maxwell shrugged his shoulders.

"What if she didn't accept your offer?"

Maxwell, again, shrugged his shoulders.

"I know who she is."

"What? You mean you have her name?" The smile showed just a hint of cracking.

"She used to be law partners with a guy who works for me at

the bookstore. He was there yesterday when you were in the store."
Langdon watched the man's face, but there was little to be read.

"The old geezer? Used to be a lawyer?"

Langdon laughed. "He had a few tough years. As a matter of fact, it's your blackmailer who sent Star spinning into the brown bottle. The stress of a career in law is not for everybody, I guess. He seems happy selling books."

"If you want to send me a bill, I will make sure you get a check for your services," Maxwell said.

"What do you mean?"

"You have done your job, Mr. Langdon. We asked that you track down the blackmailer, and you have flushed her out. We will take it from here."

"You don't want me to find where she fled?"

"No, my boy. We will take it from here." Maxwell had his checkbook out with a pen poised. "How much do we owe you?"

"I would have to put a bill together."

"Of course. Send it along when you're ready."

Langdon stared the man in the eye. It would seem that he was being dismissed, but why? "Don't you want her name?"

"Name? Oh, yes, of course." Maxwell pulled a napkin from his scone and hovered the pen over it instead of the checkbook.

Langdon's mind churned in confusion. First, Maxwell hadn't thought to ask the blackmailer's name without prodding, and second, he was surprised he was already being dismissed from the case. "Jordan Fitzpatrick. She had a law firm up in Madison in the '90s. When I first met her, she was using the name Abigail Austin-Peters and working for DownEast Power. Remember that scandal? The cracks and all? She was in the middle of all that."

Either Maxwell's face had tightened, or his glasses had suddenly loosened. "I remember that whole debacle," he admitted. "You were the one who exposed the whole hideous crime? That, I didn't recall." He scribbled the name on the napkin. "Again, thank you for your service. Just send a bill when you're ready. You still have my card?" he asked, standing up and reaching out his hand.

Langdon remained sitting, leaning back and looking up at the man quizzically. "I don't feel like I've finished the job, not quite yet."

"You found the woman. You've come up with her name. That is all I asked you to do, so there's no more need to keep poking around."

"I found her, but she seems to have disappeared again."

"Never you mind," Maxwell said. "We will take it from here."

"What do you plan on doing when you find her?"

"As I said, Mr. Langdon, we will buy her off."

"What is it she wants from you? Did you get a blackmail demand?" Langdon asked, suddenly feeling as if he were only now seeing the forest and not just the trees he'd been blindly runnung through. Maybe KJ had reached out with her exigencies. If so, what were they? It could not be anything as petty as money, not unless the woman he remembered from twenty years ago had dramatically changed.

"That is no longer any of your concern, Mr. Langdon." Maxwell's eyes were steely behind the lenses of his glasses, but the smile never left his face. "We will handle it from here on out."

"This woman is a radical. She believes in saving the environment in any way possible, even to the point of playing with sabotaging a nuclear power plant. She's not going to go away with a bribe."

"You let me handle that part of things. You've done what you've been hired for." Maxwell waved his hand dismissively.

"I believe your wife is the one who hired me," Langdon said. "I'd like to speak with her before I drop the case."

Maxwell stopped smiling and stood up. "Whatever you like, Mr. Langdon." He nodded and left the way he'd come.

~ ~ ~ ~ ~

Langdon was crossing the wide Maine Street to check in at the bookstore when 4 by Four called. He'd set up a meeting with

Tugiramhoro Mduwimana for four and wanted Langdon there if possible. Jewell had already said yes to the meeting. Langdon checked his watch as a small hatchback sped up, making him realize he was dawdling too much in the crosswalk. It was 3:00 now, and he agreed to meet at the Cumberland County Jail in Portland. Hopefully his Jeep was downtown.

The bookstore was hopping, but Jack, Chabal, and Starling had a good handle on things. Dog came careening through customers and shelves, happy to see him. Langdon was forced to apologize to three people, including a mother who had rushed to pick up her toddler before the canine swept him off his feet and sent him flying like a bowling pin. Langdon pretended to discipline dog, but they both knew better, and dog appeared appropriately chagrined for a total of ten seconds.

"I thought you were off today?" Langdon asked Starling.

"Yeah, but what else am I going to do? Go to church? I think that ship has sailed."

"Make sure you make a note of your time so you get paid for it."

"Don't worry, I already took enough cash out of the register to cover my time, and then some," Starling said smugly.

"I'm sure we won't miss that $5," Langdon retorted.

"Hey, Langdon," Jack called his stepfather of twenty years by his last name, as did just about everybody else. "I spent some time searching for that lady this morning when the store was slow but didn't have any luck. But Mom said you found her?"

"Found her and lost her," Langdon grunted.

"Did you say lost her?" Chabal turned from the customer she was waiting on.

"She came back a bit after you left, but must have seen me, or been tipped off by something. Whatever the case, she took off running, and a car picked her up on the shoulder of Route 1."

"Did you get the plate number?" Star asked. The lady at the counter didn't seem to mind waiting for her change, just as caught up in the conversation as the rest of them.

"Yeah, but it doesn't matter. Mercer dropped us from the case."

"But she's still on the lam," Star retorted. "The senator can't just change her mind like that. Damn fickle women."

"It wasn't the senator. It was Maxwell."

"He can't fire us," Chabal chimed in. "We were hired to find the blackmailer, and I'm not so sure the woman you just let outrun you and the blackmailer we're looking for are one and the same."

Outrun him? "She didn't outrun me," Langdon blustered. "I was catching up when she got in a car and drove off."

"And what do you mean 'fickle women'?" Chabal rounded on Star.

Langdon took the distraction as an opportunity. "I have to get down to the Cumberland County Jail. I can fill you all in later. C'mon dog, you're probably due a road trip." He slipped out the door as the lady at the counter asked if that had all just been an act to promote mystery books. She sounded like she was from Connecticut, where they probably actually did things like that.

Once on 295 South, Langdon called Bart. "You at the station by any chance?"

"Nope. And not at the donut shop either."

"You think you can do me a favor?"

"Is there any other reason you'd be calling?"

"I need you to run a plate for me."

"And you think the Brunswick PD is your personal one-stop info shop?"

"Remember the lady who broke 4 by Four's jaw?" Langdon knew if there were any softening the gruffness of Bart, it would be reliving this event, which never ceased to bring a smile to his broad face.

"Remember? If I ever run into her, I'm going to give her a hug, right before I arrest her."

"She's back in town. Turns out she's the woman in the pictures with the senator. Almost two hours ago she rode off in a waiting car. I need to know who it's registered to."

"Okay, then. Give it to me. But you got to keep me in the loop. I want to be the arresting officer."

Langdon chose not to tell him that they weren't arresting her. Not yet. "Maine plate, 389JK."

"You're shitting me. Don't be messing me around here."

"What are you talking about?"

"Silver Oldsmobile?"

"Sounds about right."

"I'm parked right behind it. About an hour ago a guy calls up and says his car's been stolen. He was grocery shopping at Shaw's in the Merrymeeting Plaza out to Cooks Corner and came out and the car's gone. When I showed up, I had him drive around the lot with me. Probably a half-dozen times I've had cars reported stolen and the driver just forgot where they parked. Sometimes they're not even drunk. Sure enough, we just found it, parked down by Bed Bath & Beyond."

"Don't disbelieve the poor guy. Our girl just got into that car on Route 1 South. It's all tied up in that blackmail thing I was telling you about."

Bart whistled over the phone.

"Look, I'll tell you about it later. I'm almost where I'm going."

"Yeah, and I guess I got to write this up as a stolen vehicle returned to the wrong spot," Bart said sourly, and hung up the line.

~ ~ ~ ~ ~

Langdon eyed the black clouds rolling in over Portland. The key to being in an open Jeep in a rainstorm was to keep the speed at 45 miles-per-hour, as that caused the drops to get swept over the top in the wind tunnel created by the forward motion. He wasn't a big fan of putting the soft-top on in the summer, but supposed he was going to have to do it anyway, for dog wouldn't be allowed inside the jail, and pedestrians would complain if he tied him outside in the rain, even if he had had a leash with him.

4 by Four and Jewell were already sitting in the austere waiting room when Langdon entered and checked in.

"They might not let you back out of here," 4 by Four said as Langdon sat down next to them.

"Why's that?"

"You look like shit, man. You look like a man fallen on bad times, is what you look like."

Langdon looked down and had to admit the lawyer was right. His sandals were muddy from chasing KJ through the woods, with brown splatters spotting his legs and shorts, but it was the clean white shirt he'd worn just to look good today that had taken the brunt of the day. It'd probably been doing fine until he'd been thrown to the floor of the motel by his wife, then there were the sweat stains from the chase, an errant branch likely the source of the rip in one sleeve, and then a final soaking by the storm that broke just as he was putting the top on the Jeep, the source of the droplets of water dripping from his brow.

"Yeah, well I've been chasing after your mystery girlfriend," Langdon said.

"My mystery girlfriend?"

"Guess who is back in town?"

"No idea," 4 by Four said.

"Jordan Fitzpatrick, or as you knew her, Abigail Austin-Peters, now calling herself Kamrin Jorgenson."

4 by Four sat silently for a long moment, absently stroking his jaw. "Wow. I thought she was gone for good. What were you doing chasing her?"

"Long story. I'll tell you later."

"Did she turn a fire hose on you?"

"I blame the weatherman," Langdon replied. Before he could ask what the plan was, a guard called them into an inner room. There were tables set up with inmates talking with visitors, but they bypassed these to go into a smaller room.

"I was able to get us a private room," 4 by Four said. He sat down and pulled a single folder out of his soft-leather briefcase and set a pen on top of it, steepling his hands in front of him.

"You leading this thing?" Langdon asked him. "What's the angle?"

"Simple meet and greet," 4 by Four replied. "Jewell introduces me as a lawyer willing to take his case pro bono. I introduce you as my investigator. We get him to sign some papers making it official, and get his general take on what is going on."

Two guards came in with a man in an orange jump suit that engulfed his thin body. Langdon was reminded of a Halloween costume he'd seen the previous year of a teenager in a pumpkin outfit.

"Please remove the shackles," 4 by Four said. The guards were taking no chances with a serial rapist and murderer.

The smaller guard stared at 4 by Four as if he'd threatened him to throw-down, but the taller one smiled and produced the keys that freed the man's hands and feet. "Ring if you need anything. You have half an hour." The two guards then ambled out.

"Hello, Tug. How are you holding up?" Jewell reached across and grasped his hand.

The man from Burundi didn't reply. His dark eyes stared at 4 by Four and Langdon. There wasn't a crease on his face, his skin drawn thinly across his skull so that his ears jutted out like jug handles. His nose flared as he breathed, but otherwise there was no reaction.

"Tug—these two men are my friends and want to help you. Jimmy 4 by Four is a lawyer and Goff Langdon is a private investigator."

4 by Four was slightly miffed as he'd spent an hour working on the correct pronunciation of the man's name, and now here was Jewell calling him Tug. "Can you tell us what happened?" he asked.

"Nothing happened," Tug replied in fairly unaccented English. "I returned to my room from work on Friday and the police were there. They arrested me."

"Did they read you your rights?" Jimmy asked.

"Yes. Something about Miranda."

"Did they tell you why they arrested you?"

"They said I had raped and killed those University women. The ones all over the news."

Langdon looked into the flat dark eyes of the young man, past the defiance, and saw the fear. "We're not in Burundi," he said gently.

"Why am I in jail for something I did not do?" Tug demanded.

"The police found a school ID of one of the girls and a knife with blood on it in your room," 4 by four said.

Tug shook his head. "That is what the police in Burundi would do. This is no different. Do not tell me I am not in Burundi."

"Do you know why the ID would be in your room?" 4 by Four asked.

"Maybe because the policemen put it there," Tug replied.

"Do you own a knife, about this long?" 4 by Four held his hands seven inches apart.

"I own no knife," Tug replied. "Mrs. Levesque has steak knives, but they are much smaller."

"Mrs. Levesque is your landlord?" Langdon asked.

"Yes."

"Do you have friends in Portland?"

"What do you mean?"

"Anybody that can be a character witness?" Langdon also wanted to question them, for he didn't know where else to start. If this young man really hadn't commited these horrendous crimes, then why had he been framed?

"I speak with a few people at work, but mostly I study, go to church," Tug replied.

"Is it okay if we talk to your boss at the hotel where you work?"

"I guess," Tug said, spreading his hands out to his sides. "I am sure he now knows I have been arrested and my job is gone."

Langdon looked at his notes. "Mr. Martinson is his name?"

"Yes."

"How about your cousin? Didn't you come to Portland because your cousin was here?"

"He was deported a few months ago."

Tug blinked twice as the words dropped from his lips, his features otherwise impassive. He had spent a lifetime learning to mask his innermost thoughts behind a bland, middle-distance stare. Growing up in Burundi, a misguided glance, a frown, or the slightest smile at the wrong time could get you arrested, beaten, or even killed. Being a journalist, he had had to walk a fine line every day. Printing anything negative about powerful people or dangerous gang members invited retaliation, while being critical of the government brought the wrath of the devil down on your head.

When President Nkurunziza was nominated to run for a third term, protests erupted in the streets, led by journalists such as Tug, who pointed out that the constitution didn't allow for this. This had led to a coup attempt. When that failed, Tug realized his arrest was imminent, and he fled. His mother was still in Burundi, and so far, had not been retaliated against for her son's actions. He'd never known his father, and both of his brothers had been killed. There was truly no one in his life. No woman. No friends. His only family a mother he hadn't seen in years.

There was not much to say. Tug claimed to have no knowledge of anything. 4 by Four got him to sign some paperwork and advised him not to talk to the media when he had to travel to the courthouse for the bail hearing. On the nights of all three murders, Tug had been home in bed, alone. On at least one of those nights he'd spoken with Mrs. Levesque when he got home from the hotel, but they'd both retired to their rooms by 10:00 p.m., and the girls had been murdered much later, to the best estimate of the medical examiner.

"Zero chance of bail," 4 by Four said to Langdon and Jewell in the parking lot. The shower had passed over once again, and the water rose back up like a steam bath from the hot pavement. "Tomorrow I will see what else the prosecution has, but those two pieces of evidence in his room?" He shook his head.

"Do you know the woman who rents him the room?" Langdon asked Jewell.

"Sure. She's been letting rooms to immigrants we work with for years now. Tug has been with her for almost a year."

"I'd like to pay her a visit on the way home. It'd probably help smooth the waters if you come and give me an introduction."

Chapter 9

Still Sunday

Mrs. Levesque was a doll-like, white-haired French-Canadian lady who demanded they come in and have tea and cookies with her. She moved stiffly, but her eyes were a sharp blue behind the horn-rimmed glasses. Her husband had died twelve years earlier from too much work and too much booze, and she'd been taking immigrants in ever since, no doubt thinking back to her early years as a migrant, first in Lewiston and then Portland.

Like so many Mainers of Franco heritage, the Levesques had arrived in Lewiston, Maine, in the early 1960s. Mr. Levesque had written letters home excitedly telling his relatives and friends that Maine was wonderful, he was making a dollar an hour and working ninety hours a week, and his boss said he could have more if he wanted it. A passel of relatives had moved down to Lewiston from La Beauce, the poor agricultural area bordering north central Maine, to take on this wonderful opportunity, but by the early 1970s the factory work had dried up, and they had moved to Portland so he could take a job as a plant manager.

When he died in 2006, she was left mostly alone. Both children had gone away to college and never come back, other than for holidays and a break in the summer, when she might get a chance to see some of her five grandchildren. Tug was her seventh immigrant child, and her favorite thus far. He was kind, courteous, helped out around the house, and never brought home rowdy friends or played his music too loud.

"Did the police have a warrant to search the house?" Langdon asked her. The house was on Munjoy Hill, just a short walk to where the last coed had been deposited on East End Beach.

"They showed me a piece of paper, but I didn't have anything to hide, anyway. I told them to come right in. They asked me which room was Tug's, and not twenty minutes later the street was filled up with police cars. They made me go outside and wrapped tape around the entire house. When Tug showed up from work they slammed him on the ground and handcuffed him and took him away." She said this all very matter-of-factly. This was not a woman who'd led a sheltered life.

"Can you show us his room?"

Mrs. Levesque led them upstairs. There were two doors, and she opened the one on the left. The room barely fit a single bed, a nightstand, and a bureau. The window was small, and when Langdon went to lift it, he could only get it halfway up. There was a stick that could be stuck underneath it, and a standing fan in front. "Is that your room across the hall, Mrs. Levesque?"

"Yes it is, Mr. Langdon."

"Are you a light sleeper, Mrs. Levesque?" Langdon casually opened a drawer, looked in the closet, but didn't expect to find anything left behind by the police.

"I hardly sleep at all, Mr. Langdon."

"Did you often hear Tug stirring around at night?"

"I never hear him much in his room. He has those ear things to listen to his music, and he reads quite a bit, I think. Sometimes he'd go downstairs to the washroom. I have my own, but he has to use the one on the ground floor."

"In the past few months, has Tug, to your knowledge, gone out of the house again after retiring to his room?"

"Out? Oh, no, Mr. Langdon. I'd hear that front door shut even if

I was sound asleep. It makes a terrible clunk when you pull it tight."

They went back down the stairs. It was a tiny home, with just the two bedrooms upstairs, and downstairs a kitchen, a dining room that barely fit the round table, and a living room. "Have you had any visitors in the past week, Mrs. Levesque?" Langdon tested the front door, and it did indeed shake the home when pulled shut.

"I rarely have visitors, Mr. Langdon. As I told you, my children live away. One in Pennsylvania and the other is all the way over in Oregon. I got a cousin who came over from Lewiston back in June, but nobody since then."

"If you think of anything else, perhaps you could give me a call," Langdon said, handing her one of his cards. "And if I think of anything else to ask you, would it be okay if I called or stopped by?"

"Anytime you want to stop by, please do so, Mr. Langdon. I get awful lonely sitting here by myself watching television. I got an terrible scare when the cable people came by and said there were connection issues in the neighborhood."

"What?" Langdon asked abruptly. "I'm sorry, Mrs. Levesque. Did you say that you had a service visit from the cable company?"

"Yes. Is that important?"

"When did they come by, Mrs. Levesque?" Langdon asked, shifting his gaze to Jewell.

"Ah, let me see. Today is Sunday. It must have been the day before yesterday. Friday. Friday morning after Tug had left for work."

"How did you know they were from the cable company?"

"Well, they said they were, for one. But they were driving one of those white vans with the big red letters. You know, that say Xfinity. I didn't have any reason to question them."

"What exactly did they do?"

Mrs. Levesque pressed her lips together, thinking. "Well, Larry, he was the one with the clipboard, he sat down with me in the kitchen and asked me some questions, while the other fellow, I didn't get his name, checked the boxes in the house to make sure they were working fine. I told him that there was no cable upstairs but he went up there to check the lines or something like that anyway."

"Did you tell the police about this?"

"No, Mr. Langdon. They didn't ask. Why?"

~ ~ ~ ~ ~

The sky was clear and the sun was descending over the Portland skyline as Langdon climbed into the Jeep. Dog was looking at him with disdain, wondering why he'd been brought along if he was just going to be left behind to sit in the car. He turned onto Congress and drove the half-mile to the parking lot for East End Beach. There were a few people on the walking path, and a couple still on the beach drinking wine. Dog ran from smell to smell while Langdon tried to capture the scene in his mind.

For starters, Tug didn't own a car, and the ME had determined that all of the victims had been killed one place then dumped elsewhere. This, coupled with the fact that Tug didn't seem to be the type, meant absolutely nothing in a court of law. If the Xfinity service call turned out to be bogus, that would be something. Still, Langdon knew the prosecution would shred Mrs. Levesque on the witness stand, dismantling her story as the foggy recollections of a confused elderly lady. They had a murder weapon and blood evidence found in the accused man's room—a man who had no alibi and who was an immigrant to boot.

His phone buzzed in his pocket. Unknown number. "Hello." And then as an afterthought, "Goff Langdon."

"Hello, Mr. Langdon. This is Delilah Friday."

"Hello, Miss Friday. What can I do…" he almost said you for, but quickly caught himself, "for you?"

"I'm sorry to call you on a Sunday night, but I just heard from my sister, and wanted to fill you in."

"What did she say?"

"I'd rather talk face-to-face, if that's okay?"

"Sure. I can come to you."

"I'm staying at the Bernard Hotel in Freeport. There's a tavern downstairs."

"Sure. I can be there in an hour, if that's okay with you."

As Langdon hung up the phone, he mused on what a coincidence life often was. He'd just been to the Bernard that very morning in regard to one case and was now meeting a woman there about another matter entirely. Although it was only five miles from his house, he hadn't been there before today for at least ten years.

He whistled for dog, who had made friends with the couple on the beach. They had not yet broken down to sharing whatever it was they were eating, so he was hesitant to leave, but caved in when Langdon was halfway back to the Jeep.

Once on 295 North, Langdon called Chabal to tell her he was meeting with a new client. She was on her way out the door with Jack to see some superhero movie but told him there was some leftover lasagna in the fridge if he got home before her. Langdon was relieved that his wife was in a hurry so she wasn't expecting him home soon and didn't quiz him about taking on a new case. He decided that at least dog should eat, and swung by home to feed him and drop him off. There didn't seem to be time to reheat the lasagna and eat, but he'd gone hungry before. The sun was down, and it was almost fully dark when he pulled into the parking lot of the Bernard.

Delilah Friday was at a small, round table kitty-corner to the bar. Langdon counted no less than five sets of eyes on her as he crossed over to the vacant seat, watching those eyes mirror their owners' dismay, envy, jealousy, and finally hatred for Langdon. At the same time, all the other women in the room were happy that the threat of the smoking hot blonde had been removed, and by such a normal looking, if somewhat rumpled, middle-aged man, at that.

"Miss Friday," Langdon said as he sat down.

"Please call me Del, all my friends do," she replied.

"My friends call me Langdon."

"And what does your wife call you?"

"Langdon."

"I believe I will call you Goff, if you don't mind?" she said with that smile with the suggestive little twist that hadn't given him any rest in the past twenty-four hours. "I'm glad that you weren't settled in for the night."

"I was actually on my way back from another case, down in Portland."

"I hope I didn't interrupt."

"Not at all, but as I just discovered some good news, a drink to celebrate is in order."

Langdon licked his lips. At that moment the bartender came over and Langdon ordered a double Glenlivet on the rocks. Delilah had a drink with a bluish tinge, still mostly full.

"And what was the good news?"

"Have you heard of the Old Port Killer?"

"OPK? Sure, it's been all over the news."

"They arrested the wrong man for the murders, and I'm trying to clear his name," Langdon bragged. "I just learned that the real bad actors might have been posing as guys from the cable company to plant evidence, Xfinity truck and all." He wasn't sure why he was running off at the mouth so much, but he just couldn't shut up.

"Bad actors?" She laughed at him. "What are you, Charlie Rose? I'm not sure you can call murderers bad actors."

"You said you were staying here, Del?" Langdon asked, changing the subject. Enough about him, how was she able to afford this very posh and expensive hotel? "How are the rooms?"

"Very comfortable. Maybe later I'll give you a tour."

"Do you mind if I ask what you do for a living?"

"I am in the entertainment business, Goff." She took a small sip of her drink through the straw. "Nothing as exciting as being a private detective."

"What kind of entertainment?" he asked.

"We can talk about that later, but first, let's get to why I called you."

"Go for it."

"My sister called me."

"And is she okay?"

"She told me she was fine, but then she got very flustered when I told her I was in Maine and wanted to see her." Delilah paused, thinking back to the conversation. "She told me that wouldn't be possible right now, and when I asked why not, she hung up on me."

"Did you call her back?"

"Of course, but there was no answer."

"Text me the number and I'll run a trace on it."

"Very impressive." Her eyes got very large. "I didn't think private detectives could do that."

Langdon ordered another scotch. He didn't remember getting the first one, much less drinking it. Maybe there'd been an empty glass on the table?

"I know a guy," he said, even though he was almost certain it would be a burner phone.

"Of course you do."

"What else did she say before you told her you were in Maine?" Delilah shrugged, thinking. "Any clue where she might be—like maybe from something you heard in the background?" Delilah shook her head and began to speak.

Delilah Friday wore a lacy red dress with thin shoulder straps and apparently no bra, and this may have been why Langdon had to have her repeat her answer. After a bit, talk veered to her work in the entertainment business, home in Alexandria, and even her cat, Melvin. Langdon should have ordered something to eat, but Del had eaten earlier, and he didn't want to seem awkward gobbling food in front of her, so he continued to splash cupfuls of scotch into an empty stomach.

When the bartender came over and told them it was last call,

Langdon was shocked, a quick glance at his phone showing it was closing in on midnight. One more couldn't hurt at this point, as he was most certainly taking a cab home. When the blueberry vodka lemonade for Del and the scotch for Langdon were delivered, he asked if the man had the number of the cab company.

"You'd have to call Brunswick Taxi, but they stopped running at 10." The bartender was not much more than a kid himself, his thick hair covered by a beanie. He smirked, as if to say, *I knew you couldn't be hooking up with this bombshell.* Except he wouldn't have said bombshell or probably even know what it meant, a word from Langdon's era, or actually from the books he'd read growing up.

Langdon sipped his drink, contemplating his choices.

"I did promise you a tour earlier," Delilah said. Her voice was steady, and the only indication of her alcohol consumption were eyes that shone and cheeks that glowed in a becoming flush. "Why don't you come back to my room while you sober up. I've got one of those little coffee makers in my room."

Langdon stared at her. It'd been some time since a woman other than his wife had come on to him, and probably never, not even in the prime of his prime, had one this beautiful done so. Still, he was fairly certain that this was what was happening here.

"Knock, knock, anybody home?" Her mouth twisted, and Langdon felt the thrill of a purely animal desire that caused him to grunt.

Delilah laughed, causing her breasts to move in a lovely tandem dance behind their fragile lace constraints. She put her hand to his cheek. "What did you say, darling?"

"I don't think that would be a good idea."

"Sobering up before driving?" She raised her eyebrows, her skin flawless and creamy. "I think just about everybody would disagree with you on that one."

The bartender put the tab down in front of Langdon, but Delilah grabbed it. "I believe this is on me. Are you ready for your… tour?" She stepped to the bar and slapped down a credit card.

Langdon stared at her bared back and found himself standing. Once erect, he stumbled slightly, tilting the table, which he steadied even while his mind was reeling. It had only been this afternoon that his wife had seduced him in another hotel room. His wife. Chabal. The picture of his wife from earlier that afternoon, that was the sobering splash of cold water that rinsed the worst of the fuzz from his brain. What was he doing?

Chapter 10

Monday

An alarm was going off in his jail cell. He struggled to sit upright, wondering what was going on. It was actually his phone ringing. What had he been dreaming?

"Hello."

"Langdon, my man. Are we working out today?" It was Richam.

"For sure." Langdon always hated being caught asleep. He felt it was a weakness. "Eight o'clock. What time is it now?"

"Ten minutes past 8:00."

"Damn. Sorry, I had a late night. I'll be there in fifteen minutes." He hung up, pulled on a pair of shorts and a T-shirt. His gym bag was in the mudroom.

"Look what the cat dragged in." Chabal was sitting at the kitchen island with a cup of coffee.

"Good morning." He grabbed his bag and went back into their first floor bedroom to grab clothes for later, and then into the laundry room for a towel.

"Were you drunk last night?"

"What?"

"I don't even know what time you came home, but you snored like Lil Wayne singing."

"Um, I had a meeting. I'm late for my workout with Richam. I'll tell you all about it later." He kissed her and started for the door.

"You best brush your teeth before you go out in public," Chabal scolded, making a face.

Langdon went back and dutifully brushed his teeth and swallowed a large glass of water, the refreshing liquid a balm to his dry mouth. When he emerged, dog had roused himself from the couch, so Langdon brought him along.

~ ~ ~ ~ ~

Richam was on the treadmill when Langdon clambered down the stairs of Cellar Fitness. "Morning, Brittany," Langdon said to the owner behind the desk as he scanned his membership tag. She mumbled a reply and bent to scratch dog's head and butt, while Langdon sat on a bench and changed into his workout shoes, pushing the gym bag underneath.

"Glad you could make it," Richam said, stopping the belt as Langdon came over. "Shoulder and arm day?"

They started with seated military press. "I might've had too much scotch last night," Langdon admitted, as the warm-up set tested his resolve, drunk-sweat breaking out on his brow.

"Jewell told me all about meeting with the immigrant fellow in jail, and the follow-up with his landlady up on Munjoy Hill. She didn't mention anything about you hitting the sauce, either in jail or with the elderly grandmother." Richam effortlessly whipped off the twelve reps and added more weight.

"What are you, my sponsor?" He shrugged. "So I got a call from a client on my way home and met her at the tavern over at the Bernard Hotel in Freeport," Langdon said.

"You mean the blackmail thing?"

"No, this is something else that just came up the other night."

"You going to tell me about it?"

"It's some lady from Virginia looking for her sister. Says she's gone missing from her home in Falmouth. The husband says she ran off with some guy. The lady thinks the husband might have something to do with the sister having gone missing."

Richam nodded. "And they're from Falmouth?"

"Yep."

"Money, then. No Allen's Coffee Brandy domestic abuse here. Rich wife beating is a lot harder to prove."

"I haven't made it down to talk to the husband, yet. Hoping to do that later this afternoon. But the lady who hired me has some real bank. She's staying at the Bernard, after all."

"Smoking hot, I bet."

"Why do you say that?"

"You get over-served good scotch on a Sunday night with a client? It's either Tom Brady or a very attractive woman, would be my guess. Am I wrong?"

"It wasn't Tom Brady," Langdon admitted.

Richam moved over to the dumbbells for a set of Arnies, the twisting press made famous by Schwarzenegger. "So, what's the deal?"

"What do you mean, 'what's the deal'?"

"You're not the cheating type. You and Chabal have a real good thing. Plus, she'd shoot your sorry ass if you pulled any funny stuff."

"The client invited me to her room to sober up." Langdon took his turn sitting on the bench and pumping the iron upward.

"And?"

"She is absolutely ravishing. She's got this smile with a sexy little thing going at the corner of her mouth, and the face and body of a Greek goddess. And she smells better than bacon," Langdon added, to lighten what was proving to be an awkward conversation.

"And?" Richam pushed his black-rimmed glasses back and fixed Langdon with a stare that wasn't going to let him wriggle free of this one.

"What do you think I did?" Langdon asked. "I ran. I got in my car and drove home drunk."

~ ~ ~ ~ ~

Langdon showered, gathered dog, and went through the rear door of the gym. Cellar Fitness was located in what used to be the warehouse building to a large department store in town, but that establishment had been ravaged by Walmart, and now hosted a scattering of businesses, one of which was the Coffee Dog Bookstore. There was an underground passage through which goods used to be delivered from the warehouse to the retail store, and thus, Langdon didn't have to go outside to traverse from the gym to work. He took one flight of stairs up to street level and walked into the bookshop.

Starling was waiting on a customer at the counter and merely waved as Langdon passed on his way to his office. Dog veered over to collect his customary morning snack from the man. Langdon immediately called Xfinity about the service call this past Friday at Mrs. Levesque's home, but they were unhelpful. Langdon then called Jewell to see if she were able to swing by the landlady's house and have her, as the account holder, call to confirm whether or not Xfinity had sent a truck to her house that day. He thought it best to have somebody there to make sure the elderly lady asked the right questions. Jewell agreed to stop by on her lunch hour.

Langdon was avoiding calling Delilah Friday. He had to pay a visit to her brother-in-law to get that missing person case started, but thought it best to avoid speaking with Del for another day. At that point, his phone rang, and Senator Mercer herself was on the other end of the line, wondering if he could be at Nate's Marina in thirty minutes, prepared to take a sail. He agreed, made sure Star was okay, promised to be in by 2:00 to relieve him, and he and dog were out the door.

Nate's Marina was most of the way out to Mere Point, just short of the private neighborhood that Michael Glover lived in—a gated community, so to speak, but without the gate. Langdon parked and walked down to the dock. Senator Mercer waved from the back of a sailboat, a yacht, maybe? He wasn't really sure of the correct terminology, but it was almost forty feet long, had two masts, and was called *Swing Vote*. Langdon and dog clumsily clambered aboard, and Dwayne, the bodyguard, threw the rope in behind, following them onto the sailboat.

"Welcome, Mr. Langdon," Senator Mercer said. She had on a gray windbreaker with the number eighteen on it, large maroon sunglasses, and looked altogether more sporting than her usual pants suit and demurely buttoned jacket.

"Senator," Langdon replied.

"And hello to you, dog," she said, rubbing his head.

Michael Glover came up out of the cabin and shook Langdon's hand. "Great job tracking down the blackmailer, Mr. Langdon."

"I just wished she hadn't gotten away," Langdon replied. He quickly sat down as the boat began motoring slowly away from the dock. He was across from Senator Mercer who was sitting in the right-rear corner with one hand loosely on the large wheel. Glover sat down next to him on the short bench and Dwayne sat down next to the senator.

"Do you sail, Mr. Langdon?" she asked him as they pulled away from the dock, the gentle thrum of the engine making the deck hum underfoot.

"Only when out-of-state friends visit, and we pay to have somebody take us out to look at seals or puffins or something like that," Langdon replied.

"This is an early Tom Morris design called a Justine. Thirty-six feet. Good Maine boat builder."

"As long as it floats," Langdon said after a silence dictating that he was supposed to respond in some way.

The senator chuckled. "You don't care much for the finer things in life, do you, Mr. Langdon."

"I guess a name or a brand doesn't mean much to me. I like cheap wine same as expensive, and I can't see myself paying to have a Nike symbol on my shirt to advertise for them, if that's what you mean."

Glover and Dwayne went to work raising the sails, and dog followed, as the senator pointed off to the left. "Birch Island may have been visited as early as 1525 by Europeans, but it was a summer fishing spot for the Abenaki long before that. Robert P.T. Coffin spent part of his youth there, and it inspired many of his poems."

Langdon had to admit that gliding over the slightly rippled water and past the many small islands off the coast of Brunswick was a thrilling experience. He momentarily worried that dog was going to fall overboard, but he did love to swim after all, so what would the harm be? "Where do we stand, Senator?"

"What do you mean, Mr. Langdon?"

"Your husband tried to pay me off and send me packing, but I don't quite feel the job is done."

"Maxwell doesn't always understand the bigger picture," Senator Mercer said, her face tilted to see in front of the sailboat, the sun glinting off her Prada sunglasses.

"So, you would like me to continue looking for KJ?"

"KJ?"

"Kamrin Jorgenson."

"Ah, yes. Kamrin."

Langdon had almost forgotten that this had all begun with the senator having sex with KJ. "What are your plans when I find her?"

"I got a note dropped in my mailbox this morning from Kamrin. She wants me to use my influence in Congress to force the President to rejoin the Paris Agreement on global greenhouse emissions."

Langdon contemplated that mouthful for a moment, watching the islands pass by. "Seems rather a large ask. You don't have that kind of clout, do you?" What was KJ playing at, Langdon wondered. She was too smart to think that a senator could force the government to rejoin the world agreement preserving the environment, not if the President didn't want to be part of it, that is.

"No."

"But, you can buy quite a bit of time by claiming to be working towards that end, whether you are or not," Langdon said. "Which, I hope you are doing anyway." Langdon had a feeling that the senator was not putting all of her cards on the table.

The senator chuckled. "As a sign of good faith, Kamrin has asked that I push through a current bill being bandied around that states that climate change is a scientific fact and an undeniable truth. It has language that would at least begin to implement strategies not unlike what the Paris Agreement requires."

"And this is possible for you?"

She raised a hand and waggled it while frowning. "But I'd have to use up some pretty hefty chips. Probably cost me at least a destroyer, maybe Medicaid expansion, who know what else? The Dreamers? There's a lot at stake, Mr. Langdon."

Bath Iron Works was the area's largest employer and the U.S. Navy its largest—its *only*—client, but there was a fierce competition for new ship commissions, a competition complicated by the fact that, while BIW was unionized, the southern shipyards also building destroyers were not. Langdon chewed over these thoughts, before asking, "What do you plan on doing, Senator?"

"That is Bustins Island ahead," the senator said, apropos of nothing. "We'll loop around that and come back up the coast. There are some truly beautiful homes along the way."

They flowed along in silence. Glover and Dwayne had by now returned to their seats. Dog still stood at the front of the sailboat, eagerly watching seagulls swooping overhead. Langdon had never been to Bustins before but knew people who spent months of the summer out there. The day was one of those with a perfect summer blue sky, so sharp and distinct that it almost made the bones ache not wanting to let it slide by. He supposed the senator would speak when she wanted to. He was right.

"I would like you to continue searching for Kamrin," the senator finally said. "And when you find her, I would like you to offer her

$100,000 for all pictures and images, and to sign a nondisclosure agreement."

"Was that what Max was going to do?" Langdon was relieved that the plan was not to kill her. He wasn't quite sure how big-time politics played out, and was fairly sure he didn't want to know.

"My husband's strengths do not include negotiating with blackmailers, Mr. Langdon. I think you'd be better suited for that."

"Am I negotiating or just making a flat offer?"

"Try to sell it for a hundred, but you can go fifty more if you need to."

"Is that legal?"

"Perfectly legal. Do you read the news, Mr. Langdon? The President has done it many times."

"Not exactly a moral high-water mark to measure yourself against, Senator."

Senator Mercer chuckled.

Langdon rolled it around in his mind. "Haven't a bunch of congressmen gotten in trouble recently for this kind of thing?"

"They were using taxpayer money to buy the silence, and while they were legally justified to do this, it did bring up some ethical issues."

"And this money would come from where?"

"It is my money, Mr. Langdon. Not campaign money. It was my indiscretion, and I will pay for my mistake with my own check."

"I'll give it a whirl," Langdon said, as the dock at Nate's Marina came back into view, sending Glover and Dwayne scrambling to lower the sails once again. "But I don't think KJ will go for it."

"I heard you knew her from back when. Quite a scandal that was. '96 wasn't it? I was a friend of the chief, you know."

Langdon stared at the impassive face of the senator. She was telling him that she knew KJ had used blackmail before, and that back then it'd resulted in the death of a man in a position of power, similar to her situation. She was saying that she knew the woman had ideals that she held more dearly than life, death, freedom, and most certainly, money.

"Time changes things," Senator Mercer continued. "She's in her fifties now, and from the sounds of it, she's been living on the edge of the wild, probably a hand-to-mouth existence. It's gotten harder to be cold, to be hungry, to get out of bed every morning. Hot flashes shooting through her body like vandals, intent only upon wreaking havoc. When we face our own mortality later on in life, our youth seems like a distant dream, and security and comfort a much more tangible reality." They pulled up to the dock and Dwayne jumped out to secure the line. The senator took off her sunglasses and fixed her grey eyes on his. "Offer her the money, Mr. Langdon."

Chapter 11

Still Monday

Langdon was almost back to the bookstore when he realized how hungry he was. He hadn't eaten anything since yesterday morning's breakfast, and his system, while usually slow to remind him of such basic needs, was suddenly blaring away that a crisis was imminent. Instead of continuing straight past the First Parish Church at the top of the downtown, he veered the Jeep to the right onto the Bath Road, and seconds later was pulling into a parking spot at Hog Heaven. He put his lights on to indicate he was ready to be served. There was a text from Missouri saying she was going to come a day earlier, and could he still pick her up? He pecked out a quick 'of course', just as the waitress came up to his window.

"Hello, Goff. What can I get for you?"

"Hi Susie, How've you been?" She was a few years younger than Langdon, a two-pack a day smoker, and he suspected some sort of opiate addict, was relegated to menial summer employment, went from man to man, but there was still a fire in her dark eyes that smoldered with an enjoyment of life.

"Like shit, Goff. But it's a beautiful day and a big tipper just pulled in." She bared her brown teeth in what may have passed as a smile. Langdon had helped her out of a jam with an abusive boyfriend a few years back, and she had a sweet spot for him.

"How about you bring me a McDonny burger, a fried clam basket, some onion rings, and a Coke. And a hamburger and a water for my friend here." He nodded at dog who was quite excited to be at the drive-up restaurant, even if the wait staff wasn't on roller skates.

"All for here?" And when he nodded, "Don't forget to turn your lights off."

She was no sooner gone then the back door opened, and somebody slid into the seat directly behind Langdon. "Hello, Mr. Langdon. Do you have any idea what a Glock 43 with a silencer looks like?"

Dog whined low in his throat. "Nope," Langdon said, reaching slowly over to pet dog's head and let him know it was okay.

"It's pointed at your back as we speak."

"If you hand it up to me, I can get a gander at it, you know, improve my knowledge of such things."

"I'll show it to you when I leave," the voice offered. "Hopefully you'll still be alive to see it."

The passenger door opened, and the Matt Damon look-alike with glasses from a few nights prior was standing there with a carton of fries. "Hungry, dog?" he asked, dropping a few of them on the ground. Dog jumped down to gobble them up, and the man sat down and shut the door. He looked like he might have been wearing the same tie and suit from the previous visit.

"You again," Langdon said.

"I'm sorry I didn't introduce myself the other night. My name is John, and the fellow behind you is Pete."

"What can I do for you… John?"

"Well, apparently I wasn't clear…"

"We weren't clear," Pete interrupted from the backseat.

"Apparently we weren't clear the other night when we stopped by your house," John said. "I thought you being a detective and all, you'd be able to fill in the blanks, but perhaps I overestimated you. We would appreciate it if you'd stop searching for the lady in the pictures."

"Kamrin Jorgenson?"

John tossed a french fry to dog outside the window, who caught it without standing up. At least he wasn't running in traffic, Langdon thought with a wry smile.

"I told you he was a smart guy," Pete said.

"Or do you mean Jordan Fitzpatrick?"

"Either one will do," John said. "Just don't find her. Hell, if you want, you can keep collecting your fee from the senator, but you got a little too close yesterday."

"That was you in the car on Route 1, wasn't it?"

"Us," Pete said. "That was us."

"I have a cash offer from the senator for KJ," Langdon said. "Maybe you could have her give me a call?"

"She isn't interested in your offer," John said.

"You haven't heard the offer," Langdon replied.

"When the U.S. rejoins the Paris Agreement, Miss Jorgenson will return all the pictures and will be willing to sign an agreement to keep her mouth shut."

Langdon thought this was interesting. A blackmailer not interested in an offer, without even hearing what it was. For all these two knew, perhaps Langdon was here to tell them that the senator had agreed to their demands. Maybe the proposition was something slightly less, but a blackmailer who didn't want to hear the proposal on the table just didn't quite ring true. But he didn't say anything. There was, after all, a gun pointed at his back, and he could almost feel the bullet severing his spinal cord.

John opened the door and got out. He threw a couple fries on the seat, and once dog had scrambled back in, he shut the door and walked off. Pete waited until he was around the corner of the building, and then stepped out of the back. He had a light windbreaker draped over his arm, and he stepped to Langdon's window and showed him the Glock, complete with silencer, underneath.

"The lady stays missing," he said.

"What lady?" Langdon asked.

Langdon watched him walk off, thinking he perhaps should be

following, but the pistol had been ugly and ominous as promised. "Way to go, dog," he said to his companion. "Some sidekick you are. Sherlock had Watson, Nero had Archie, Batman had Robin, and I'm stuck with a mutt who sells me out for a couple of fries." A GMC Yukon Denali pulled around the kitchen part of Hog Heaven, and Langdon took out his phone and snapped a picture, making sure to get the license plate, as well as the faint image of the two men in the front.

Susie came back over with his food and set the tray on his window, and Langdon was reminded how hungry he was. "Those guys friends of yours?" she asked, nodding her head towards the disappearing sports utility vehicle.

"Not so much," Langdon replied.

"They came in here two days ago for lunch and left me zero tip," Susie said. "So, you know, I memorized their license plate to tell the other girls to watch out for the cheapskates. Maybe add a little something special to their food, if you know what I mean?"

Langdon winced. "That's why I always leave a good tip," he said.

"Funny thing is, I saw them pull back in today without turning their lights on. I thought it was kinda strange that they was just sitting there without ordering, and then I noticed the license plate was different from the other day. I walked over to check on them, just to see if they were the same guys, and sure enough they was."

"What was the plate number from the other day?" Langdon asked. Susie told him.

Langdon left a twenty-dollar tip on a fifteen-dollar bill.

~ ~ ~ ~ ~

Langdon tried to make sense of all that was happening as he drove the five minutes to the bookstore. By the time he got there, he had a plan. Sitting in the parking lot, he called Jewell back. She'd left a message on his voicemail he hadn't had time to listen to.

"Langdon, it's about time you called me back," she answered on the second ring.

"Sorry, Jewell. I've been sailing with senators and dining with Boy Scouts all day. What'd you find out?"

"Xfinity has no record of a service call to Mrs. Levesque's residence for over a year. She got them to check and see if anybody in the neighborhood had a call, and that came back zilch as well."

"So we got a fake service call from a couple of guys. Gee, I wonder why?"

"First of all, there were three of them. Mrs. Levesque remembered she noticed one man stayed by the van. He stood outside smoking a cigarette. Second of all, it's pretty obvious to me, as well as you, that they were there to plant evidence."

"Is Mrs. Levesque sure they said they were from Xfinity?" Langdon was playing devil's advocate, even though he was as excited as Jewell that this could be a possible lifeline for Tug.

"She is certain that the van had Xfinity on the side in large red letters, and the man with the clipboard was quite clear in identifying them. She may be growing a bit frail, but her mind is still pretty darn sharp. Sharp enough to know the man had an accent."

"Accent? Like from another country? Or just a good Maine brogue?"

"Foreign, she said," Jewell replied. "Not French or Canadian, obviously. Not one she's heard before, except maybe on television. Don't forget she's housed quite a few immigrants from a variety of African and Central American places."

"What do you mean, maybe on television?"

"She told me he sounded like the villain in the last Bruce Willis *Die Hard* movie. She couldn't remember his name, but we looked it up on my phone, and she confirmed that Yuri Komarov was who she was talking about."

"Sounds Russian to me." The film is called *A Good Day to Die Hard*, and Langdon knew it well. Of course, he didn't want to admit it, but he'd seen it five times.

"You got it."

"So, what's that mean?"

"It means… I don't know what it means."

"Can't be too many people with Russian accents in Portland. I'll call Jimmy, and have him get the police on this. I doubt they'll listen to me. But if they do lend this any credence, they'll probably send a sketch artist over to Mrs. Levesque."

"Does this mean they'll let Tug go?"

"Not unless we can track down the guys who really did it. Police are like anybody else, they don't like to admit mistakes. When and if the real murderers are revealed—let's hope we can make that happen—only then will the cops let up on Tug."

Langdon hung up, checked the time, and called 4 by Four to fill him in on the latest update. Tug's bail hearing had been set for Wednesday, and it would go a long way to getting Tug out of jail if they could substantiate any of their suspicions.

Once Langdon had filled him in on the false service call and suggested he put the police on it, 4 by Four changed the subject. "Did Jewell say anything about having Cary Stockton over for a dinner party? One that I may also be invited to?"

"What are we, in seventh grade?"

"Just asking, is all."

"I got another question for you," Langdon said. "Is it legal for me to offer a woman money for somebody else, just to keep her mouth shut?"

"Who's in seventh grade now?"

"No, seriously. This other case I'm working on involves Senator Mercer, and she wants me to negotiate a settlement with a woman who's blackmailing her."

"How much we talking?"

"Hundred thousand. Maybe a bit more."

"You're in the big time now," 4 by Four said. "But no worries. It's perfectly legal to contract with somebody to keep their mouth shut."

Bart didn't answer his phone, so Langdon left a message asking him to do a search on the plate number Susie had given him at Hog Heaven. Then, as an afterthought, he asked that Bart check to see if any Xfinity vans had been stolen recently. With that completed, he and dog lurched out of the seat and headed into the bookstore. Chabal and Starling were splitting a burrito from Large Z's, the mammoth creation more than they could finish together, but dog was more than willing to help. A few customers loitered, wandering slowly up and down the aisles and pulling books from the shelves. It was two minutes before 2:00, so at least he wasn't late, for a change.

"Hi, babe," Langdon said.

"Don't you 'babe' me," Starling retorted. "Chabal says you got in late last night, and you were drunk."

Was nothing private between husband and wife? "I wasn't that drunk," Langdon muttered.

"Who was this client that kept you out to all hours and plied you with alcohol?" Chabal asked.

"A woman looking for her sister."

Chabal sighed. "A woman?"

Starling decided he'd best not get any further into the middle of this conversation and went to check and see if anybody needed help looking for a mystery.

"Tell me about this woman."

"Not much to say. Her sister up and disappeared. She suspects the husband might be involved in some foul play, and he says she ran off with some guy, but the woman can't get ahold of her sister to verify either version."

"Is she good looking?"

"I don't know… She looks okay in the picture, but I'll let you know the real deal when I find her."

"I mean the woman who hired you?"

"Her? Yeah, she's a pretty young lady. Am I allowed to comment on how women look in this day and age?"

"How old is she?"

"Maybe thirty-five."

"Is she married?"

"No."

"Where did you meet with her?"

"At the tavern at the Bernard."

Chabal nodded. "So you met an attractive single woman much younger than your aging ass at a hotel and drank into the night with her before coming home to pass out in our bed?"

"That about sums it up. I'm sorry, but I had an empty stomach from not eating, so the liquor hit me hard, and I lost track of time. I'm sorry."

"Yes, it does," she said. "Pretty young filly and horny old man. Didn't you get enough yesterday as is?"

"I said I was sorry. And I'm not that old."

Chabal grabbed her clutch, a bright red purse big enough for her phone, wallet, and keys, but no more. "Will you be home for dinner? Or will you be dining with your new strumpet?"

"I plan on coming home as soon as I close up shop."

"Maybe you could pick up some Thai on the way home?"

"Absolutely."

Chabal gave a low whistle for dog and waved to Starling. "C'mon, dog, you're going with me." Dog padded faithfully out the door behind her.

"Tell me about the chick," Starling said, returning to the registers as soon as the coast was clear.

"What do you want to know?"

"Is she any good in the sack?"

Langdon shook his head. "Why do I continue to pay you?"

"So you can go get drunk with random women, apparently."

Langdon was rescued by a woman coming to the counter with a toddler clutched in her arms. With her free hand, she dropped a Mary Higgins Clark book on the counter and finagled her wallet from her purse.

Once she was gone, Starling nodded at the door. "Speaking of cruise ships, did the senator take you out sailing this morning?" The book had been *You Belong to Me*, a mystery set at sea.

"She did. Quite the skipper, she is, by the way. Seemed very comfortable behind the wheel."

"Nice boat?" Starling had no more knowledge of sailing than Langdon.

"She said it was a Tom Morris."

"Ahh." Starling drummed his fingers on the counter. "What'd she want?"

"She wants me to negotiate a bribe to shut up your old law partner."

"Jordan, or Kamrin, or whatever she's going by, she'll never do it."

"That's what I told her, but she said something about changing priorities as you get older."

"Change is part of every day," Starling agreed. "Guess you never know."

"Just had lunch with my buddies who stopped by the house the other night," Langdon said.

"The Boy Scouts?"

"Our friendship seems to be progressing. Pete and John, they call themselves now."

"What'd they want?"

"For me to stay away from KJ."

"Seems to me she's got a couple of boys backing her play."

"I guess so," Langdon replied.

"You guess so? That doesn't sound all that certain."

"Not quite sure it's her play, is all, or what the play really is. It's only that, well, they didn't seem interested in me having a conversation with her on behalf of the senator. Don't you think if they were working with her to blackmail the senator that they'd be interested in what Mercer has to say?"

"That does seem a tad suspicious," Starling agreed.

Chapter 12

Langdon ran the store by himself for the afternoon, keeping busy with a steady flow of customers. He was pretty beat from a late night and long day, and was looking forward to a quiet night eating takeout, so as six o'clock approached, he started easing himself over to lock the door before any last minute people squeezed in and spent fifteen minutes browsing before deciding they didn't actually want a book.

Before he could get there, though, Delilah Friday breezed through the opening. She wore a red floral dress with spaghetti straps that was tight, sexy, and classy. A choker around her neck held a simple jade pendant, and she held a shocking yellow vinyl handbag that matched her high heels.

"Goff, I'm glad I found you here," she said before he could open his mouth. "I'm going to pay a visit to Paul this evening, and suddenly had the thought of, 'what if he did kill her?'"

Langdon shook his head to clear unseen cobwebs. "Paul?"

"My sister's husband." She placed her hand on his chest. "Will you please go with me?"

Langdon stepped around her. "Let me lock the door, so I can finish closing up."

"You do like locking me in, don't you?"

"I don't think you'd do very well in confinement," he said, locking the door and returning to the cash register to close out.

"Because I'm a free spirit?" She giggled. "Speaking of escaping, what happened to you last night?"

It was getting difficult to count the money, but Langdon plowed gamely on. "I thought it best that I just go home."

"I think it would've been best if you'd had some coffee, and then went home. I woke up this morning with a screeching headache. It must've been the blueberries, don't you think?" Delilah leaned forward over the counter, all but releasing her enormous breasts from their fragile captivity.

The hell with counting the money, Langdon thought. He'd come in early and tally up, vacuum, and what not.

"Why did you take off without saying goodbye?" she asked.

"I, um, I'm a married man, Del, and it didn't seem right going up to your room with you." He grabbed his keys and motioned for her to follow.

"What did you think was going to happen?" she asked in a breathy voice.

He stopped to unlock the door and she ran into the back of him, her arms encircling him, before stepping back.

"I had no idea what was going to happen."

"Did you think I was trying to seduce you?"

"Were you?"

She laughed, a noise not unlike wind chimes. "I was far too drunk to get randy."

"Are you parked in front or back?"

"I'm out back."

"Good. I can follow you to your hotel and pick you up, if you're okay riding in my Jeep? Their house is in Falmouth, right?"

The Bernard was just off the mile 22 Exit in Freeport, and before Langdon had quite organized his thoughts, he was pulling in behind the hotel. Delilah stepped out of her Mercedes-Benz, looked at the open Jeep, and reached over to grab a jean jacket that had a well-worn look.

"I just have to run up to my room for a minute. Do you want to come?" She leaned in the passenger window, and Langdon hurriedly turned his eyes forward. "I'm just funning with you," she said, pulling open the door and sliding in.

He reached into the backseat and pulled a Gettysburg College baseball hat from the floor. "You might want this to keep your hair from blowing all over."

Delilah pulled the cap brim low over her cat's-eye mirrored yellow sunglasses. "You know, I've been hit on countless times in my life, but this is a first for me."

"Route 1 or the highway?"

"Let's go the slow way. I'd like to see some of the coast. Will we go through Yarmouth?"

"Not downtown, but we'll catch a slice," Langdon said, turning left and driving past L.L. Bean and the other factory stores of Freeport. "What is a first for you?"

Delilah punched an address into her phone, and it tried to redirect them to 295, but eventually succumbed as Langdon continued along Route 1. Once it aligned with their destination, she replied to his question. "Having a man think I'm hitting on them, and refusing me, even though I'm not."

"You probably don't get refused very often, Miss Friday," Langdon acknowledged.

"I don't get refused *ever*," she replied.

The blood flushing his face was a mix of embarrassment and desire, a messy tangle of emotions. There was something about this woman that just plain put him off kilter. "I just want to keep a professional distance," he said. "And I thought visiting your room in the wee hours of the night might be stepping over that boundary."

"I think that you probably stepped over that boundary when you began having lascivious thoughts about me," Delilah said.

How long could the blood remain in one's head before he passed out? "I'm sorry." There'd been an awful lot of apologizing to women today.

"No worries, Goff. Let's just find my sister."

The Springer home was the last house on the right of a small development that looked like it had never moved past phase one. The road ended ten feet past the driveway, and the few trees in the yard couldn't be more than five years old. It was a modular cape, with a two-car garage. Nothing special, but in Falmouth, it was probably worth at least 500 grand.

Paul Springer answered the doorbell before the chimes finished echoing within. "Hello, Del," he said as if inviting her to brawl. He was thin, like a taut spring, with a balding dome, and hard eyes.

"Hello, Paul," she replied. "This is Goff Langdon. He's helping me look for Amy."

"Little old to be your boyfriend, isn't he?"

"He's a private detective. Can we come in?"

"Sure." He opened the door wide and gestured them inside. "Let's sit at the kitchen table, back on the right."

Langdon wasn't sure if he was supposed to be running the show or was just along for protection, but as the three of them sat down and an awkward silence invaded the room, he realized that the role of at least facilitator was necessary. "When did you last see your wife, Mr. Springer?" He thought it odd that there were no pictures on the walls, not a single book or magazine on a coffee table, no clutter of any sort for that matter. Paul Springer must be anal-retentive, or perhaps it had been his wife that was the neat freak.

"Ten days ago."

"How were you getting along?"

"About normal."

"What do you mean by normal?"

"She was a bitch and we rarely talked."

"Were you fighting about something particular?"

"I didn't say we were fighting."

Langdon desperately wanted a beer, but he had an inkling this wouldn't be offered. "So, you weren't fighting. In what way was she being a bitch?"

"I'd work all day, come home, and make myself a sandwich for dinner because she'd be off with friends at a movie, or a book club, or some such thing. She spent all my money getting her hair cut, nails painted, and buying throw pillows. We have thirty-nine throw pillows in this house. Can you imagine?" Langdon glanced around, seeking but not finding a plethora of pillows. A plethora or anything, for that matter. He wondered what he'd see if he opened the fridge.

"Did Mrs. Springer work?"

"She conned her friends into hosting parties so she could foist jewelry and other junk on whoever was dumb enough to show up."

Langdon could picture the scene. Amy Springer was most likely your typical pampered, but bored, suburban housewife. He'd filmed many of these women over the years, stepping out with anybody who paid them any notice, not for love, but for the thrill. "Were you and Mrs. Springer still… intimate?"

"Yeah, sure, we had hallway sex."

Langdon knew this was a joke he'd heard somewhere before, but before he could stop himself, the words spilled out. "Hallway sex?"

"Yeah, every once in a while we'd pass each other in the hallway and say 'fuck you.'"

"Don't be an ass, Paul," Delilah spoke for the first time since entering the house.

"How often did you visit with your sister, Del? You don't like her much more than I do, you just had the luxury of not putting up with her shit every day." Paul slammed his hand down on the tabletop.

"We just went our separate ways, is all," Delilah retorted. "She had her thing and I had my gig."

"She was a royal class-A bitch, and you know it."

"What did you do to her?" Delilah stood up and leaned her face into Paul Springer's. "What did you do with her?"

He licked his lips, his eyes fixated on her breasts. "She, uh, she took off with some jackass she met at the gym. They're probably, um, pumping each other right now."

As they confronted each other, Langdon looked from one hard face to the other, feeling as if he were watching a play—and not a very good one—in which the actors were reciting their lines forcefully but without any real emotion.

~ ~ ~ ~ ~

There was no real information to be gleaned from Paul Springer, and with the sun descending in the west, Langdon and Delilah climbed back into the Jeep. "Are you okay?" he asked her.

"I can't stand that man. I know he did something to Amy."

"There was a little something odd," Langdon said.

"Odd? Other than him being an asshole?"

"Yeah, I kept wanting to glance over my shoulder to see if there was a teleprompter there. His answers definitely felt scripted. And the house looked more like a show model, you know, one of those things that gets propped, not something anyone ever lived in."

Langdon backed out of the driveway, but only went as far as the next house. "I'll call him tomorrow and find out what gym she worked out at. If she really hooked up with some dude there, people will know about it. Then we'll have a name, and it should be as easy as paying the guy a visit. Either Amy will be there, or she won't."

"What are you doing?" Delilah asked.

"Investigating the disappearance of your sister."

"Why are we here?" She nodded towards the house.

"I figure we'll ask the neighbors if they know anything. There's gotta be one nosey gossip monger in one of these places that can tell us something."

There were only seven houses in the development, and of the three people they spoke with, nobody knew the Springers. Delilah had told Langdon that they'd only just moved in at the beginning of the summer. A Mrs. Beede was surprised anybody was even living there, thinking it'd been vacant for a few years. Apparently, it was not a close-knit neighborhood.

Langdon dropped Delilah at the front of the Bernard. She opened the door, but then paused, and turned back, placing her hand on his knee. "Won't you come up to my room for a nightcap?" she asked in a throaty purr, and then laughed loudly, and climbed out.

He cursed in his head and pulled his cell phone from where he kept it in the Jeep, which was under the emergency brake. Somehow he had forgotten that he was supposed to pick up Thai food and be home right after closing the shop. There were three voice mails from Chabal. He'd turned the ringer off while at the bookstore, and never turned it back on. The first message was asking if she should place the Thai food order. The second was wondering where he was, and what time would he be home. The final declaration would have made a sailor blush and caused Langdon to seriously consider the idea that never returning home was the only option that would allow him to see another day.

Chapter 13

Tuesday

The Blue Cat Café in Westbrook was a place where working people could get a cup of coffee before going to work, but its main business was imported food items from Europe, Russia, and Asia that could not typically be found in much of the United States, especially this Maine mill town, a Portland suburb. The proprietors were a gregarious man and his surly wife, both from the town of Arkhangelsk in Northern Russia.

People in the know might whisper behind closed doors that the real owners of the establishment were the three men sitting around the small table in the corner. These men had known each other in Chechnya in the 1990s, two brothers and their best friend, and had fled the brutal wars for independence taking place at that time. The Greater Portland area had developed a surprising Russian population as those first pioneer immigrants had settled, begun to prosper, then sent home for, first, their parents, then siblings, nieces and nephews. Customers were more likely to hear Russian spoken in the Blue Cat Café than English.

Oleg Popov was considered in the local area to be what his last name signified; he was the Pope of Westbrook, and no decision large or small was made without his consent. His younger brother, Boris, was fiercely loyal and would do anything his brother asked him to. Albert Volkov was a flat-out killer, a man whose approach made men, women, and children cross the street, eyes downcast. Whereas Oleg and Boris were large jovial men, Albert was a thin blade, with eyes the color of steel.

These three controlled the Russian syndicate in Maine. While it wasn't Brighton Beach, it was their slice of the American Criminal Dream. They pimped some prostitutes, had a lucrative opiates business, and ran a small gambling empire. Thus, they and their families were well taken care of, if not rich. So, when they had been approached with an offer of ten million dollars to do a long but not particularly complicated job, they'd been unable to say no. That kind of money would mean winters in the islands, respect from New York, and a whole new avenue of business expansion, brighter options indeed.

At just past 6:00 in the morning, two men came through the door of the café. This was a dead period between the early risers off to do shift work and the regular crowd that would begin drifting in an hour later. The two slender men were expected. This was the second and final installment of the money owed, nothing more than a simple exchange of bank information. Gone were the days when the briefcase would've been filled with bundles of actual cash.

The Russians might have been more on guard if the two men weren't such obvious lackeys. They were thin, dressed like pretty boys, with manicured nails and coifed haircuts. How was it even possible to style such short hair? They were certainly not men to be feared.

Oleg, Boris, and Albert had discussed it amongst themselves and come to the conclusion that these two men must be some kind of assistants to the real bosses. Certainly, the Russians had no clue as to the real purpose of their tasks, only that those tasks were precise and detailed, clearly part of some plan they were to know nothing of. Albert was certain that it was some African king reaching his wealthy hand out to exact revenge upon the Black fellow currently sitting in a prison cell for murder. Oleg thought it was drugs. Boris didn't much care.

All they knew was that they were being paid a great sum of money to rape and kill three young women and then frame a man up to take the fall. Boris was the only one who felt remorse for setting the African up, but his share of the money certainly helped erase that guilt. Oleg had rather enjoyed the violation of the young girls, and Albert had happily snuffed out their souls when the time came.

The two fops came in and walked over to their table, as if coming to pay a ten-dollar bet on the previous night's baseball game. The one with the glasses set a briefcase on the table and sat down across from them, while the man with dark eyebrows stood loosely behind him with his hands clasped at his back.

"My employers are very happy with you," the one with glasses said.

"Our employers are very happy with you," the other man corrected.

"They have set up an account for you in the Cayman Islands. It is a different bank than the first one, just to split your eggs into separate baskets."

"And then we are done?" Oleg asked.

"After today, we will never see each other again."

"Let's finish up then." Boris leaned forward over the table.

The one with glasses took a small key, unlocked the briefcase, and opened it. He looked at the Glock 43 sitting there, raising his eyes for a brief moment to measure the three men. He knew that the dangerous one was Albert, who was standing, watching intently, to the right of the two brothers, who sat next to each other. While Albert's hand was not on a weapon, the thought was most definitely on his mind. There was something unsettling about the slender Russian that concerned him, even if he hadn't already run a background check on the man and discovered his brutal and callous nature.

Glasses reached his hand into the briefcase and grasped the handle, the weapon complete with silencer barely fitting into the space, so he had to pull his hand back as he tilted the pistol and shot Albert Volker in the forehead. Glasses shifted the pistol, firing twice more. Oleg had not even registered what had happened when his own life ended, and Boris was just leaning forward with widening eyes when the bullet split the distance between them.

At the same time, the other man, with thick eyebrows, turned and shot the gregarious proprietor once in the forehead. The two men retrieved three listening devices from the store, carefully wiped down anything they might have touched, and walked out the door. The proprietor's wife would come into the Blue Cat Café ten minutes later and discover the four dead bodies. Her screams would attract a passer-by, and eventually somebody would think to call the police, but this would be long after the two Boy Scouts were gone.

Chapter 14

You up? **The text** message was from Bart. Langdon checked the time. It was barely six in the morning. He'd been up for the past two hours. His peace offering of Thai takeout the night before had been met with stony rejection. It was, after all, three hours late, and he hadn't had the courtesy to remember to call, and yes, there appeared to be that thing about being out with the young lady he'd gotten drunk with the previous night. The bedroom seemed devoid of air to breathe, and Langdon had tossed and turned the night through, finally giving up and getting out of bed two hours before the paper was even delivered. He pecked out a quick reply: *Yep.*

The phone rang almost instantly. "Hey, Bart," Langdon answered.

"That plate you gave me to run? Enterprise. Tracked it down to the airport, but the guy on the phone was giving me a bit of a run-around. Said his manager came in at seven."

"Rental car place that opens at seven?" Langdon asked.

"It's the one at the airport. Gotta open when the people are coming through."

"You working today?" Langdon asked. He'd come into the bookstore to finish closing and cleaning from the night before, but was not on desk duty for the day.

"What do you know? First day off in the past two weeks. We need to seriously hire some more policemen."

"I bet you don't mind all the overtime you're getting."

"I'm not getting rich. You want to take a ride down to the Jetport?"

"Sure. You eat yet?"

"Thought you'd never ask. Why don't you pick me up and buy me breakfast at Rosie's on the way down?"

~ ~ ~ ~ ~

Langdon and Bart lumbered into Rosie's just as an exodus of first shift workers at BIW spilled out through the door. Luckily, this meant there was plenty of counter space available, but they did have to wait for Rosie and the one waitress to try and catch up from the morning rush.

"So, what's going on with this missing woman case? The one where you want me to see what I could find out about this Amy Springer?" Bart asked.

"Her sister is up from Virginia and thinks there might have been foul play by the husband. Did you turn up anything?"

"There are a lot of Amy Springers in Maine, bub, I'm gonna need an address."

Langdon read him the address off of his phone. "Talked to the husband last night. He said she ran off with the guy she works out with."

"You been to the gym yet?"

"I forgot to get the name," Langdon admitted. "I have his number, and I'll call him later. I got a couple of other questions to ask that I didn't want to touch upon with his sister-in-law there."

"I hear she's a real hot tamale."

"Who told you that?" Was Langdon destined to never have any degree of privacy in his entire life?

Bart shrugged. "I play cribbage Monday nights with Star."

"Hey, Langdon, I talked to that lady who was the press secretary for the senator," Rosie said, laying her bulging forearms on the countertop. "Afraid there's not much on that angle. Susan said she'd signed on to work with Senator Mercer when she was a moderate Republican, but she seems to be falling into step with the President along with the rest of them conservatives in the Senate."

"Thanks, Rosie," Langdon replied wearily.

"She had about enough when the senator voted to abolish Obamacare with no substitute plan in place, but hung on until the beginning of the summer, and that whole Dreamers fiasco."

"I think I have a line on the blackmailer," Langdon said. "So you can stop your snooping around."

"Yeah, Star said it was that lady who broke Jimmy's face," Bart said with a guffaw.

Rosie squinted. "You mean that lady who tried to blow up the whole state?"

"I think she was just trying to close the nuclear plant down," Langdon replied.

"By not reporting cracks in a nuclear reactor? Sounds like a piss-poor way to accomplish that goal, is all I got to say." Rosie moved down the counter to take the order of a young couple who looked like they were on their way to the beach.

"I think those two guys who threatened Chabal are working for her."

"Her?"

"Kamrin Jorgenson." As they ate, Langdon filled Bart in on his visitors at Hog Heaven the day before.

"Even back in the day, she had herself an army with the Flower First Party," Bart said when he was done. "But why did they refuse to let you talk to her?"

"Just protecting her?"

"Could be, but weren't you bringing her an offer?"

"Not the one she wanted, obviously. They did say Kamrin would return the photos once the President rejoined the Paris Climate Accord." Langdon watched in awe as Bart shoved an entire pancake into his mouth.

"How likely is that?"

"Zilch."

"So, Kamrin can release the photos and get nothing, or compromise, and to do that, she needs to negotiate?"

"The woman I remember from twenty years ago doesn't compromise," Langdon said.

"Okay, let me see if I got this correctly. Kamrin Jorgenson—who we previously had a run-in with under another name—is back in town blackmailing Senator Mercer with photos of an intimate nature, the ask being a political action impossible for the senator to meet? I remember that woman being a hell of a lot smarter than that. Maybe she's actually after something else." Bart shoved another pancake into his mouth.

"Yeah, maybe, and she's got foot soldiers backing her play."

"You have a point there." Bart's eyes widened almost as large as his mouth had to accommodate the flapjack. "You think they might actually be soldiers? Or former soldiers? What you've told me about them fits the type."

"Yeah, they could be, but that doesn't help us get any closer to knowing what KJ actually wants."

"Let's get back to the hot tamale," Ray finally said from his booth. There were four regulars who sat and nursed coffees every day, but he was the only one Langdon had ever heard speak. "What's she doing with a bloke like you?"

"Let's get out of here," Langdon said to Bart. "If we can find out who those Boy Scouts are, well then, we might actually have a chance of untangling this mess."

~ ~ ~ ~ ~

Langdon and Bart bickered all the way down to South Portland about a variety of topics, from sports, to country music, to the Big

Bang Theory, and finally, when they could avoid it no longer, the sorry state of the current political arena. Thus, Bart was suitably worked up when the manager at Enterprise gave them a hard time about client confidentiality and the need for a search warrant.

"What's your last name, Harold?" Bart asked him, reading his name tag.

"Jankowski," the man replied.

Bart held up a finger, pulled out his phone, and made a call. He looked back over at Harold. "34 Blackwell Lane in Windham. Is that you?"

Harold nodded, his face losing some of its bluster.

"Marijuana bust two years ago?" Bart shook his head. "Just before it was legal to possess. You smoke on the job? Does your boss know?"

"I don't smoke on the job," Harold muttered.

Bart held up his finger again and listened into the phone. After a bit, he looked gravely at Harold. "I think you best give me what I want."

They walked out of the Jetport with the name of the company that had rented the car. It was called Priority Z, with a Boston address and phone number.

"Who'd you call at the station?" Langdon asked him as they returned to the short-term parking lot.

"Angela was on duty. She's a sweetheart."

"What'd she tell you at the end that you didn't share, but caused Harold to cave?"

"Nothing. She'd hung up two minutes earlier."

"So, you bluffed him?" Langdon laughed.

"The guy was a turd. He had to be hiding something. I just had to let him think that I knew what he was hiding, or that I might at least be interested in looking further into his situation."

"If it's okay with you, I'd like to stop by a house up on the Eastern Promenade and ask a lady about some fake cable company men."

"Is that why you had me check and see if there'd been any stolen Xfinity vans?"

"Ahh, yes," Langdon concurred. "I forgot all about that. What'd you find?"

"Nothing," Bart said, settling his bulk into the passenger seat of the Jeep with a grunt. "Guess it wasn't that important if you don't even remember asking me."

"Trying to clear an innocent man, my friend. Sorry if I made you log into a computer for no reason, but I'm grasping at straws here."

"What's this cable van have to do with your case with Jewell? You know, the one with the black-skinned fellow who killed those girls?"

"I believe you can just say Black," Langdon said gently, knowing the explosive temper of his friend, but feeling it his duty to at least introduce him to the grosser nuances of political correctness. He, after all, came from a different age, had no kids, had never been married, and his friends could be counted on one hand. He just didn't always know any better.

"Yeah, the immigrant," Bart barreled on. "What's going on with that?"

Langdon told him about the fake service call from Comcast on the day of the anonymous tip that led to Tug's arrest.

"Did you say he had a Russian accent?" Bart honed in. "I got a buddy works in Westbrook. He tells me Russian gangsters are starting to become a real problem in the greater Portland area."

"You think you can give him a call?" Langdon asked. "See if he can give you some names of men with a Russian accent that are big enough players to be involved with murder, and smart enough to set somebody else up for it."

Langdon pulled the Jeep into a strip mall parking lot for Bart to make the call. It was hard to have a conversation on a cell phone with the open top. He decided to make a few phone calls of his own, and got out for some privacy. Mrs. Levesque did not answer, which was odd, but she probably had to get out for groceries at some point. Paul Springer's phone went directly to voice mail, his condescending tone filling Langdon's ear with a request to leave a message.

A text popped up from Missouri: *I am getting in to Portland tomorrow at 3. Are you still good to pick me up?* He hastily pecked out a quick reply to the affirmative and asked how she was doing. He gave it a minute, hoping he'd caught her able to communicate, but when no reply was forthcoming, he walked back to the Jeep.

Bart was waving out the top. "C'mon, we gotta go."

"What's the hurry?" Langdon asked, as he opened the door.

"We need to go back the way we came, back towards Westbrook," Bart said impatiently.

"What for?" Langdon turned left onto ME-22.

"There was a quadruple murder."

"In Westbrook? What's that got to do with us?"

"You ever hear of the Blue Cat Café?"

"Nope."

"It's a Russian grocery, deli, and coffee shop. Take this right."

Langdon curled to the right at the Tate House Museum. He knew better than to pepper Bart with questions, for that just caused the man to clam up.

"They just found four bodies there. The czar of Little Russia and his top two generals, as well as the proprietor."

"Holy shit."

"Left here."

It was a neighborhood joint, not quite in downtown Westbrook. There was side-of-the-street parking only. The police had closed down one lane of traffic with cones and yellow tape. Bart was able to flash his badge and get them through. They were stopped at the doorway by a police officer with stern directions to let nobody in.

"Is Lieutenant Moss inside?"

"Who the hell are you?"

~ ~ ~ ~ ~

It took some finagling, but Moss came outside to talk to them. He and Bart had known each other for years, and while he wasn't sure what his friend was doing here, he agreed to give him a few minutes. Forensics had just arrived and was kicking him out anyway.

"What's going on?" Bart asked.

"What's it to you?" Moss and Bart had a mutual respect for each other, but it only extended so far.

"I have reason to believe that your dead men inside may in some way be tied to the Old Port Killer," Langdon said.

"And who the fuck are you?"

Bart inclined his head. "This is Goff Langdon. He's a private detective from up in Brunswick."

"I certainly don't need a private detective poking around in the middle of this shit storm," Moss exploded.

"I might be able to help you out, Lieutenant," Langdon said.

"I got four dead guys and you might be able to help me out?" Moss rolled his eyes. "I'll give you one minute."

"I was hired to clear the name of Tugiramhoro Mduwimana who was recently pegged as the OPK. The man is an immigrant from Burundi, but he's as clean as a whistle. On Friday, the police got an anonymous tip and searched the house he is staying at. They found the murder weapon, and the ID of one of the girls in his room."

"I could get all that from reading the newspaper if I wanted to give myself a headache in the morning," Moss retorted.

"I spoke with the landlady and she tells me there was a visit by the cable company that day, even though she had no knowledge of an appointment. Comcast has no record of a service call."

"And what does that have to do with the fucking mess here?"

"She said the man she spoke with had a Russian accent."

"Just tell us what you got inside?" Bart said. "It's not like it's a secret."

Moss sighed. "I got four vics in there. All with bullets in the forehead. Oleg Popov, the Pope of Westbrook, his brother, Boris, and their enforcer, Albert Volkov."

"I thought you said four?" Bart asked.

"The owner. Wrong place, wrong time."

"All four in the forehead?" Bart asked incredulously.

"A professional hit, for sure," Moss replied.

"Anything missing?"

Moss shook his head. "Not that we can tell."

"You should see if they have alibis for the coeds killed by OPK," Langdon said.

Moss stared at him. "I'm in the middle of a quadruple murder and you're wasting my time telling me some cable man had a Russian accent? I'm sorry, Bart. I don't have time for this. Get out of here." He waved his hand dismissively and turned back to one of the medical examiners.

They stepped back to the sidewalk. Police cars filled the street. The media was being held back, reporters and cameramen yelling questions. Pedestrians surged in the midst of all of this, something deep inside of them drawn to gore, to misfortune, and to death. A seagull flew overhead, unperturbed by the machinations of man.

Right in front of the store was a white van. As they started to walk past, Langdon suddenly stopped, and stared at the vehicle. He then moved to a different angle, and craned his neck sideways.

"Bart, do you think you can get your buddy to come down here?"

It was not easy, but Moss was persuaded to come down and look at the van from the angle Langdon had. "What am I supposed to be looking at?" But then he paused, sidled a bit closer, and stared along the side.

Barely discernible, seen only with the right angle and light, were two shades of white. Slightly cleaner than the rest of the van were the letters X-f-i-n-i-t-y. The 'X' covering the front door under the window and angled up to the 'y' at the back.

"Who do you suppose owns this van?"

Moss walked slowly towards the rear doors. "More important, what do you think we'll find when we see what's in it?"

Chapter 15

Still Tuesday

At the end of Maquoit Road was a boat ramp with a small parking lot with only enough room for five or six cars. The access was mostly for the clammers—at low tide, much of the bay was a mud flat. At high tide, on a sunny day, it was a great place to come and sit, eat a pastry from the Lenin Stop and sneak a latte, while reading the *Bath Daily News*. As long as the black flies or mosquitos weren't in season—or worse, the greenies that took a chunk of flesh—Jonathan Starling liked to bring a beach chair out and enjoy the beauty of the Maine Coast. Starling had never taken a smoke break once since working at the Coffee Dog Bookstore, but the rest of the time, he smoked ferociously.

There had been a time when he had strutted around in expensive suits, and thought that ideals were more important than realities. When he graduated from Maine Law in the early eighties, his path was neatly laid out before him—to do battle to save the environment. He and his best friend, Harper Truman, moved to Madison where they could stare Big Paper in the eye, and still be close enough to Augusta to lobby the legislature. They rented a house and hung out their shingle, sleeping in the back and practicing in the front. They worked day and night, and one night, when out celebrating a victory, even if only a temporary restraining order on cutting a parcel of land, they had met Jordan Fitzpatrick.

Starling had sex with her the first night he met her, but it wasn't until much later that he realized his friend and partner, Harper, had also been sleeping with her regularly. She joined their small law firm, and in a town built by Big Paper, they were the three musketeers, one for all, and all for one against everybody. At some point, Starling had realized they'd begun skirting the edge of the law, and that ethics for his partners had become merely what one could get away with. As the firm grew more radical, their house became first a meeting spot, and then home and center to a growing number of hippies who were into drugs, free sex, and nature. They had been groomed by Jordan Fitzpatrick to be her strike force, but it wasn't until years later, after countless drunken nights, that Jonathan Starling realized this. By then, the group was sabotaging skidders and vandalizing worksites.

The paper companies brought in guards and dogs to protect the equipment, so the group's next logical step was spiking trees. After they'd done their clandestine work, the group would send an anonymous letter to the company telling them what had been done, but not where, with the intent of preventing them from cutting. And then the day came that a man from Madison that Starling knew fairly well ricocheted his chainsaw off a spike and into his own forehead.

With no way forward, and no way out, Starling had taken the coward's route and disappeared into an alcoholic haze, and slowly slid from his own firm to a barstool and then a curb. It was here that Bart and Jimmy had retrieved him some years ago. When Langdon gave him the menial job of clerk in his bookstore, Starling had managed to clean up his act, if not all at once.

With these thoughts reverberating in his head, a shadow suddenly blocked the sun, and then a woman sat down next to him. She was dressed casually in capris, a white tank top, sandals, and dark glasses. A baseball cap covered up her short, sandy-brown hair. It was as if his imagination had conjured her from thin air.

"Hello, Jonathan."

"Hello, Jordan. What the fuck do you want?"

"I just wanted to say hi. It's been a long time."

"Not long enough, I'd say, and I doubt you ever did anything to just say hi, so let's have the real reason you've tracked me down."

"It's been a long time since I've been called Jordan."

"Langdon calls you KJ."

"KJ will do."

"I take it you showing up here has something to do with Langdon?"

"We'll get to that. You still boozing?"

"No. Gave it up the last day I saw you."

"Good for you. I'm sorry if I was the cause of all that."

Starling shrugged. Of course, she had been the sole reason for his disintegration all those years ago. "What have you been up to since I last saw you?" he asked.

"Trying to do what we both wanted back in the eighties. Do you remember what that was?"

"We were young."

"Did that make us wrong?"

Starling ground his butt out and dropped it into the jar he kept in his old Ford truck just for this purpose. "It's not wrong to want to save the earth, but it is wrong to hurt people to achieve those aims."

"Who have I hurt?"

"Tommy Peters when the chainsaw cleaved his head in two?"

"We told them we'd spiked the trees. He knew he was taking a chance."

"He was trying to make a living."

"Not my problem."

"How about the Chief?"

"He committed suicide, that wasn't me."

"Whatever helps you sleep at night." Starling wasn't going to give her the satisfaction of his own name being bandied into this conversation. At least he'd survived.

"He didn't have to cheat on his wife with me."

"It seems you're up to your old tricks," Starling said, lighting another cigarette. "I suppose the fallout from this one won't be your fault either."

"The woman shouldn't have cheated on her husband."

"They have an understanding, or so I've been told." Starling turned and looked at her for the first time. "You've cut your hair and lightened it up since your last photo shoot."

She grinned wickedly at him. "So, you saw those pictures. I'm doing okay for a woman in my fifties, don't you think?"

Starling blushed, as those pictures and this visit had brought back a rush of erotic memories with this woman. "What are you playing at... KJ?"

"I'm not playing, not one little bit, but I think I might have gotten in over my head, or at least, into the wrong game. I'm not sure I even know whose game it is, to tell the truth, and that's got me a bit worried."

"What do you really want from the senator?"

"I was hoping that she would use her influence to save the Paris Climate Agreement, but I'm not sure that someone doesn't have another agenda, one I know nothing about, in fact." She shook her head, a preoccupied look on her face. "I knew it was too fantastical to be true."

"What do you mean?"

"A month ago, these two guys paid me a visit, said they were part of Earth First, and that I could be useful."

"And?"

"I don't know. I was so desperate to, to escape the shitty circumstances I was living in, I'm not sure I was thinking that clearly. That was then, but now, something seems off."

"Are they the two that have been warning Langdon away from you?"

KJ ran her tongue over her lips, which were suddenly dry. She didn't actually know what those two men had been up to, other than creating the opportunity for her to meet and seduce the senator and getting her out of South Dakota. The night at the Bernard had been the fourth time she'd managed to bump into Senator Mercer, and KJ knew she'd hooked her the minute Mercer's eyes had widened at the light blue off the shoulder evening dress she was wearing. "Do you think Langdon will talk to me? He's not just going to finger me so that the senator's private assassins can kill me?"

"You think the senator has private assassins on the payroll?"

"Don't they all?" KJ didn't think that Margaret would kill her. She had been a gentle and conscientious lover, and it was hard for KJ to believe the tender woman she'd made love to at the Bernard was really a stone-faced killer, or that she lacked morality so completely as to order murder commited in her name. The senator, however, wasn't necessarily in control of the whole thing it seemed, and who knew what those around her were capable of?

Starling contemplated that. He considered himself a confirmed cynic. But, while he believed that government agencies, such as the CIA, certainly had mercenaries and killers working for them, he'd never considered that senators might, as well. "I guess they might, at that," he finally concurred.

"So, I need to know, is the plan to negotiate with me, or to kill me?"

"As I understand it, Langdon has an offer from the senator that he wants to discuss with you."

KJ looked across the blue shimmering Maquoit Bay, watching what may have been an eagle circling gently high above. She pushed a tuft of hair back under the rim of her baseball cap. "You know I can't be bought, Jonathan." A breeze sprang up, tipping the water in whitecaps. "But I don't like to be used either."

"What do you mean? Aren't you the one using people? Like the senator?"

KJ stood up. "What's Langdon's number? I need to talk to the man."

~ ~ ~ ~ ~

"Four dead Russians?" Chabal asked. It didn't seem plausible, not here in Maine, especially after there'd already been the Old Port Killings. She and Langdon were on their back deck, overlooking the Brunswick Commons, a parcel of woodlands crisscrossed with town paths. Chabal was drinking a glass of white wine and Langdon had a beer, and while it was not yet five o'clock, it was close enough.

"Each one shot in the forehead. It was more of an execution than a murder. The dead men were part of the Russian mob in Westbrook." Langdon was glad to divert the focus of the attention away from Delilah Friday. "Hell, they *were* the Russian mob in Westbrook."

"The Russian mob is in Westbrook?"

"Not anymore," Langdon replied. "Although, I'm sure somebody will step forward to fill the hole."

"And this helps in your immigrant case, how?"

"There was a white van out front, and still faintly discernible was the silhouette of Xfinity on the side. The van was registered to Oleg Popov, who was one of the dead men, and also the head of the Russian mob in Maine. This would suggest they were involved in planting the evidence on Tug with that false cable service call. The police seemed convinced enough to keep their eyes open for any sort of connection to the murders of the USM students."

"There's suspicion, but you have no motive or actual evidence."

"This is true," Langdon admitted. "But once the ball starts rolling it usually hits something."

"Unless it's a gutter ball," Chabal responded. "So, why were these men abducting, raping, and killing college students?"

"I don't know," Langdon shrugged his shoulders.

"I suppose it could just be because they're horrible, evil men, but let me float another idea by you," Chabal said.

"Float away."

"What if the Russians were doing this on orders of their government?"

Langdon snorted, took a second look at his wife, and chewed his lip.

He was not yet so far out of the doghouse that he could be disdainful. "You think Putin ordered them to rape and kill young women?"

"Why not?" Chabal asked. "It's a proven fact that he has close ties to organized crime."

"To what purpose?"

"Let's say you're right, and these Russians did kill those girls, and then tried to frame an immigrant from, where did you say he was from?"

"Burundi."

"They frame an immigrant from Burundi. Who stands to gain?"

"Nobody?"

"That's your perspective as a rational human being," Chabal said. "Now put on your MAGA cap. Think about the President's policies of halting immigration from Muslim countries and building a wall on the Mexican border. Don't you think that if an immigrant is convicted of raping and killing a bunch of young women that it is one more step towards the country going ape-shit and falling in line with the President's wishes?"

"Putin is going this far to support Trump for the next election? Really?"

"It wouldn't be the first time," Chabal said grimly. "He helps get him elected, promotes his polices, and in turn, controls their relationship."

"On the one hand, it just seems so fucking crazy!" Langdon observed. "But on the other, our fearless leader has been known to do some pretty crazy-ass stuff. You might be right. I can see how, with something like Tug's arrest, Senator Mercer might be more inclined to yield to pressure to support some of the more conservative polices she has avoided," Langdon mused. "But Putin?" He shook his head.

"Why not?"

"Why were they, in turn, murdered?"

"I guess it sounds pretty far-fetched."

"We have to consider every possibility," Langdon said, even though his tone suggested that no, some notions need not be followed up on.

"Maybe by CIA operatives?" Chabal was well aware that this was starting to sound like an episode straight out of *The Americans*, the series they'd recently finished about Russian spies, but why not?

"It was certainly professionals," Langdon admitted.

"Or maybe they knew you were on to the Russian connection?"

"Who do you mean by 'they'?"

"The Russians. The FSB."

"You mean they were covering their tracks?" Langdon stood and walked to the deck railing. "They couldn't have known we were even looking for a Russian. The only person that even knew other than me was Jewell." But a fleeting memory of bragging to Delilah Friday about being suspicious of a Russian connection was knifing through his thoughts, though he was not going to bring this up to his wife.

"Just trying to think outside the box," Chabal came up behind him and slid her hands under his shirt and pressed her cheek to his back.

"Hmmm. You certainly pose some good points." He was watching a squirrel boldly scampering into their yard.

"Maybe I watch too much television."

"Get the squirrel," Langdon said to dog who was immediately off the deck in a flying leap that in no way surprised the rodent as it escaped up a tree. "CIA. FSB. Wow."

"What about the young man who is suspected of being the OPK?"

"4 by Four has a meeting with the judge and the prosecution before the bail hearing tomorrow. I doubt they'll set him free, not without more evidence." Langdon pulled a beer from the bucket of ice where two Stowaways from Baxter continued to reside. He popped the can and poured the cold beer into his glass.

"And where are you at in the blackmail case? The senator hired you to negotiate with KJ, but the two men who work for her have warned you to stay away? That seems a bit odd."

"It is strangely odd. Not that I've worked on many blackmail cases, but in all the books it's always pretty clear-cut. If you don't pay or do something, we are going to reveal something. In this case, the pictures were sent first with no demand. Then when the demand was made, the goons working for the blackmailer warn off the negotiator hired to handle the situation."

"Has KJ said she wants to deal only with the senator?" Chabal leaned over the railing, her tanned legs stretched out as she looked left and right wondering where dog had gone. She wore a white tank top that was one of Langdon's favorites. It was the simplicity of the cotton-ribbed shirt that left little to the imagination and was almost, but not quite, see through—that spurred his imagination.

"Not that I know of, but I have a feeling that the senator isn't telling me everything."

"I wonder how her husband—what is his name? Maxwell?—I wonder how he took the news that she was overriding his decision to let you go." She whistled, wondering if dog had perhaps gotten carried away in his pursuit of the squirrel.

"It's obvious who wears the pants in that family," Langdon replied. "It's Glover who kind of freaks me out. He's always lurking in the shadows."

"Missouri comes in tomorrow?" Chabal wondered that perhaps Langdon should convince his daughter to stay away, with all the intrigue and violence that seemed to be swirling around them. "Do you think she might want to postpone her visit until…?"

"I already tried. If anything, my mentioning danger seemed to stiffen her resolve to come visit. I pick her up at 3:00."

Chabal had figured as much. She wouldn't have mentioned danger to Missouri, but might have just left it at it was not a good time. "Jewell wants to know if we'll have a barbecue tomorrow night."

"Why?"

"They're in the middle of remodeling their kitchen, and something about a promise to 4 by Four to set him up with her friend, Cary Stockton. She thought it could wait, but you know how much of a pest 4 by Four can be. She said her and Cary had plans for tomorrow night already, so it'd be easy to swing her through here instead."

"Really? We are in the middle of a mess that includes serial killers, Russia mobsters, framed immigrants, death threats from mercenaries, and we have to pander to 4 by Four's social life and throw a barbecue?"

"Be a good chance to get everybody together and talk it through. Invite Bart and Star. Jimmy, Jewell, and Richam will be coming already."

"Who's working the bookstore tomorrow?"

"You're opening, and then Star comes in at noon. You pick up Missouri at 3:00? I can shop for food as I'm off all day."

"You getting hungry yet?" Langdon asked.

"Where did dog get to?"

"He's gotta be around somewhere," Langdon replied. "It's almost his dinner time so I can't imagine he's wandered off too far."

"Dog!" Chabal called. She went down the steps and across the lawn to the woods and called again.

Langdon decided to check the front since the neighbors across the way sometimes left their garage doors open and that happened to be where they kept their trash. Not that the mutt would rip into it, but the smells emanating from the waste were an irresistible pull on the canine.

Dog was in the center of the road wolfing something down, and Langdon hoped that it wasn't a dead rodent of some sort. Eating roadkill was one of dog's favorite pastimes. Langdon called his name, just as he heard the racing of a car engine. He called again louder and more insistently, and dog picked his head up just as an old Mercury came barreling into view, easily going twice the posted speed limit of twenty-five.

With horror, Langdon watched dog take two steps, and then the left front fender cracked into him, sending him tumbling head over heels down the street. Langdon broke into a run, yelling curses that he wouldn't remember, anger and worry erupting as he crossed the front yard and into the street. He didn't think to get a plate number, and he considered giving chase, as the car turned a corner and whizzed away, but his first priority was to dog, who lay crumpled in the road.

Chapter 16

Michael Glover sipped his scotch. It was only noontime, but he felt that he'd put in a good day's work already. Years of planning were finally coming to fruition. Late the night before, he'd picked up the CEO of MacLeod Brandt at the Brunswick Executive Airport. He'd spent most of the night, and all of the morning, discussing strategy with her.

Marisa Wilkes had recently become the head of MacLeod Brandt, the largest military contractor in the world, rising with the appointment to become one of the most powerful people who walked the earth. With a $50 billion dollar annual turnover and given its role as the main supplier of weapons in the United States, the company was a juggernaut with a power all its own. She wore a black-knit sweater with a rounded collar and all three buttons buttoned. Gold plated steel huggie hoops clutched her ears on either side. Her hair was pulled back in a bun.

Just an hour earlier, her predecessor at MacLeod Brandt, Deputy Secretary of Defense, Randall Ryan, had arrived. Ryan had flown into Portsmouth and driven up to Brunswick, so as to not be spotted meeting with, or having a flight log record similar to, Marisa Wilkes, as this was all highly unethical. His schedule said he was taking a vacation day on the southern coast of Maine. It was said that this slender man would soon be assuming the top position of Secretary of Defense, as the man currently in that position was being not so gently prodded to resign. When that happened, it would be much more difficult to disappear from the public eye for a day of back-room dealing.

Just ten minutes earlier, Senator Margaret Mercer had shown up with her husband, Maxwell. The five of them, plus two personal assistants, now sat in the living room, all with glasses of Macallan eighteen-year-old Sherry Oak. It was not every day that people hosted a luncheon of this magnitude, and Glover allowed himself to revel in the moment. The kitchen counters held sandwiches, soups, green and pasta salads, and a variety of desserts from Wild Flour down on Maine Street. He only hoped that he was allowed to stay for the guts of the conversation. Glover wondered who carried the second most clout in the room, the contestants being the soon-to-be Secretary of Defense and a United States Senator. There was no doubt in his mind that Marisa Wilkes firmly held the number one spot.

Deputy Secretary of Defense, Randall Ryan, was sitting on the couch conversing with Maxwell Mercer. His blond hair was receding, leaving a gleaming patch of scalp up front. This gave his face an unnaturally long look, offset by his wide mouth and piercing blue eyes. It was said that he often golfed with the President, but knew enough not to shine too much on the course. That might have been his greatest gift, knowing when to hide his light under a bushel, all while carefully advancing his way through promotions and power plays almost undetected, rising to the top while other flashier candidates had fallen by the wayside to petty jealousies and offended enemies.

Maxwell Mercer also knew well the art of camouflage, and Glover was one of the few who were aware of how deep his influence ran. Glover doubted that even Maxwell's wife, the senator, knew the duplicity he was capable of. He had done everything there was to do in the political arena except to be an actual politician. He'd been chief-of-staff, personal assistant, campaign director, and most recently, head of a political consulting firm that was renowned in Washington. He wore that goofy smile on his face and stabbed people in the back once they'd been disarmed by his "harmless fellow" act.

Marisa Wilkes was conversing with Senator Mercer, and Glover wondered about the changing world, a place in which these two women held such positions of power. He could remember a time when the fairer sex silently supported their husbands, and while they may not have cooked and cleaned, had certainly kept their opinions to the confines of their own homes. Glover had never married, but rather, liked to hire the women he slept with to ensure they kept to their place in his world.

Glover's face remained impassive, and he wondered how it was possible that a woman held this position of power. Wilkes was a very plain woman, perhaps the problem, Glover thought. Her face was broad, her features plastered on it like a toddler's attempt to assemble Mr. Potato Head, and her bulky sweater equally unbecoming. Glover supposed that her $20-million-plus salary a year made up for her homeliness. But he knew full well the agility of her mind, with its keen perception and ability to read the basic nature of people, himself included.

There were not many people in the world who scared Michael Glover, but Marisa Wilkes was one. She was probably meant to be a man, was how he rationalized that she was absolutely superior to him in the power she'd amassed. He did not much go in for that genetics stuff, people being born gay, and/or trapped in the wrong body, or feeling the need to dress as the opposite sex. It was all a bunch of phooey devised by communists masquerading as liberal democrats, as far as he was concerned. Except for Marisa Wilkes. Of course, Michael Glover knew enough to not share any of his innate prejudices with the world. His only counsel was himself, and to this he was true.

MacLeod Brandt supplied missile defense systems, helicopters, combat ships, and spacecraft for NASA, but their primary source of income was the P-38 jet fighter, which had opened up the

Saudi Arabia weapons market to MacLeod Brandt production, dramatically increasing their stock price, and substantially distancing them from their closest competitor. Finally, the Saudis would have the advanced weaponry to destroy Yemen once and for all, and then the war with Iran could begin, a decade of conflict making the world's arms manufacturers and dealers even wealthier and more powerful, especially those whose former CEO would soon become the U.S. Secretary of Defense. The profit that MacLeod Brandt stood to reap from war with Iran made Halliburton's yield from the Iraq war seem trivial, a mere pittance in comparison.

Glover knew that the lobbying efforts of MacLeod Brandt were second to none, as they donated to over 250 congressmen and women in their campaigns, regardless of their party affiliation. He also knew that they went above and beyond the typical lobbying efforts. Cash was a lubricant to make even more money, and they were not afraid to spread it around, patiently waiting for the moment when it started the machinery moving. Think tanks and institutes and endowed chairs at no-name universities, scholarships and summer internships for Congressional offspring, reams of peer-reviewed papers in fusty journals and hot-button white papers commissioned from the Bains and the McKinseys of the world—Brandt MacLeod's ocean of dollars found its way into every corner of the Washington decision-making establishment. What were millions when you were dealing in billions?

"Should we eat first, or talk first?" Senator Mercer asked the room at large. There had been another blackmail letter, this one far different than the first, but certainly aligned with Mercer's political philosophy. If all went well, she'd have the negatives back soon, and the whole ordeal would be over.

"I could use a bite," Deputy Secretary Ryan said. "But I do have to be back in D.C. early tonight, so perhaps we can talk while we eat?"

Glover took that as his cue to go to the kitchen and tell his own assistant to put out the food on the dining room table and then take a break for a couple of hours. Once she had everything set out, he beckoned the others into the long room that held a table for twelve. There were no windows and two doors, which Glover made certain were shut. A single painting on the wall, an original by Andrew Wyeth, of an open window spilling out onto a field that stretched into the distance, offset the confining nature of the space.

"Congress is set to vote on the budget once summer recess ends." Senator Mercer saw no reason for idle chitchat if Ryan had a plane to catch.

Ryan nodded. "How does it look?"

"I think it needs some work, a few changes to be made," Mercer replied.

"To the defense budget?" he asked.

Mercer helped herself to a carton of soup that was labeled *ropa vieja*. She looked over at Glover. "Is this from Wild Flour?"

"It sure is, Senator."

"I love their soups, but I've never heard of *ropa vieja* served as a soup."

"I assure you, its excellent," Glover replied. "The peppers especially."

Ryan looked at his watch. "What are your thoughts on that, Senator Mercer, the defense budget?"

"It's a bit steep," she said.

"I would say that $750 billion is a compromise," Ryan replied, his face impassive.

"This isn't the media, Randall. We both know the real number is 200 billion more than that." Mercer dipped into her soup. "Wow, that is good."

"What exactly do you have trouble with, Margaret?" he asked, tight-lipped at her comment, manner, and use of his first name instead of title.

Glover smiled inwardly, his face utterly blank, blending in to the point of invisibility. Tomorrow, most of the people here would not remember that he'd even been present. His esteem of Senator Mercer moved up a notch, surpassing his opinion of Ryan, and placing her squarely just behind Wilkes among all the power brokers at the table.

"Well, I guess the seventy-billion-dollar slush fund for, how shall we call them—war games?—yes, that would be a place to start." The senator took another spoonful of the soup.

"I don't know what you're talking about," he replied. Ryan hadn't touched the sandwich corner he'd grabbed as soon as he sat down.

Mercer raised her thin eyebrow in a high arc. "No? I guess I should clarify I'm talking about the OCO funds. The money that is supposed to be slated for Overseas Contingency Operations, but we all know the DOD really uses it for a variety of things, both domestic and foreign, don't we?" She touched a corner of a table napkin to an invisible spot of soup on her chin.

"Again, I don't know what you're talking about. As far as I know, the OCO fund is earmarked for war operations against foreign threats."

"How much of it goes to Goldenrod?"

"We hire them for security operations in many foreign countries," Ryan said.

"As well as domestic missions, as I understand it, but nobody knows what any of it is about or what the heck they're up to, as there is no oversight of exactly how that money is spent."

"I assure you that that money is used only for what it is intended for, and every operation is of a legal and ethical nature."

Mercer held his stare for a long moment, letting him know she wasn't fooled in the slightest. The OCO fund was a separate entity with little to no oversight, and she knew full well the Defense Department was able to direct that money to whatever was needed, including operations by private mercenaries within the borders of the United States, something highly illegal on many counts. "Well, the number seems high to me, but who is going to argue against the safety of our nation?"

"What are you saying?" Ryan asked. He knew that she was a crucial swing vote, and that to garner her support was critical to the passage of the defense budget. He expected to compromise, so was visibly surprised by her next comment.

"I might be able to cast a 'yes' vote," Mercer said in a low voice.

"As it stands?"

"We've had some troubles here in Maine over the past month," Mercer replied, thinking that scotch was a good chaser to *ropa vieja*, but perhaps wouldn't compliment a pastry. "The police arrested an immigrant from Africa for the serial rape and killing of three college girls. Just yesterday, there was a gangland killing of four men, all Russian, who my sources tell me might have been working for Putin, spreading disinformation."

"Your constituents would be happy with a firm vote in favor of their safety," Ryan concurred. He took a bite of sandwich, immensely pleased.

"Putin developing hypersonic rockets by 2020 is a good selling point for the budget. I'm sure that MacLeod Brandt will continue to develop weapons that can travel at five times the speed of sound to match them." Senator Mercer had the line out and was carefully reeling it back in.

"We hope to hit twenty times the speed of sound by 2021," Marisa Wilkes said. MacLeod Brandt had worked with BIW on various projects including laser systems and the P-38 jet fighter.

"And some of these missiles will be deployed on destroyers?"

Ryan finished off another corner of a sandwich, chewing carefully. Here was the rub, he thought, but doable. "How many?" he asked.

"We are already making five DDG-51s that will be completed by the beginning of 2020. Give us five more to carry the hypersonic missiles."

Ryan made a steeple of his fingers and frowned. "Huntington Ingalls beat BIW's last bid by over a hundred million per ship. You're lucky to have any contract, much less five more."

"What price do they have to hit to make it happen?" Mercer knew the numbers and had fully expected this, having prepared the day before in a conversation with Phebe Novakovic, the CEO of General Dynamics, BIW's parent company. Novakovic would not be happy to know Senator Mercer was currently cutting a deal with the Deputy Secretary of Defense that included the CEO of her competitor, MacLeod Brandt, but that which she didn't know, couldn't hurt her.

"I could get you three more for, ballpark, 900 million apiece."

"I help pass the defense budget that includes money for the wall, the slush fund money to be used as you want, the continuance of the astronomically-priced P-38 program, the expansion of the hypersonic weapons program, and you give BIW five destroyers for 900 million apiece."

Ryan appeared to consider the counter, gazing deeply at the Wyeth. Finally, he nodded. "I will see to it," Ryan agreed, nodding and smiling. It was, he thought, after all, a good deal, everybody made out, and isn't that what negotiations and politics was all about?

"Can you guarantee it?"

Ryan looked at the two aides, and then Maxwell Mercer, and finally at Michael Glover, and shrugged his shoulders, as he came to some internal decision. "I have it on good authority that Secretary Mathis will either resign or be fired very soon, and that I will be the pick to replace him. If that happens? I can guarantee it."

"You get me the contract, and you can count on my vote," Senator Mercer said.

Chapter 17

Still Wednesday

"Hi, Dad." Missouri Langdon walked across the pick-up section in front of the Portland Transportation Center terminal to where Goff Langdon leaned against the front of his Jeep in short-term parking.

Langdon noticed that her hair was redder than the streaks of blond and auburn that were her normal mix, inherited equally from each parent. She'd let the wild curls follow their own path, and they cascaded down to her shoulders in a gorgeous chaos. Her red and black speckled yoga pants complimented her hair, and a flowing black top helped give her the appearance of a runway model. There was a bright inquisitive shine to her eyes, a hint to the nature of a mind that wanted to learn everything about everything, a trait she'd been born with.

He gave her a hug. "Hi, E. I missed you." This was his nickname for his daughter, Missouri. When her mother, his wife at the time, started calling her Missy, he went the opposite direction, and started calling her E. That might have been the first hint of issues in their marriage.

"I missed you too, Pops."

"You've dyed your hair."

"Yep, do you like?"

"Yes, and I also like it when you let it go like this. You look more and more like me every day."

Missouri laughed. "Just what I wanted." She was tall at 5'8", but too thin, probably because she refused to spend money on food when there were many better things to do with it.

Langdon took her bag from her hand. "How was the trip?"

"After I almost missed the bus?" Missouri laughed. "Smooth. One movie, two naps, and some social media browsing." She was rarely without a book, but reading while moving gave her a queasy stomach.

"Why'd you almost miss the bus?"

"I knew it left at 9:00, and I knew the subway ride was thirty minutes, but somehow I forgot I had to walk ten minutes to get there, and my cats were so cute that they were hard to leave," she said with a rush. "I grabbed a coffee on the way, and then went back in and bought a breakfast sandwich for a homeless man on the corner, and before I knew it I was running. But I made it, and here I am."

They climbed into the Jeep and Langdon pulled around and exited the bus terminal. "Dog had an… accident last night, but don't worry, he's going to be okay."

"What? What sort of accident?"

"He was hit by a car. He got banged up pretty good, but the vet said there were no broken bones, though he does have a pretty good limp." Langdon choked up just thinking about it, but the anguish was passing, slowly being replaced with a growing rage.

"Did he run out into the street?" This was not unthinkable. Dog had once chased the UPS truck down the center of Maine Street for a good half-mile, just because the driver always made sure to bring him a treat when he delivered books to the shop. Unfortunately, this was a different driver, and he had been quite surprised when this brown thunderbolt bounded into his truck in search of sustenance.

"Not really," Langdon replied. "It was out front of the house, and he was standing in the street."

Missouri wrinkled her nose. "In the neighborhood? The car can't have been going that fast. How did they not see him? What did they say?"

"They didn't stop, and they were going quite fast."

"They didn't stop?" Missouri repeated in disbelief. "They hit a dog and just kept going?"

"They did it on purpose."

Missouri digested this information silently. Even with living in the city, she was still quite naïve about the evil that could reside in mankind. This was a constant concern for Langdon, the latest worry coming from stories of false Uber drivers picking people up then sexually assaulting and murdering them. Was that what had happened to the USM coeds, he wondered?

"I came around the side of the house looking for him, and he was standing in the middle of the road eating something. The car seemed to accelerate as it closed in on him, and luckily he took a couple steps when I called him, so the bumper just caught him a glancing blow, otherwise I'm certain he would've been killed."

"Are you sure they did it on purpose? Couldn't it have been some kids out messing around, and then they panicked and kept going?"

"After we got back from the vet, I went out to the street to see what he'd been eating. There were parts of a few hamburgers still sitting there."

"You mean some fucker baited him into the road with food and then ran him over?" Missouri asked incredulously. The skin on her face was matching her hair and she was staring at her father like she was going to smack him.

"It looks that way."

"Who would do such a thing?"

"I think it may have to do with a case I'm working on." Langdon pulled onto 295 North, his ire building even as he tried to calm his daughter.

"What case?"

"It's a blackmail case."

"Whoa, moving up in the private detective business, huh, Pops?"

"Oh, I've got several exciting cases going right now," Langdon said, a hint of irony in his voice. "There have been a couple of men warning me off of looking for the blackmailer."

"Why do you think it was them?"

"The last time they threatened me off was out to Hog Heaven. The man calling himself John tricked dog out of the Jeep with french fries." Langdon pictured the scene in his mind of the man casually dropping fries and exchanging seats with dog. "There was a bit of McDonny Burger wrapper still in the street last night."

"You've been hired to track down the blackmailer?"

"Yes."

"So, what? You think that two men who work for the blackmailer are sending a message that you should leave well enough alone?" Missouri hit the dashboard with her fist. "And the message was to hit my dog?"

"I'm not so sure they're working for the blackmailer."

"Who else wouldn't want you to hunt down the blackmailer?"

"That's where it gets strange. I know who the blackmailer is, and I am trying to set up a meeting to negotiate a settlement with her."

"And they respond to this by trying to kill dog?" Missouri had an uncanny ability to get right to the marrow of a subject. "That doesn't make any sense."

"No. No it doesn't."

"So, who do they work for?"

"That's the nub of the whole thing, right there," Langdon replied.

They rode in silence for a bit, Missouri looking out the window at Portland as it passed by on their right, and then over at Back Cove on the left. She liked all that New York City had to offer, sure, but she did miss Maine. Not now, but someday, it was in her life plan to come back here and live. Maybe not Brunswick, but Portland certainly had a bit to offer, and was cleaner, safer, and less crowded than NYC.

"How is the new apartment?" Langdon asked once Portland disappeared behind them.

"It's nice. Better than I could get for my money in Brooklyn, that's for sure." Missouri had recently moved up to Morning Side Heights to be closer to Columbia University where she'd be attending graduate school starting the next week.

"I'm excited to see it and meet your roommates."

"You've met Karalana a few times," Missouri reminded him. "And I'm sure you'll like Jocelyn. Maybe you can drive me back down on Monday? That way I don't have to take the bus. I've got an air mattress you can sleep on, or we even have a couch and a living room now, if you prefer that?"

"I am actually investigating three cases," Langdon bragged. It was not often he got to blow his own horn to his daughter, as most of his work involved taking pictures of cheating spouses, and really, how much could you go on about that with your own kid? "So I don't know if I'll be able to get away, but once they wrap up I will definitely come down."

"Wow, Dad. Three? Way to go. Tell me about them." She'd been just a toddler when her father had been shot in the head, and a couple years older when he'd been used as a dartboard, but she'd heard all the stories over and over from various members of Langdon's unofficial band of helpers—casually known as "the group"—usually after they'd consumed too much alcohol.

Langdon wasn't quite sure if she was being sarcastic or not, but plunged gamely forward. "I've got the blackmail case I was just telling you about, I'm trying to clear an immigrant of murder charges, and I'm also looking for a missing person," he said proudly.

"Not the OPK dude I've been reading about?" she asked.

"That's the one. The police arrested an immigrant from Burundi, but Jewell knows the young man through the immigrant social services agency she works for and didn't believe it, so she brought me in to investigate and got 4 by Four to represent him." Langdon knew that Missouri, who volunteered for a New York City program mentoring new immigrants seeking asylum, would not need an explanation of where Burundi was, that there would be no wrinkling of the forehead and repeating of the country's name in puzzlement like everybody else he'd told.

"And have you had any luck?"

"Actually, I'm waiting to hear from 4 by Four and Jewell. The bail hearing is supposed to be this afternoon. I've found out a few things that raise a reasonable doubt that it was him, but we'll find out soon what the judge thinks."

"Like what?"

"There was a fake Xfinity service call that went to the house where he rented a room. Later that day there was an anonymous tip, and the police found evidence in his room implicating Tug, that's his name, in the murders."

"So you're trying to track down the cable impostors?"

"Well, I found them, but I'm not sure they're going to be much use." Langdon wasn't sure he needed to tell his daughter that these men had just been killed in a grisly execution.

"Why not?"

Luckily, his cell phone buzzed, saving him from answering that question. Langdon wrestled it from the pocket of his shorts and barked into the phone, "Hello, Jimmy. What happened?"

"They dropped all charges," 4 by Four said excitedly into the phone. "The judge pulled us into his chambers, and the prosecution said that due to new evidence, they no longer wanted to pursue the case against Tug."

"Fantastic," Langdon replied. "Did they say what evidence?"

"No, but they must have found something in the van, or even in the Russians' homes. Bart told me they'd gotten search warrants after the suspicious Xfinity outline on their van."

"So, he's free and clear?"

"Yes. We're dropping him off at home as we speak."

"We? Are you with Jewell?"

"Yep. She picked me up and brought me down. Thanks, by the way, for inviting me to your barbecue tonight."

"I don't think I had much choice. My understanding is that Jewell is bringing a friend."

"Is that so?" 4 by Four asked, and Langdon could feel the smarm drip through the phone.

"Any time after six," Langdon said.

"Oh, shit," 4 by Four said. "Jewell, keep driving, don't stop."

"What? What's going on?"

Langdon could faintly hear frantic words on the other end, the commotion rippling with a suggestion of danger.

And then 4 by Four came back on the line. "Fucking ICE crawling all over the place. Find the guy innocent of all charges and still want to deport him. What a system."

"Do they have him?"

"Fuck no," 4 by Four replied. "We kept going. We're swinging around the promenade trying to figure out what to do."

"Take him to your house, or Jewell's," Langdon suggested.

"Yeah, we can't do that. Jewell is his caseworker and I'm his attorney. I'm pretty sure we will be getting our own visits from ICE very soon. You, on the other hand…"

"I'm not connected to him in any official capacity," Langdon finished for him. "Fine. Bring him to my house. He'll enjoy the barbecue after jail food, I imagine."

Langdon hung up the phone. "Looks like we have a house guest for a few days."

"Did I hear 4 by Four say ICE was crawling around his house?" One of Missouri's central roles in life had always been as crusader for the underdog.

"Yeah. They can't do anything if he has been granted asylum, can they?"

"You said the charges against him were dropped?"

"Yes. They didn't say what, but more evidence was found to exonerate him."

"Does he have a criminal record?"

"Not in the United States."

"In Burundi?"

"Yeah, there were some charges against him for inciting riots through inflammatory journalism. He left just in time. They wouldn't send him back to face imprisonment for disagreeing with the ruler of Burundi, though, would they?"

Missouri might have a naiveté about her, but that did not extend to the shenanigans of the government, whether it be the President, Congress, the judicial system, or what she deemed to be their Gestapo agency, ICE. "Suspicion is the new guilty, as far as immigrants are concerned," she said.

"What can we do?"

"I guess it's time for Uncle Jimmy to see how good of a lawyer he actually is," Missouri replied. "But if they get their hands on him, he'll be gone before any sort of motion to protect him ever makes it into the courts."

Langdon gazed fondly at his daughter, a twinge of regret growing to a dull ache that once again he had brought her into a potentially dangerous situation over which he had no control. Her first visit in some time, and dog was laid up after an assassination attempt on his life, most likely by the two Boy Scouts who'd threatened Langdon and Chabal as well. Now, they were harboring a fugitive from ICE. Perhaps he should send her away? But he knew that would not happen. She was a Langdon after all, and when people hurt your dog, you don't run away.

"Can we stop by Beans?" Missouri asked. "I need to see if I can get my old boots replaced."

It was strange in the midst of all of this to run such a mundane errand as a visit to L.L. Bean, but that is what they did before continuing on home, passing by the Bernard Inn and Tavern on their right. Luckily, Missouri hadn't made it around to asking about his third case, Miss Delilah Friday's missing sister.

Once they reached home, dog met them in the mudroom, his tail wagging furiously, beyond happy to see his sister. Of course, this made him fall down on his bad leg, whacking his scraped side in the process and letting fly a yelp of confusion and pain. Missouri fell to the floor beside him, and the two of them lay right there reconnecting as Langdon went inside to check on the preparations for the barbecue. It was nice to have his daughter home, Langdon thought, even if it was in dangerous times.

Chapter 18

Still Wednesday

The first chore of the barbecue had been to fill a cooler with beer and ice. Knowing there would be free beer, Bart showed up early, as Langdon figured. 4 by Four and Jewell had dropped off Tug and then gone on home to freshen up, or at least get out of their courtroom clothes into something more comfortable.

Tug had thanked Langdon for his help in freeing him, but Langdon could see the lingering concern in his eyes that was created by the ICE agents. Going back to Burundi would not be a good thing for him, not that his stint in America had been all that great so far, but at least he was still alive. There was something to be said about the democratic process of trial, judges, juries, and mostly fair play, especially if you had money or good people in your corner.

Missouri had stolen Tug away, speaking French with him, excited to have somebody to keep her language skills keen. They were sitting in chairs in the far corner of the yard bordering the Commons, and a few minutes earlier, Jack had joined them.

Jack was living at home as he developed his video production business. The idea was to create short promotional videos for companies to post on their websites. He had a degree in audio media and had spent eight years working for Channel Six, but was now hoping to leverage his computer skills in a direction that he more enjoyed.

It was strange to think that he was the oldest of the three, and that Missouri was not much, if any, younger than Tug. Missouri and Jack had certainly led sheltered lives compared to Tug, who had fled his home country in fear for his life, been granted asylum, then framed for horrific murders and just as abruptly found innocent only to find himself in danger of being deported to almost certain death.

"It was a Glock that killed those Russians," Bart said. "Moss called me himself, this afternoon. He asked why I was so interested."

"What'd you say?" Langdon took a swig of beer.

"I wasn't sure if you were keeping it secret that you had a Glock pointed in your direction recently by two mysterious figures. Are you?"

"I'm not sure. If I go to Lieutenant Moss with this, he's going to want to know what case I'm working on, and I can't really tell him that it's some lady blackmailing Senator Mercer about an illicit lesbian affair, now, can I?"

"Aren't you protected by client confidentiality?"

"Not as iron-clad as lawyers. Moss could make things pretty sticky for me, and I can't blame him. He's trying to solve a quadruple homicide, and I'm keeping secrets from him."

"I told him I was just curious, but I'm not sure he bought it," Bart said.

"What'd you find out about John Smith?" This was the name on the driver's license used for the car rental.

"About what you'd expect. Nebraska address. About four billion John Smiths in the world, and our technology is not as good as you see in the movies."

"Maybe I can see if Jack can dig up anything. He's pretty good with that internet thing."

"How's his business coming along?"

"He's currently looking for investors and clients. To be fair, he's actually started making money doing something with online gaming cheats, or something like that. I'm not sure I understand it, but it seems to be paying a few bills."

"And how's Missouri?" She had not yet seen Uncle Bart sitting up on the deck, even though there were three empty beer cans next to him. Langdon was still on his first.

"Doing great. Loves her new apartment and roommates. All signed up for classes."

"Master's program in English? What's she planning on doing with that?"

"Maybe she'll write mystery novels," Langdon said with a chuckle. "I'd be ebullient to have a shelf at the shop dedicated to my own daughter's writing."

Bart shot him a look. "Ebullient? You buy one of those word-a-day calendars or something?"

Chabal came out on the deck. "You think you can get the grill going while you drink that beer and entertain the guests?"

"Sure enough," Langdon replied. "I was just waiting for the go-ahead." He had the charcoal chimney already filled and just had to light the paper on fire, which he did as he got himself a second beer. "Did you buy any salads?"

"I am making a green salad, but I also bought a pasta salad. I might add a few things as it doesn't look all that exciting."

Langdon checked the time on his phone. "Eat at seven?"

"Perfect," Chabal replied.

They were interrupted by the arrival of Jewell and Cary Stockton. Langdon knew her faintly, as she had a son close in age to Missouri, but had only seen her in passing in quite a few years now. They made the perfunctory small talk, introduced Bart, and then Chabal swept the two women back inside to help her prepare the salad.

Ten minutes later, Langdon was spreading the charcoal out to heat the grate when Richam and 4 by Four arrived together. 4 by Four immediately spotted Tug, Missouri, and Jack, and walked across the yard to where they were sitting, while Richam pulled up a chair on the deck.

"Hanging out with 4 by Four?" Bart asked.

"He called to see what the driving situation was. When I told him Jewell had picked up Cary earlier, he suggested he come get me, that way I can go home with my wife," Richam said with a straight face.

"Mighty nice of him," Langdon said.

"But, who will give the newly single friend a ride home?" Bart asked.

"I suppose you could?" Langdon suggested to Bart, who threw a glare his way.

"Had a fellow into the bar today who works out on the airfield at Brunswick Landing," Richam said, moving the topic away from the philandering ways of their friend. "Don is always sharing the who's who of the important people that are on the flight lists. Guess who came to our little town last night?"

"Jeff Bezos?" Bart asked.

"Close," Richam replied. "Marisa Wilkes, the new CEO of MacLeod Brandt."

"The airplane company?" Langdon asked.

"Weapons manufacturer," Richam replied disgustedly. "Only the biggest in the world. I guess they develop and produce airplanes too, but that's only the tip of the iceberg."

"Yeah, they make those P-38s that have all the problems, but we just keep paying for," Bart said. "You're telling me some woman heads up that company?"

Richam ignored Bart's sexist remark. "Her private jet landed late last night and flew out this afternoon. Not much of a vacation."

"Sounds like a business trip. BIW?" Langdon asked.

"Perhaps," Richam agreed. "But it certainly could have included your client. Do you suppose the senator met up with her?"

When no answer was immediately forthcoming, Langdon went in to grab the steaks from the counter. He'd considered just burgers, but they hosted barbecues all too rarely, and so he had suggested Chabal pick up some tips from Bow Street.

Jonathan Starling had just walked in carrying some tortilla chips and salsa, which he claimed he'd made. He beckoned to Langdon, "Hey, you know that thing I needed to talk to you about earlier, but then those people came into the store and you had to head out to get Missouri?"

"Sure, but can it wait until later? I need to put these steaks on."

"Just give me a minute," Starling said, stepping back out the front door onto the porch.

"What is it?" Langdon asked, following him out.

"Have you heard from KJ?"

"No, not a word. Why?"

"I saw her yesterday. She must have followed me out to the boat ramp on Maquoit. Came walking up like we'd just seen each other a few days earlier, instead of twenty years ago."

"What'd she want?"

"I don't know," Starling said, shaking his head. "She was all over the place. She was wondering if the plan was to kill her, and talking about not liking to be used. But mostly, she said she needed to talk to you, and I gave her your number."

"Did she say who wanted to kill her?" Langdon asked.

"I think she was talking about the senator."

Langdon had wondered the same thing, if only idly, so this seemed to be a fair-enough concern. Even with the assurance of the senator, he had his doubts. It was not like she was going to come right out and say she was ordering a murder, even if she was. Not to mention the complication of the Boy Scouts, whose presence suggested there might be another puppet master pulling some strings. "And who is using her?"

"I don't know, she walked off before I could get that out of her."

"You're waiting until now to tell me this?"

"I called you last night, but you didn't answer. I figured I'd tell you at the store when I came in today, but it was so busy I never got the chance."

Langdon remembered noticing a missed phone call from Starling, but he hadn't seen it until this morning, because of the whole rushing dog to the vet thing. "Okay, not much we can do, except wait for her to call."

Langdon went through the house, grabbing the steaks from the counter, and returned to the deck where he went about laying them carefully on the grill. He had the charcoal raised up to sear the outside, flipped them after a minute, and then after another minute, lowered the tray to cook them with the ambient rather than the direct heat. Richam had brought a bottle of Glenlivet, and Langdon decided to allow himself one scotch as he cooked.

"What the hell happened to your mutt?" Bart asked, his eyes wide. Dog had decided that, injuries or no injuries, it was high time to check out the food situation on the deck, and limped his way out the door. In addition to the gimpy leg, there were several spots on his body rubbed raw by tumbling ass over teakettle across the asphalt road. He was supposed to be wearing a halo, one of those plastic cone things, to keep him from licking the raw flesh, but Langdon couldn't face his mournful eyes and had taken it off.

Starling knelt down and gave him a chip, scratching the top of his head. "He looks like he met his match, that's for sure."

"You know he's a lover, not a fighter," Langdon responded. "But in this case, he lost to a two-ton car."

"Told you to keep him out of the street," Bart said. "People don't much pay attention to driving anymore. Too busy with phones, food, and makeup."

"I believe this was done on purpose," Langdon said, and told them of the hamburgers in the street and the racing car.

When the steaks were almost ready, Langdon asked Jack and Missouri to get the folding table from the garage to set up on the end of the cast-iron outdoor table, and gather the scattered chairs for the meal, while Chabal, Jewell, and Cary brought out dishes from inside, and Langdon set Jimmy the task of opening a few bottles of red wine.

Once they were all seated, Langdon raised his glass. "I'd like to welcome Tug to our home, to our family, and to our friends. I am glad that justice prevailed." He'd barely spoken with the young man, other than to show him to the spare bedroom and to tell him to make himself at home.

Once they'd drunk to the toast, Jimmy piped up, "First thing tomorrow, I will see if I can find out why ICE was looking for you. Jewell gave me your paperwork, and at first glance, everything seems to be in order. Don't worry, we'll get them off your back."

Langdon guessed he was speaking more to Cary Stockton than to Tug, showing her what a fine man he was. Whatever the motive, he didn't care if the end result was positive. They ate and talked of everyday things instead of blackmail, murder, and deportation. The sun was gone by the time they finally cleared the plates, and Langdon went about building a fire while the others cleaned up. Once the blaze was going, they moved the chairs in a circle around the flames, the warmth welcome as the night brought a coolness with it that promised the approach of fall, and soon after that, winter. Here in Maine, after all, there were three short seasons, and one long, cold one.

Langdon found himself back to the Glenlivet, the brown liquid soothing, as were the friends and family around him. Jimmy and Cary were huddled in conversation across from him. Chabal was setting up the speaker to pipe some music out, and soon The Kinks were belting out "You Really Got Me."

"Bart was saying those guys who were in our house the other night threatened you out to Hog Heaven?" Jack asked. He was sitting to Langdon's immediate left. "And Missouri said they might have been the same men who hit dog?"

"Threatened you how? They pointed a gun at you?" Missouri asked. She was sitting to Langdon's immediate right.

Langdon silently cursed Bart. "They showed me a pistol," he admitted.

"Bart said you got the license plate number and it was a rental registered to some company called Priority Z, and that the driver was John Smith from Nebraska."

"Yeah, that's all we have so far."

"Can you give me the photocopy of the license?" Jack asked. "I can see what I can dig up."

"I'll help," Missouri added.

Tug leaned forward from the other side of Jack. "I'm pretty good with a computer, Mister Langdon. Maybe I can be of some assistance."

"Sure, why not?" Langdon replied. "That'd be great. When do you want to get started?"

"Might as well be now," Missouri said. "It's better than hanging out with old people getting drunk by a fire."

"Whatever," Langdon said, standing up. "Send the girl off to the big city, and she comes back scared to be outside in nature after dark. Let's grab that photocopy."

By the time he got back to the fire, the conversation had grown more raucous. Richam had lit up a cigar and was plowing through the scotch, still no match for Bart, who was efficiently knocking back the beers and throwing them over his shoulder. He'd moved the cooler next to him for easier access, and so that he didn't have to get up. Langdon wasn't sure how the man didn't ever seem to need to take a piss, even after consuming a twelve-pack in a sitting.

Judging by the pile behind him, he was approaching that number. This didn't include what he'd consumed before sitting down to the fire. Starling did his part by matching Bart's drinking with smokes, flicking a cigarette into the fire every time Bart tossed a can.

Cary Stockton seemed quite smitten with the dapper, smooth-talking, and fit Jimmy 4 by Four. She was about average height with short blonde hair, an athletic rangy build, and was a good ten years younger than 4 by Four. Langdon wondered if she knew that this whole affair had been set up for the two of them to meet. It made him think of Delilah Friday, and the fact that he'd neglected her case, whether busy with other matters or shying away from the temptation that she was, Langdon was not quite sure. He made a mental note, looked at the glass of scotch in his hand, and pulled out his phone to set himself a reminder first thing in the morning to track down Paul Springer.

Chabal sat down next to him. "Good times, Langdon."

"We don't do enough of this," he replied.

"Do you think 4 by Four will score tonight?"

Langdon looked over where Cary Stockton was laughing and tossing her hair at some story 4 by Four was telling. "I'd bet on it. They leave together within a half-hour."

"Half-hour? You're on. What's the bet?"

"You know what," he replied.

"Why is everything sex with you?" she asked.

"Are you in?"

"Of course, I'm in. The woman just left her husband."

"My thinking exactly. 4 by Four is like a vulture when it comes to vulnerable women. See?" Langdon nodded and half-pointed. "He's circling right now, getting ready to tear at her carcass."

"You're sick," she said, picking her head off his shoulder and poking him in the side. "But you're right about 4 by Four. Why do you suppose we're friends with a man of such low morals?"

"Maybe because we live in a glass house and know better than to throw stones?"

"Okay, point taken." Chabal agreed.

Jewell pulled her chair closer to Chabal as Richam stood and moved over to the empty chair next to Langdon.

"Do I need to untangle my friend from the tentacles of that hipster lawyer?" Jewell asked.

"Don't you dare," Langdon replied.

"Why not?"

"We've got a wager, and if," Chabal checked her phone for the time, "the two of them don't leave together in the next twenty-two minutes, my man will be giving me a back-rub later and getting nothing in return for his troubles."

"And if they leave in the allotted time?" Richam asked.

"I will sleep the rest of the satisfied," Langdon said.

"Christ, Jewell, why don't we make wagers like that?" Richam asked his wife in a tone made loud by drink.

"Will You Still Love Me Tomorrow," by The Shirelles, came drifting out of the speaker. "This is it," Langdon said. "Make or break time for 4 by Four. This is too good of an opportunity to let pass." The four of them watched 4 by Four and Cary across the fire as unobtrusively as they could, the lyrics caressing the night air.

4 by Four rose to his feet, holding his hand out, and then helping Cary to rise beside him. Hand in hand they moved around the ring of chairs surrounding the fire. "I'm going to give Cary a ride home. Thanks for having us over." He wasn't quite sure why this was met with suppressed laughter, but gamely continued on, "I'll touch base with you first thing in the morning, Langdon."

Once they were gone, the four of them broke into loud laughter, surprising Star and Bart, who'd been deep in some joint philosophical rant, a continuing conversation between the two of them on the context of spiritual beings, a topic that shifted and changed as often as the wind. Generally speaking, nobody had any idea what they were talking about most of the time.

Langdon stood up and clapped his hands twice. "That's a wrap. We've got to get to bed."

"It's like that, is it?" Richam asked, rising unsteadily to his feet.

"Absolutely. Jewell, I can help get him to the car if need be?"

"You're an asshole," Richam muttered.

"Okay if I leave my Caddy here and pick it up tomorrow?" Bart asked.

"Of course. You fine giving him a ride, Star?"

"Ha," Richam interjected. "Goodnight, Bart Star," he said, saying it all as one name like the old Green Bay Packer quarterback, a common, if overused joke in the group.

~ ~ ~ ~ ~

Around the corner from the Langdon home, Pete climbed into the luxury Volvo van with curtains pulled carefully around all the windows. Inside, John Smith was just removing headphones. There were eight computers in the back, most of them running sophisticated audio equipment. There were a total of sixteen bugs in the house, and another eight in the backyard furniture, grill, and various spots. These had been added earlier that day after they listened to the recording of Chabal telling Langdon that they were having a barbecue.

"That sounds like it for the night," Pete said, pulling his night vision goggles from his head. He was dressed all in black, but had not gone so far as to smear his face, as he doubted the wariness level of those present at the cookout. "They say anything important?"

John had been monitoring the different devices, trying to stick with Langdon, but it was all recorded and the computer was running a program for key words now. In minutes they'd know if they'd missed any trigger words. "They've connected the killing of the Russians to a Glock, which you told Langdon you had, and then, showed him."

"Shit," Pete said. "I didn't know we were going to be doing OG stuff a few days later, or I wouldn't have done it."

"I think you sometimes miss the point of our work. We are hired and paid to be inconspicuous. To fly under the radar. And yes, sometimes we have to do Old Gangster stuff, and then disappear into the cracks. We provide a service, and it is not an entertainment service."

"Not like that gal Friday, huh?" Pete winked at John, and when he was met with stoicism, decided to get serious. "So, we lose the Glocks. They should be gone already. I don't know why you had us hide them instead of making them disappear, anyway."

"I have an idea on that." John began shutting down the computers. The listening bugs would be emitting bursts to a receiver they'd put in the woods behind Langdon's house. Every couple of hours, the information would be downloaded into a two-second clip in a microchip, which they'd pick up daily and have the computers check for key words. "We didn't bug Jack's computer. That was a mistake."

"Jack?" Pete's face showed puzzlement.

"Chabal's son who lives there," John said. "He's going to do some digging to see if they find out anything about me or Priority Z. Him and that African fellow, and the daughter, Missouri."

"I told you not to use your real license when renting the car."

"My real, fake license, you mean? John Smith from Nebraska with a false address and birth date? Good luck hunting me down. I'm more worried about Priority Z."

"Jesus, you're a Nervous Nellie! There are government hackers who couldn't trace that back," Pete said. "They're kids, they won't find a thing."

"There's one more thing," John said.

"You always save the best for last," Pete commented, sliding into the driver's seat.

"The old codger who works down at the bookstore? Jonathan Starling? Seems that Kamrin Jorgenson contacted him and told him she wants a confab with Langdon."

"I thought this job was supposed to be a piece of cake," Pete said. "Summer in Maine will be like a vacation, you said. Get out of the office, enjoy lobster rolls, watch the leaves turn... now, it seems like we're killing somebody every other day."

Chapter 19

Thursday

Langdon woke early and slipped out of bed, careful to not wake Chabal. Once he finished his first cup of coffee, he called Paul Springer, and was again directed to voice mail. He had left messages Tuesday and Wednesday to no avail, so he didn't bother now. He was starting to believe Delilah Friday in that there was something suspicious in the man's wife being missing. It was just past six in the morning. Maybe the man wasn't up and turned his ringer off at night. With a sigh, Langdon poured a to-go cup full of coffee. He would just have to pay the man a visit. Who doesn't like getting a knock on the door before seven?

He made sure his ringer was on and turned all the way up as he got in the Jeep. With the top down, even at full volume, it was often hard to hear incoming calls, not that he usually cared. If it was important, people could leave a message, and he would get back to them. In reality, probably ninety percent of his calls were one politician or another asking for money, sales calls, and the buggers who seemed intent on wearing him down to buy an extended warranty on his Jeep. But now, he was waiting for a call from Kamrin Jorgenson, and she most likely would not leave a message, even if it were of the utmost importance. Langdon wondered if he'd be able to call the number back, or if it would show up on his caller ID as blocked.

She must be reaching out to him for a reason. Langdon mused on the possibilities, the obvious one being that she was willing to make a deal. What had Senator Mercer said? Everybody does it. Blackmail, extortion, and payoffs were just part of being a politician. Who, out there, lived a life that had zero blemishes or missteps or failures they were not embarrassed about, some type of muck being uncovered? He, himself, had just spent a night drinking with a strange woman he barely knew, and had been tempted to sleep with, an offer in retrospect, that according to Delilah, had not been on the table. But it *had* been, Langdon knew in his core, it was real, even if Delilah Friday claimed she was only offering to let him sober up before driving.

So what if Senator Mercer didn't want it revealed that she was a lesbian, and that her marriage was more of a business and social arrangement rather than a personal one? No, that wasn't quite correct. What was it that Maxwell had said? They had an intellectual love that transcended the physical. They enjoyed each other's company, if not each other's flesh. It was not a concept that he understood, but it was a changing world. Plenty of people had a best friend that they didn't sleep with. Often, these people lived together, but at some point in time society dictated it was time to move on and get married and settle down, though the why of that eluded him.

Langdon didn't think that her marital relations or sexual proclivities diminished Senator Mercer's ability to be a good senator, not that he much cared for her politics as of late. He'd always voted for her in the past, but had begun to have his doubts. He couldn't care less about the sex of her bedmates, but rather, he was concerned because she was leaning evermore in a conservative direction. As for her preferences, as long as her husband, Max, was fine with the arrangement, then why was it anybody's business?

If KJ had decided to abandon her rigid ideals of saving the earth at any cost and would take a cash payout, well that was her business, too. Somehow, Langdon wished she would say no, and hold to her position. Not that blackmail was right, but at least harnessing its evil for something good instead of for personal gain spoke of some kind of integrity, however twisted. Still, Langdon was being paid to persuade her to take the money and turn over all photos and copies, and he would do what he'd agreed to do. Did that cheapen him? He was damned if he did and damned if he didn't. He certainly didn't think the senator should have her sex life publicized, but he also didn't like buying the silence of a blackmailer. He wasn't Michael Cohen, after all.

Of course, there was no answer at the door when he reached the house. He peeked through the window of the garage, and there was no car. Not only was there no car, but no trash cans, no mower, no rake or snow shovel. Not even an oil stain on the pristine concrete floor. Was Paul on vacation? It was the start of Labor Day weekend, after all. Did he have a girlfriend?

He walked around back and peeked in the French doors into the dining room. There was no sign of life. There was no sign that anybody even lived there. He went to another window that looked into the kitchen. It was bare. There was nothing on the island. Not a Keurig, or fruit, or bowls, or even mail. Nothing. When he'd been here before he remembered vaguely thinking the house looked unlived in, but now it seemed absolutely barren.

Langdon went around the house, peering in windows without shades, testing to see if any of them were open, but they weren't. He checked for signs of a security system, and seeing none, chose a rock and broke a window in the back door. He quickly reached his hand through and unlocked the door and slipped inside in case any of the neighbors had heard the breaking glass.

Paul Springer had fled, leaving no trace that he'd ever been there. Perhaps he had killed his wife? But Delilah had just spoken with her. Maybe he'd been holding her captive and made her make the call? Langdon went from room to room, afraid of finding a body, until only the door to the basement remained. With tentative steps he eased his way down. Half of the lights seemed to be out, casting shadows across the walls, but the basement was just as empty as the rest of the house.

It was certainly beginning to look like Paul Springer was involved in the disappearance of his wife, Amy.

After Langdon had ascended back up the basement stairs, he left the way he'd come, and walked to his Jeep. In case there was some sort of silent alarm he hadn't noticed, or a neighbor had seen him breaking in, Langdon drove down to Route 1 and pulled into a parking lot fronting a strip mall. He called Delilah, but there was no answer. He then called the Planet Fitness across the street, saying that he was Paul Springer, and wondering if his wife was there? And if not, had she been in? They told him he must be confused, as they did not even have an Amy Springer as a member. He called fifteen more fitness facilities in succession using the same ruse, but not a single one of them had an Amy Springer as a member. So, Paul Springer lied to him, disappeared… and most likely, killed his wife?

~ ~ ~ ~ ~

Chabal ran her tongue over her dry lips. She probably shouldn't have drunk so much the night before, but it had been so much fun having everybody together again. It'd been too long since the gang had hung out. Life had a way of appearing busy even when it wasn't, and friends needed to make the time but often didn't. She unlocked the door to the bookstore and slid the sign to open. Starling had left the starting cash in the register and prepped the coffee, so all she had to do was turn both on and she was good to go.

She wondered if she looked as bad as she felt, but avoided checking the mirror in the hallway, not really wanting to know. The entire evening had been magical, and the night had ended as well as it went, but the morning had certainly come too soon. She remembered her daughter, Darcy, had texted her late and she had to reply, something about getting a dog, her first pet. Chabal would have to go visit if she did get a dog, and a trip to Charleston was always a pleasure, above and beyond getting to see Darcy. She thought about the shrimp and grits at 82 Queen, which she and Darcy often frequented during their visits together. Thinking of this comfort food was soothing to her hangover.

She smiled, as she thought of pleasing Langdon the night before, happy that she'd lost the bet, feeling a bit naughty, and wanting to make her man happy. She was surprised that he'd been up and gone before she even rolled out of bed, but that was not unlike him. He didn't appear to need either food or sleep to survive, and in fact, could probably subsist on alcohol alone, usually with no discernible side effects. She, on the other hand, had had four glasses of wine and her head was throbbing. Had Langdon and she had a baby together, what and who would the child look like, she wondered for the umpteenth time. She tried to imagine a cross between Jack and Missouri, but that wasn't quite right, as they both had traits of their other parents.

She couldn't have scripted her life any better if she was an author, one of those mystery writers adorning the shelves. Her first marriage had been bland, careful, a check on her impulsive nature and predisposition towards trouble. She'd reined that crazy streak back by marrying a man who was responsible, reliable, and restrained. Together, they had three beautiful and wonderful children, and Chabal had reorganized a life that was, well, so devoid of real life as a couple that it had been on the verge of descending into self-destruction.

And then Langdon had come along. A spark in the recesses of her soul had glowed briefly, brightened, and then ignited, showering her insides in a roaring blaze. He was her rock, her stability, her passion, and the center of her universe. There had been a disconnection over the past week, a piece of Langdon swirling just out of her reach, and she had overanalyzed why that was, much like she did with most things in life. Last night, however, the pieces had dropped back into place, and the stars shone brightly from their appointed spots in the sky.

A blonde woman with a shockingly tight halter-top that bared her stomach, shoulders, and much of her chest—basically only covering her mammoth breasts—walked through the doorway. Chabal watched as the woman went down an aisle, looking around, but not at books. She moved like a tigress, even with stilettos strapped to her feet. Her shorts were just that, *short*, like the young girls liked to wear them these days, though this woman was definitely past the age when Chabal deemed it acceptable. She found herself disliking this woman not for her beauty alone, but for flaunting her voluptuousness. Chabal was glad that she had not looked in the mirror, because this was not the day to compare herself to this provocative stunner. The woman approached the counter with a smile, and Chabal fought the urge to make a snarky comment.

"Is Goff here?"

"No. He has the day off. Can I help you?"

"Oh, I don't know. I have something for him."

"You can leave it with me. I'll make sure he gets it," Chabal replied. Who was this woman and what did she have for her husband?

The woman gave a twisted smile, proving herself mortal, and not actually a goddess. She reached into her handbag, and Chabal realized with horror that it was an authentic Louis Vuitton. Did people actually own genuine Louis Vuitton?

"It's a gift," the woman said, placing a picture frame on the counter.

Chabal turned it over to see a picture of her husband with his cheek pressed to the cheek of this woman, his arm around her back. "Who are you?" she demanded, but she thought that perhaps she already knew.

"Delilah Friday," the woman said, sticking out her hand. "And you are?"

"Chabal. Chabal Langdon."

"Oh, are you Goff's sister?"

"No. I am his wife."

"Wife?" Delilah Friday seemed dumbstruck. "He didn't say he had a wife."

"It must have slipped his mind."

"But, he doesn't have a ring, not even a tan line."

"Jammed his ring finger about a year ago, or so he said, playing basketball. Hasn't been able to get it on since, or so he says."

"Are you two separated?"

"Not as of last night."

"But, why did he…" Delilah trailed off, her eyes looking up in the air, before dropping back to the counter. "Men."

"Why did he *what*?"

"Come to my room this past Sunday and make love to me." A small sob escaped her perfect lips. She turned on her heel and walked out the door.

~ ~ ~ ~ ~

Langdon stopped by the house on his way into the bookstore. His living room had been turned into a command center. The folding table was in the center with three computers on it. There was a large whiteboard scribbled with words although Langdon could see the remnants of squares on the edges, leftover from the Super Bowl wager, the hundred boxes each costing a dollar, and the lucky winner of each quarter and final score, Star and Bart in this case, leaving with money in their pockets. A bulletin board leaned against the wall with pieces of paper tacked to it, and the printer was busy spitting out more.

"Wow," Langdon said. "How's the search coming?"

"Slow going, but Tug is brilliant on a computer," Jack replied. "He thinks Priority Z is just a shell corporation, so we are trying to backtrack to find out who really owns it."

"Shell corporation?" Langdon knew he was outside his comfort zone, and was hesitant to sound stupid, but realized he needed to understand what they were doing.

"It's a business without any real assets or activity," Missouri said. "People use them to hide who they are and what they are doing."

"All perfectly legal," Tug said.

"But very shady," Jack added.

"Anything on John Smith?"

"There are a lot of John Smiths in the world," Missouri said.

"Did you say you have a picture of him?" Jack asked. "His driver's license looks to be an old picture, doesn't match any addresses or birth dates of any John Smith we can find. An updated photo might help."

"Yeah, not very good, but I can text it to you," Langdon replied, looking up the picture he'd taken of John and Pete as they'd driven out of Hog Heaven.

Jack's phone buzzed as the text arrived. "We should be able to enhance that," he said.

"Can you add another name to your research?" Langdon asked. He gave them Paul Springer's name and address in Falmouth, and then added Amy as well. "And how about Delilah Friday, while you're at it?"

"Is that a real name?" Missouri asked.

"As far as I know," Langdon replied.

"Is she involved with the blackmail?" Jack asked.

"No, it's another case I'm working on."

"Do you have a picture of her?"

"No," Langdon replied. He opted against giving a description. "She lives in Alexandria, Virginia, and works for some sort of entertainment company."

"She should be easier to track down than John Smith."

Langdon turned to Tug. "Have you heard anything from Jimmy?"

"Mr. 4 by Four has not contacted me today," he replied.

"Do you need anything?" Langdon realized that the man had come straight from the jail, and probably didn't have clothes, bathroom essentials, and the like.

"Jack and Missouri have promised to take me shopping, but I'm afraid my bank account might not be accessible."

Langdon pulled his money clip out and dropped the hundred-dollar bill he kept for emergencies. "This will get you started. Perhaps Jack can loan you some clothes?"

Dog was fine with being left behind, for already snacks were falling from the table, and the bonanza was only likely to increase. His injuries had already elicited a great deal of sympathy in the form of food. Langdon had some calls to make, but decided he'd do it from his office. He wondered about stopping to buy flowers for Chabal, or maybe a pastry, or some other token of his appreciation of her, but the idea slipped his mind, blown away with the rushing wind as he drove the open Jeep into town.

He parked in the municipal lot behind the bookstore. The firemen were sitting outside eating lunch, and one of them called out, asking where dog was. Sometimes, Langdon felt like he was just a sidekick to dog, and that without the adorable animal, he'd be a nobody. With a dismissive wave of his hand, he crossed to the back door of the building and went in. He did not like the look on Chabal's face when he walked into the store.

"What's wrong, babe?"

She stared at him with hard eyes. His phone suddenly rang, and he pulled it from his pocket and looked at it, before turning off the ringer. It was Bart, and he meant to call him in a few minutes anyway.

A woman came up to the counter to purchase *Winter in Paradise*, an Elin Hilderbrand book. Langdon's phone began buzzing again in his pocket, and he hit the side button to stop it. His eyes were suddenly drawn to the picture frame on the counter, and with a lurch, he realized it was a picture of him and Delilah Friday. Like the flash of a camera at night, his rusty recollection of the night drinking with the woman at the Bernard was illuminated for a split second. "Here, come closer," she had said. "I want to get a selfie with my private dick." Langdon was laughing when the phone clicked the picture, his cheek touching hers, his arm around her back, the alcohol lowering his inhibitions, her perfume filling his head with waves of adrenalin.

"Where did you get this?" he asked dumbly, his tongue thick in his mouth.

Chabal gave the woman her change and waited for her to leave the store. "Your client dropped it off. Said it was a gift."

"It's not what it looks like."

"What does it look like?"

"She wanted a picture of us, and we had to squeeze together to fit in the screen."

"She said you told her you weren't married. Seemed quite surprised to find out I was your wife, as a matter of fact."

"That's not true. I told her all about you."

"Why would she lie?"

"Maybe she forgot? We were drinking."

Chabal measured him with her eyes. "She said you fucked her. You know, the night you went drinking with her at her hotel?"

"What?" Langdon raised his hands as if to ward off an attack. "We had drinks, nothing more."

"She was quite upset. Ran out crying."

Langdon had the feeling of being in a subway tunnel, the roaring of the train approaching, the stifling stillness preceded by the rushing wind, everything dark and dangerous. "I never laid a finger on her. That's the truth."

"There's a picture right there that says you did. Your hand on her back and your cheek on her cheek. She is quite stunning."

An older man came up with three books and while Chabal was ringing him up, Langdon's phone started buzzing again. It was Bart again. Langdon clicked the accept call button and said woodenly into the phone, "I can't talk right now, Bart. I'll call you back."

Before he could disconnect, Bart told him not to. "The police are coming to arrest you. Where are you?"

"What? What for?"

"Some guy down in Falmouth has video of you breaking into his house. Paul Springer? Does that ring any bells?"

"Paul Springer?"

"Do you know the man?"

"I've been hired to find his wife by that woman, Del." Langdon froze, but it was too late, he could see Chabal's lips press into a tight line. "My client thinks he may have hurt her."

"He says you stole his laptop and some money."

"What? You know better than that."

"Did you break into his house?"

"I think I better call Jimmy." Langdon hung up. "I did not have sex with Delilah Friday," he said to Chabal, and the man who was in the process of leaving. "But I can't talk about it right now. I have to go."

"Go? You have to go?"

"The police are looking for me. I have to clear up something before they find me. I love you." Langdon turned and walked out the door. He'd made it as far as opening the door to his Jeep when the police cruiser pulled up behind him.

Harry Daigle, an officer he knew slightly, stepped out of the passenger seat. "Hello, Langdon." He was a rotund man with a ready smile, but one wondered how he, and Bart for that matter, kept up. Another cop, younger and fitter, stepped out of the driver's side.

"Harry," Langdon replied.

"We have a report on you breaking into a house," Harry said.

"Are you here to arrest me?"

"Do you mind if we look in your Jeep?"

Langdon knew that if an arrest warrant had been issued, that this was not a request, but otherwise, they had no rights to search his parked vehicle. But, he had nothing to hide. "Go ahead."

The smaller officer proceeded to look in the backseat, while Harry stood back and watched. Meanwhile, Langdon's mind raced. At best, they had him on breaking and entering, and he should be able to get out on bail today, as long as he was able to reach Jimmy. Stole the man's laptop? There was nothing in the house. No clothes in the bureau or closets. The fridge was empty. The house was obviously not being lived in, yet his breaking in was immediately reported. Had somebody else robbed the house, and it was just his bad luck to come along and get filmed going through a cleaned-out house?

"What's this?" The officer was running his hands underneath Langdon's seat.

There was the sound of tape pulling loose from fabric, and then he stood up holding a gun that was very familiar to Langdon. It was the Glock 43, complete with silencer, that Pete had shown him a few days prior at Hog Heaven. It was also, most likely, the weapon used to kill the four Russians. Nobody would believe his story of being threatened by Pete, not now, not after he'd had an opportunity to go to the police but had chosen to keep the threat to himself.

These were the thoughts that stampeded through his mind in the smallest possible fraction of a second, and then he ran. He heard Harry curse, and then yell, "Don't shoot!" There was a wire fence at the far-end of the parking lot, and Langdon went over that in one glorious tumble. He risked a quick glance and saw the younger officer in pursuit, and the cruiser pulling out, presumably with Harry at the wheel.

He darted through the lot of the 55 Plus Center and across Union Street, and up the hill into the neighborhoods of Brunswick, running through backyards. A woman was hanging clothes on a line, stopping to gape at a sight not usually seen in Brunswick. Down the driveway, Langdon saw the police car pass up Cumberland and he ran across the street behind it.

"Stop!" a voice yelled behind him. He ignored it as he flung himself over another fence. The wire at the top caught at his pants and raked his leg, but he broke free and stumbled on.

He heard the cruiser up ahead with sirens blaring and he changed direction. He emerged onto a street and crawled under a car, and as soon as he saw the running legs of the police officer go by, he crawled down the driveway. Two men sat on the steps smoking a cigarette, but didn't say anything. He could hear more sirens growing closer. His plan was to cross over the swinging bridge into Topsham, but then he remembered Danny T. lived very close by on Swett Street, and in seconds he was at the man's apartment. Danny T. lived on the home's second floor, but had his own staircase to access the small unit carved out by the owner to create additional income.

The door wasn't locked, and Langdon slipped in, hoping that none of the neighbors had spotted him, not that anyone here would go running to the cops. Swett Street had a certain, very bad, reputation to maintain.

Danny T. was sitting on a ragged couch watching television. "Hey, Langdon," he said. "Did you come to give me that twenty bucks you owe me for the game the other day?"

Chapter 20

Still Thursday

Senator Margaret Mercer stared out the window. Maxwell was driving, and for once, she didn't have Dwayne hanging over her shoulder. He was in the car directly behind, of course, but a bit of privacy was like a slice of heaven. They'd just come from the Windsor Fair, where she'd hung a few blue ribbons, tousled a few cute heads, and given a talk about the upcoming budget. She had expressed outrage over the violence of the Old Port Killer, blaming the Russians. Once off the stage, however, Dwayne had whispered to her that the police were searching for Goff Langdon in connection with the Russians. Langdon? It was all very convoluted.

"Penny for your thoughts, dear?" Maxwell asked. When he smiled, his two front teeth protruded, making her think of a chipmunk.

"I am confused," she replied. "And that is something I rarely say."

Maxwell took his eyes from the road and stared at her. He did not believe he had ever heard her confess confusion, or any sort of weakness before. Although this trait of showing only clear-headedness and strength was frustrating at times, it was one that he admired greatly in her "Confused? About what?"

"I meet up with a woman in her hotel room, and she takes pictures of us together and blackmails me to change my vote on climate change. I hire a detective to find her, which he not only does, but also identifies her. OPK is arrested, an immigrant, but is then cleared by the very man I hired to aid me in identifying and negotiating with my blackmailer. Then, it is uncovered that three Russian gangsters, who have just themselves been killed, are actually the Old Port Killers. And now, supposedly, the man who I hired to get me out of *my* mess is being pursued as a person of interest, and perhaps, the killer of these very same Russians. What part of that is not confusing?"

"Langdon is a person of interest in the killing of the Russians?" Maxwell asked.

"If you believe the latest news," the senator observed.

"I find that highly unlikely."

"Why?"

"I rather like the man, don't you?"

The senator stared out the window as they went over the bridge that crossed the Kennebec River. She thought about asking to stop at the A1 Diner but didn't feel like shaking hands and smiling. When had everything become so difficult?

"I don't know who to trust anymore," she said.

"The world is becoming crazier and crazier, that is for sure." Maxwell stroked his chalk-white mustache.

"It used to be much easier," Senator Mercer agreed.

"I wanted to talk to you about that," Maxwell said.

"About what?" she asked, absently.

"Not running for reelection in 2020."

"Not run?"

"It's just everything has gotten so, well, crazy. You said it yourself. Blackmail. Serial killers. Private detectives killing Russian gangsters. All for what? So the media can rake you over the coals and tear you apart? What if they find out that you are a lesbian? Do you think our marriage can stand the feeding frenzy that would follow?"

"What would I do? Take up knitting?"

"Why not become a lobbyist? I know you need to stay busy."

"I don't know. I like what I do. I feel that I make a difference."

"Michael says that Marisa Wilkes at MacLeod Brandt would hire you in a heartbeat. The pay would start at around a million dollars, and the best part? Nobody cares about the personal life of a lobbyist. You'd be outside of the public eye."

"There is an appeal to that, for sure," Senator Mercer agreed. What she left unsaid was Maxwell's insensitivity to the politics. First, his seeming offhand remark was yet another instance showing how closely Michael Glover was to Marisa Wilkes. Second, who was this Glover that he could know this, never mind her vague recollection of his presence at their impromptu summit a few days earlier? She made a mental note to run a background check on the man. How was it that she'd become friends with him in the first place?

~ ~ ~ ~ ~

"So, what have we found out so far?" Tug asked.

Tug, in his previous life as a journalist, had been very active in tracking corruption in the Burundi government. A typical way to hide, steal, or launder money was through the creation of shell corporations in far off places. At the moment, he had a website up in front of him called draw.com. This provided a framework for tracking down the connections that led back to the real owners of these phantom companies. And Priority Z was definitely a ghost, with little of substance in the public eye about the company's identity or activities.

"Priority Z was incorporated seven years ago, but had been dormant for the past five years, until just recently, when money began coming in and out of their coffers from a third party," Jack said.

"I've managed to track the domain ownership from their website back to a company called Pistachio. Their address is listed as 103 Sham Peng Tong Plaza in Victoria, Seychelles." Missouri had been searching a website called whoisology.com, looking for actual names, addresses or dates. Priority Z's own site had been conspicuously absent of any real information.

"That sounds familiar," Tug replied. He entered the information into the mapping site and went to a new tab to bang away at some keys. "Hmmm. I thought I remembered that address. As of a few years ago, there were over 900 companies listed with that particular location."

"How can that be?" Missouri asked.

"Obviously, somebody in the Seychelles is providing a service," Tug replied. "I ran across that address several times investigating corrupt politicians in Burundi."

"Isn't it illegal?" Jack asked.

"As I told you, shell companies are perfectly legal. There are no laws dictating transparency, or I guess in the United States there are some, but they are very weak. It's easy to provide the bare minimum of information and list a nominee or straw man as the boss. Then they bury the name of the authorized signer in paperwork. So, while it is legal to set one up, they are usually used for illegal purposes. When the companies start buying and selling each other and transferring assets and changing names and countries of origin, well then, it is almost impossible to untangle the web they weave."

"I did come up with a contact person from the archives website you gave me," Jack said. "Peter Yeager." This particular website stored snapshots of other websites over periods of time, which came in handy, as information was often scrubbed from the sites once business officially began to flow through, or upon incorporation.

"Peter Yeager?" Missouri piped in. "Why is that familiar?"

"There was a contact number, but it's disconnected."

"What was the area code?"

Jack looked at his notes. "402."

Missouri punched the numbers into her search. "Nebraska."

"Which is where John Smith is from," Jack replied.

"Didn't my dad say the other man, the one who pointed a gun at his back, called himself Pete?"

"There are only 227 listings for Peter Yeager in the entire United States," Tug said, reading from his screen. "Seven in Nebraska."

"I've got an article on a Peter Yeager who was court-martialed from the U.S. Navy SEAL program a few years back," Jack said, his eyes scanning the article, before reading the highlights aloud. "Chief Peter Yeager of SEAL team 4 Alpha Platoon has been found guilty of aggravated assault. The charge of premeditated murder has been dismissed. The military judge presiding over the case has determined that Chief Yeager, under psychological duress, did commit the crime accused of him, that of cutting off the head of a fifteen-year-old wounded ISIS soldier. The incident occurred in Mosul, where the platoon was operating alongside the Iraqi Emergency Response Division. The captured Iraqi soldier had been taken into the medical tent with shrapnel in his leg and side. The attending medic said that the man was stabilized when Yeager walked in, pulled out a large hunting knife, and plunged it into the man's neck. He then posed for pictures with the dead body, holding the head up, with the caption—'I got him with my knife.'" Jack went back to scanning through the article. "Chief Yeager has been ordered into a military psychological program for evaluation." Jack turned the computer around to show an enlarged photo of Peter Yeager, an image that was clearly the same as the one now tacked to their bulletin board, enhanced from the cell phone pic Langdon had captured at Hog Heaven.

"Former Chief of U.S. Navy SEALs, Peter Yeager, has just accepted a position working for Goldenrod. Yeager was recently in the news for having been found mentally unfit after killing a wounded ISIS fighter with a knife, then posting the image online." Missouri read from her computer. "Transparency Media goes on to say how Yeager was only in the psyche ward for three months, and once released, was immediately hired by this company called Goldenrod."

"Goldenrod?" Tug asked. "I've heard of them."

"Says they're a private security firm," Jack said.

"Ahh, yes, of course," Tug said. "They were the ones who killed all those civilians in Baghdad a few years back. They were called something else back then—here it is, Marshland—but it's the same people, same company, just a different name."

"Mercenaries for hire," Jack read from his screen.

Missouri looked up from her screen. "Holy shit," she said. "Goldenrod is based in Nebraska, where they have a training facility and offices. They have over a thousand acres."

Each of them was clattering away on their keyboards as fast as they could, in what now seemed like a race, to skim all of the information out there.

"Goldenrod was initially started to train military personnel in 2001, but when 9/11 happened their business exploded. Suddenly, private military operatives were needed in Afghanistan, Iraq, and Africa," Jack said.

"Six men who were supposedly working for Goldenrod were captured in Yemen just last year," Missouri said.

"The CEO, Alek Rex, has a home in Abu Dhabi, and is developing a paramilitary strike force for the Crown Prince there," Tug said.

"Bingo," Jack chortled. He turned his screen so the others could see it. "John Smith, Assistant Vice-President of Operations." It was an exact likeness of the man who had been threatening Langdon along with Pete Yeager.

"Wow," Missouri said. "Assistant Vice-President of Operations? Sounds like he's a big gun, as well."

"Not necessarily," Tug said. "Typically, in a corporation like this, the Vice-Presidents—and there can be dozens—are pretty far down the ladder, and the assistants are more like lieutenants, men and women who head up a small strike force, if you will."

"So, what does it all mean?" Missouri asked. "What is the lieutenant of a major black ops military contractor doing threatening my father?"

~ ~ ~ ~ ~

Langdon—his checkered golf shorts torn and muddy, as was the T-shirt he wore, the slogan 'Vote for Pedro' barely visible from rolling under the car and tumbling over fences—stood gasping in Danny T.'s living room. There were blinds on the window of the door, and he carefully closed these. The other windows had the shades pulled already, as obviously, Danny had an aversion to light. Langdon took stock of the room. He'd been here a few times before, but usually only to pick Danny up to take him to a Sea Dog's game, or maybe the Red Claws. Minor League sports and Bowdoin College games were the majority of their interaction.

There were two doors, partially open. The one on the left was the single bedroom, while the other was the bathroom. The kitchen rested in the right corner of the living room, a small card table with two chairs serving as a separator. Danny reclined in an old beat-up armchair, the worn yellow fabric thick with dust and mold. There was one other wooden chair, probably a cast-off that had been brought home in case the man ever had a guest.

Langdon pulled his money clip out of his pocket and plucked a twenty from it. "You're a hard man to find," he cracked, explaining away his sweat and grime, paying up for the recent bet that he didn't even know whether he'd won or lost.

"What's going on?" Danny asked, popping a Funyun into his mouth.

Langdon walked to the window and peeked through the shade. He could see the police cruiser trolling down Cushing Street. Swett Street was just a slice, not much more than an alley, connecting High Street to Route 1, no more than two hundred yards long in an L shape. "The police are after me."

"You drinking and driving again?" Danny had many a vice, but alcohol was not one of them.

"Do I look like I've been drinking?" Langdon turned and stared at the man.

Danny was steadily feeding Funyun after Funyun into his mouth.

In between bites, he noisily chewed the crispy fake onion rings. After almost a minute of contemplation, he slurped down a large slug of Dr Pepper. "Yes."

"Shoot," Langdon said, a thought slicing through his hyperactive consciousness like a lightning bolt. He pulled his phone out and dialed a number.

"Hey, Dad," Missouri answered. "You're not going to believe what we've found out."

"Hi honey, I don't have time to explain right now, but the police think I did something I didn't, and they're probably going to come to the house. I'm thinking it'd be best if Tug was not there."

"What are you saying?"

"Why don't you and Jack take him to…" Langdon began racking his mind for where, but was coming up empty. They couldn't go to Jimmy's or Jewell's. Bart would throw a fit if they brought a man wanted by ICE to his house—fair enough, as harboring a fugitive would be enough to get him fired. "How about Star's place? Do you have his number?" Langdon hurriedly gave the number.

"What's going on, Dad?"

And then another thought went ricocheting through the recesses of his head. "I'll tell you later, E, but I've got to go now." He hung up the phone and turned to Danny. "The police can track my phone, can't they?"

"I think if you turn it off they can't find you," Danny replied.

"I heard somewhere they can still find your last location before you turn it off."

"Yeah, as a matter of fact, that reminds me, I read somewhere, maybe in *The Washington Post*, that the NSA can track a phone that's turned off. I don't remember how, but it claimed they have the power."

"You need to get rid of my phone."

"Me?"

"I can't go out there," Langdon said.

"What do you want me to do with it?"

Langdon walked to the kitchen window. Just across the way was the Androscoggin River. "Throw it in the river."

Langdon locked the door behind Danny as he waddled his way down the stairs and across the street. He lost sight of him as he passed behind an apartment building, but in ten minutes he was back, sweating profusely from the walk. Once he'd settled his bulk back into the recliner, he looked at Langdon with a measuring glance. "You gonna' tell me what's going on?"

"I broke into a house down in Falmouth," Langdon replied.

"What'd you do that for?"

"I'm investigating a case and haven't been able to get in touch with the husband of a missing woman. So when he wasn't there?" Langdon shrugged. "I broke in."

"What'd you find?"

"Nothing." Langdon walked over to the kitchen window and peered out, but could see nothing out of the ordinary. "And I mean nothing. The house was empty. Not even a dust bunny."

"How'd they know you did it?"

"I don't know," Langdon admitted. "I didn't see a camera. The neighborhood was empty. Bart called and warned me they were looking for me. Said they had me for B & E, as well as theft of property."

"Bart? You mean that big asshole cop friend of yours?" Danny didn't try to hide his dislike of the policeman.

"Yeah, that's the one." Langdon briefly considered upbraiding him but sighed, just not having the energy to play facilitator right then.

"But you didn't steal nothing?"

"There wasn't anything to steal."

"So, to avoid a breaking and entering charge, you've become a fugitive from justice? You going to Canada to live in a yurt?"

"There's a little bit more," Langdon admitted. He thought of not telling Danny, but the man would know soon enough. He was definitely plugged into everything that happened in town, and

Langdon wouldn't have been surprised if he already knew, even though the discovery had only come minutes earlier. "When the police came to arrest me, they found a pistol under the driver's seat of my Jeep."

"Was it yours?"

Langdon went to get a drink of water, eyed the glasses, and then carefully drank from the tap, before going and sitting down in the rickety wooden chair. If the police came knocking at the door there was nowhere to hide anyway. "Nah, mine was locked in the center console."

Danny grunted and sat forward with effort. "So, whose gun is it?"

"I don't know for sure, but I have a sneaking suspicion." Langdon stood and walked to the window to peer out again. "You hear about those Russians who got killed down in Westbrook?"

"Sure," Danny replied. "Real gangstas!"

"Well, they were killed with a Glock. It so happens that a couple of days ago I was threatened by a couple of Boy Scouts with a Glock 43."

"What'd they threaten you for?"

"I thought it was the blackmail case I'm working on, but now I'm not so sure."

"The thing with the senator?"

"Yeah. I thought they wanted me to back off finding the blackmailer, who I thought was Kamrin Jorgenson, but now I'm not so sure."

Danny finished off his Dr Pepper and burped loudly. "So, you're thinking there might be a connection between the blackmailer and the dead Russians."

"I also think the Russians were responsible for the Old Port Killings."

"And not that immigrant fellow the police let go yesterday?" Danny again proved he was up on the gossip. Perhaps, he even knew that Tug was currently at Langdon's house.

"No. The police let him go. I think they found evidence implicating the dead Russians."

"Who they now think you killed?"

"That's about the gist of it."

"So, what are you going to do now?"

"I haven't figured that out, yet," Langdon said.

"I might have something for you," Danny replied.

Langdon had been preoccupied, or he would have noticed the careful way in which his friend had baited the hook and let the line out to just within his fish's reach before beginning to reel it back in. "If you got something, I sure could use it," Langdon said, his hands wide in exasperation.

"Orioles are coming to Fenway tonight. How about we bet fifty bucks, and you give me ten runs?"

Langdon fought back the urge to curse. He was on the run from the police on murder charges, and Danny was trying to force him to take the last place Baltimore Orioles and give up ten runs? Langdon thought about just offering up the Grant on the spot, but he knew this was not how the man operated. There was a very rigid set of rules to be followed, probably flowing from some form of autism that Danny T. had never been diagnosed with because he stopped going to school when he was fourteen. "Sure," he said tightly.

"You know the lady you had too many drinks with out to the Bernard? The hot one with the big knockers?"

Again, Langdon fought back the urge to vent. He was pretty sure he hadn't told the man about Delilah Friday, once again proving that there were no secrets in Brunswick, or Freeport, for that matter. Of course Danny knew all about Langdon and his client Delilah Friday, except, perhaps, for the fact that she had just gone into the bookshop and told Chabal that she'd slept with Langdon. "Sure," he said again.

"I got a buddy who bartends at Moretti's, you know the Italian restaurant down on Depot Street in Freeport?"

Langdon knew better than to rush the story, and thus, merely nodded.

"Well, they have trivia in the bar on Wednesday nights, and even though that's over by 10:00 p.m. or so, the place keeps rocking until 1:00 in the morning. He makes a bundle on tips, he says."

"Can you please get to the point of the story?" Langdon asked, again peeking out the window.

"Okay, okay," Danny raised his hands. "He calls me up a little bit earlier to place a bet, and in the middle of it, starts talking about this knockout who comes in about midnight and meets two guys. He describes your gal, Friday, and I'm thinking, can't be two women like that in all of Maine, right?"

"There're probably more beautiful women in Freeport than you can imagine," Langdon said, suddenly tired. The town—with the L.L. Bean headquarters and more outlets than you could shake a stick at—was a shopping destination for buses of tourists from all over North America, Europe, and even China on their way from Boston to Acadia National Park.

"Okay, so he told me it was her. He asked for her ID when she came to the bar, not because he thought she was underage, but just so he could get her name. He said he wished that drivers' licenses required you to put your phone number on 'em." Danny laughed.

"Please," Langdon said in a low voice.

"Okay, okay, so he says to me, 'You're never gonna guess what this dame's name is!' Rick, he likes his old movies, so he actually says dame." Danny leaned forward, coming dangerously close to toppling to the floor. "And of course, I guess 'Delilah Friday,' because I've been hearing all about you and her from some people. Rick, he didn't say anything for half a minute, and then finally he says, 'Damn, you *do* know everything! Who should I bet on for games this weekend?'"

"Okay, so Delilah Friday meets two guys in Freeport. So what?"

Danny T. pushed himself to his feet and walked over to Langdon. He was a good foot shorter than him, even if he weighed about the same, and his breath stank of Funyuns. Yet, his lively eyes indicated a level of intelligence one would never guess, given his appearance. "Susie was into the store last night just before I kicked off my shift, so we had a cigarette together."

Langdon wracked his mind to keep up with Danny's twisted logic. "Susie, who works out to Hog Heaven?"

"Yeah," Danny agreed. "She was telling me all about the run-in you had there with two guys in suits. She described them to a T. Right down to their clipped hair, red and blue ties, glasses, and eyebrows."

"Maybe I should hire her as an investigator," Langdon replied.

"And you know what? They sounded an awful lot like those two—what did you call 'em?—Boy Scouts that met up with Delilah Friday at Moretti's last night at midnight."

Chapter 21

"Star? Hey, can you come in and cover for me at the shop?" Chabal held the phone pressed to her ear, heedless of the customer at the counter, her thoughts spinning out of control. "Great," she managed to say. "See you in a bit."

On autopilot, she rang up the sale of the two mysteries. Her husband had cheated on her. What had she done wrong? How could he be such an asshole? And why were the police after him? It served him right.

"Jewell?" She didn't remember dialing. "Are you at work? You're working from home today? Do you think you could meet me for a drink? I know its only noon, but I've had a rough morning. Great. Why don't you swing by the shop and we'll go across to Goldilocks."

Four or five more people came through, buying books, asking questions, making small talk—it was all a blur. The phone rang. She answered it. Jack was calling, wanting to know why the police were after Langdon, and if she knew where Starling was. She bluntly said no to the first, and almost said no to the second, then remembered that he was coming into the store to cover for her, and like magic, Star walked through the door. She handed him the phone and went to get her purse from the office. How long had he been cheating? Chabal looked at the couch, the desk, the armchairs, and wondered if they'd had sex on any of them... or all of them. Why?

"What's going on?" Star asked when she came back.

"Nothing," she replied. "I just have a few things to take care of."

"Jack was wondering if Tug could hide out at my place for a bit. He said something about your husband being wanted by the police."

"Oh, that? I don't know what he did now." *He cheated on me*, her inner voice screamed.

"Are you okay?" Star asked, his worn features creased in worry.

Chabal was saved from answering by Jewell who came striding into the store like a gladiator ready to do battle. "What's going on, girl?" she asked.

Chabal didn't want to cry. She wasn't going to cry. Then two policemen came in. "Are either of you Mrs. Langdon?"

Jewell looked at her, and then at the two cops, and then over at Star, but he merely shrugged his shoulders.

"I'm Chabal Langdon."

"Hello, Mrs. Langdon. I am Lieutenant Moss. Do you think we could ask you a few questions?"

"Sure. Why don't we go in the office?" She started to retrace her steps to the back, paused, and asked, "Is it okay if my friend Jewell comes along?"

"That would be fine, Mrs. Langdon."

The four of them went in back and shut the door on a very puzzled Jonathan Starling. Lieutenant Moss looked around the room. He thought of the man who'd showed up at his crime scene two days earlier. The man didn't seem like a killer, and had, in fact, said he was trying to clear that immigrant, Tugiramhoro Mduwimana, of the charge of killing those college girls. Still, it was quite suspicious that Langdon had shown up at the crime scene, as criminals were typically drawn to the scene of the crime like moths to a hot flame. How had he known the Russians were the killers? Moss wasn't buying the story of the fake cable men with Russian accents leading Langdon and Bart to the real killers and the scene of some, if not all, of their predations. But Langdon had indeed been correct, for the Russians were most definitely the murderers.

The men had been very careful, cleaning each of the girls with chemicals after their deaths, even meticulously combing out their hair, all of their hair, and leaving no semen inside them, obviously having used sturdy condoms, and most likely not finishing inside of them, just in case. One girl, who must have put up a fight, had had her fingertips clipped off.

But they had made a mistake—as crooks almost always did—actually, several mistakes. One of the girls had tooth marks on her shoulder that matched Oleg's bite imprint. While that might not have been enough to hold up in a court, coupled with traces of his saliva in her mouth and another victim's fingerprint on the bottom of the van seat, these all together were certainly conclusive enough to justify a search of their homes.

In Albert Volkov's basement, they'd found an intricately carved cane that was more like a totem, with strands of all three girls' hair wrapped around it. There was also more hair that had not yet been identified. Moss was fairly certain that it would match various missing persons dating back as long as the man had been in the U.S.

So, Moss was quite convinced that the three men had, indeed, been the murderers, not only of the three college girls, but probably of various other people as well. If Goff Langdon had in turn killed them, the world was a better place for it, but it was still his duty to arrest the man and make a case against him.

The only problem with that was that Moss didn't believe Langdon had done the crime. True, he'd only briefly met him, but his instincts were usually good about people. Nothing about Langdon announced the kind of psychopath who could cold-bloodedly execute three gangsters and a store proprietor. First, he had no motive, and second, nothing in the man's background suggested that he was a cold-blooded killer.

They'd only just delivered the Glock 43 to forensics, but Moss knew it was going to be the murder weapon. That left one burning question—what was it doing taped underneath Langdon's seat?

Especially when the guy already had another handgun locked away in the Jeep's console.

"What's this about?" Chabal asked.

"We're looking for your husband, Goff Langdon. Do you know where he is?" Lieutenant Moss asked. The other man appeared to be along just for show.

"No." Chabal decided not to tell him that Langdon had left there just a half-hour earlier after getting a warning that the police were looking for him. "Why are you looking for him?"

"When did you last see him?"

"She's not saying anything until you tell us what this is all about," Jewell broke in heatedly.

Moss sighed. "We have a video of a man that looks to be your husband breaking into a house in Falmouth. It was delivered to the police department there with Goff Langdon's name and address on it, as well as a note listing several stolen items including a laptop. Brunswick police were notified and approached your husband in the parking lot behind this building. At the time, they only meant to question him and check for stolen items from the house. Upon searching his vehicle, the officers discovered a pistol underneath his seat that may have been the weapon used in a quadruple homicide earlier this week in Westbrook."

Chabal gaped, as did Jewell. "You think he killed those Russian gangsters?"

"We only want to question him, Mrs. Langdon. We don't know that the weapon is the murder weapon."

"A tape was anonymously delivered to your station and then a weapon was found in Langdon's Jeep? Oh, man, we've already heard that one, and quite recently haven't we, Chabal?" Jewell said.

Moss turned and looked at her for the first time. "What's that?"

"Are you familiar with Tugiramhoro Mduwimana, Lieutenant?"

"Yes. The guy falsely jailed for murdering the three young ladies."

"And why was he jailed?" Jewell demanded.

"The police were tipped off and when they searched his room, they found implicating evidence," Moss said, his words slowing the further he went.

"*Anonymously* tipped off." Jewell added.

"Did you speak with the person who accused my husband of theft?" Chabal asked.

"We went to the house, but there was nobody home," Moss admitted. "In fact, the house didn't look as if it were lived in at all, come to think of it. I agree that this all sounds sketchy, Mrs. Langdon. That's why we need to talk with your husband."

"And why isn't he in your custody right now?" Chabal asked.

Moss was still tussling with the similarities between these two connected events, and answered absently, "He ran, Mrs. Langdon. We are doing our best to locate him, but he seems to have disappeared from the face of the earth."

Chabal went to say something, opening, and then closing her mouth. Of course he ran, she thought, for that was just like him. He didn't like to be pinned down, and would prefer to do things his own way than to work within the confines of the bureaucratic structure of the law. Of course, if the pistol did turn out to be the murder weapon, nobody would believe his claims that it was planted because he ran.

"I'd like your permission to search your house, Mrs. Langdon," Moss broke into her thoughts.

"Search the house for what?" she asked.

"For him, first of all," Moss replied. "As well as for items that the anonymous note said were stolen."

"No," Chabal said.

"I am trying to help, Mrs. Langdon," Moss said. "If your husband is innocent, then we need to prove that. To do that, we will need yours, and his, cooperation."

"I have nothing more to say, Lieutenant Moss. I will walk you to the door."

Chabal opened the door and gestured for the two policemen to precede her. Missouri was at the counter, presumably getting a key from Star to his house for Tug to hide in. Now, Chabal understood what that was all about. So, at least that piece was being taken care of. She had no doubt that if the pistol turned out to be the murder weapon that Moss would have no problem getting a search warrant, but she needed to make sure that Langdon was not stupid enough to be hiding out at the house, and she had to check and see if incriminating evidence had been planted there.

Star said something in a low voice to Missouri, who turned and walked out the door before the policemen reached the front of the store. It would be the worst of luck to have them walk outside and have Moss recognize Tug sitting in the car.

"Tomorrow, Lieutenant Moss," Chabal said.

The man paused, "Tomorrow?"

"If you would like to come by my house at 9:00 in the morning, I would be only too glad to let you search my house with the supervision of myself and my lawyer."

Moss turned this over in his mind. He doubted he could get a search warrant based solely on the video. It would be hours before forensics could match the Glock to the murder scene. "We'll see you in the morning, Mrs. Langdon," he said.

~ ~ ~ ~ ~

"I guess you *are* having a bad day," Jewell said. She'd driven both of them to Chabal's house, Langdon thankfully absent, but they were now combing the place for anything that didn't seem to belong there. So far, they'd only discovered that their computer and printer were missing, but Chabal assumed that the kids had taken them to Starling's for researching the blackmail case.

"The police looking for Langdon wasn't the worst of it," Chabal replied.

"There is other bad news worse than your husband being wanted for murder?"

"One of Langdon's clients came into the shop first thing this morning and told me that my husband is screwing her."

Jewell had already been contemplating wine, but this cemented the deal, and she went into the kitchen and poured two large glasses of red, returning to the living room. "Let's sit for a moment," she said gently.

Chabal was rocking back and forth on the couch with a faraway look on her face, but allowed Jewell to press an alarmingly full glass of red wine into her trembling hand. "She is absolutely gorgeous," she murmured.

"Who is this woman?"

"She hired Langdon to find her sister. He came home absolutely smashed the other night after drinking with her at the Bernard, where she happens to be staying. He's been awful strange about her, as if he's hiding something, but I didn't think much about it."

"What exactly did she say, this woman?"

"Her name is Delilah Friday. Doesn't that sound like a fuckable name?"

"Why was she telling you they slept together?" Jewell nudged forward.

"He told her that he was single. She was just dropping off a gift for him, a picture of the two them framed and all cozy together. She seemed to be shocked when I told her I was his wife."

"But that doesn't answer my question. Why did this woman come into the bookstore and tell you that she'd slept with your husband?"

"I suppose it was because she was shocked to discover he was married."

Jewell contemplated this. "No," she finally said.

"No?"

"That man of yours loves the ground you walk on. He is also a good person who tries to do the right thing at all times, even if he's a bit of a lug and stubborn as a crow eating roadkill. No, he did not cheat on you."

"Why would she lie about that?"

"I don't know. Have you talked to him?"

"He came into the store and I told him about it, but before we could get into it, he got a phone call, I think warning him the police were looking for him, and he left. I tried calling just now, but his phone is going straight to voice mail." Her wine glass was empty, and Jewell took it from her and went and filled it up in the kitchen.

"The police were initially seeking him for breaking into a house in Falmouth?" Jewell asked, returning with the glass and the wine bottle, which she set on the table in front of Chabal.

"Yeah, I think that's what the cop said," Chabal agreed.

"It seems to me that Langdon told me the other day he was investigating a missing woman in Falmouth. Does that sound right?"

"Yep. Delilah Friday hired him."

Jewell looked at Chabal, waiting for a reaction, but when there was none forthcoming, she helped fill in the cracks. "So, this morning, Langdon is accused of breaking in and stealing shit from a house in Falmouth, and while this is happening, the woman who hired him comes into the store and tells you she's sleeping with him."

"Does kinda sound like a soap opera when you put it that way, doesn't it?" Chabal asked, a ray of hope piercing the gloom enveloping her. "But why the set-up?"

Jewell shook her head. "I don't know why, but I plan on asking that bitch what she thinks she's playing at."

Chapter 22

Still Thursday

Langdon used Danny's phone and spent the rest of the daylight hours texting with Chabal, Missouri, Richam, Jimmy, and Bart about what was going on. He made plans with Chabal to meet up with her later that night at Starling's home where the kids had set up the command center. She was rather curt with him, and several mispronounced words suggested she might have gotten into the wine. At the same time, she was relieved to have heard from him, as she'd been unable to reach him on his phone, which was currently floating down the Androscoggin. As soon as the sun descended over the horizon, Richam pulled up in his car and Langdon slid discreetly into the passenger seat, a Red Sox cap pulled low on his head.

"Where to?" Richam asked, all business. He had considered lecturing Langdon to turn himself in… or leave the state, or any number of other things, but in the end, realized that Langdon's sheer stubbornness would prevail, and he'd do whatever the hell he wanted, so why waste his breath?

"The Bernard," Langdon replied. "Danny heard a story about Delilah Friday speaking with our two Boy Scouts, Pete and John."

Richam snuck a sideways look. "Jewell says that Friday woman came into the bookstore and told Chabal that you and she were shagging."

"She had a real nice framed picture of us drinking together to back it up," Langdon said.

"I just spoke with Jewell, speaking of drinking, and I think she and your wife are plowing through the wine, or so her voice seemed to indicate. Anyway, they're not buying the woman's story, just so you know."

"I've been texting with Chabal. She might not quite believe it, but trust me, she's not too happy with me."

Richam eased the car onto 295 South, keeping well within the speed limit. It wouldn't do to get stopped by the police with a wanted man in the car. "What's her deal? Delilah Friday, I mean."

"I don't know, but I'm starting to think there is no sister to find," Langdon replied.

"Everything seems to be spiraling back to your senator's blackmail case. You get threatened to drop the case by those two fellows, who show you a Glock, which is later used to kill four Russians who framed Tug, and then—surprise, surprise—a Glock turns up in your Jeep, and now these two are meeting with a woman who hired you to find her sister."

"Missouri told me they work for Goldenrod."

"Goldenrod?" Richam turned his blinker on for Exit 22. "Aren't they the people who shot up all those civilians in Baghdad a few years back?"

"You got it. They are a private mercenary army that will do anything for money. Of course, the largest budget in the world for their type of work is the United States Department of Defense, their primary client."

"It kind of stands to reason that if the two Boy Scouts are Goldenrod agents and they've been speaking with the mysterious Delilah Friday that she also works for the company," Richam said.

"You might have something there," Langdon said. "So, KJ, or whoever she is representing, hires these mercs to threaten me, and when that doesn't work, they bring in Miss Delilah Friday to wreck my life so that I can't focus on the case."

"Goldenrod is working for Kamrin Jorgenson? That doesn't make sense."

"The night I got hired by Senator Mercer, they paid me a visit and threatened me, suggesting I shouldn't look too hard for the blackmailer."

"Front or back?" Richam said, stopping at the stop light directly across from the Bernard.

"Let's go out back to the parking lot. She drives a Mercedes."

"So, Kamrin Jorgenson has hired operatives of a paramilitary organization to dissuade you from finding her. Sounds a bit… unlikely if you ask me."

"There's been something bothering me for a few days and I couldn't quite figure out what it was until this afternoon. When Chabal and I tracked Kamrin down to the Greenlander Motel, it was as if she'd been warned. How did she know I was onto her?"

"She didn't see you or the Jeep?"

"Chabal had driven the Jeep away. There's a small chance she saw me, but I don't think so."

"So, what then?"

"She fled about twenty minutes after I called Maxwell Mercer to tell him where she was."

"Mercer and Kamrin are working together?"

"That's Del's car right there," Langdon said, pointing at the silver Mercedes. "Why don't you park over in the corner, backed in, so we can keep an eye on it."

Once Richam had shut off the car, he turned his full attention to Langdon. "Are you suggesting that the senator and Kamrin are working together? That doesn't make any sense at all."

"No, no it doesn't, but not much about this blackmail case has made any sense from the get-go. First, there is no demand, and then, when a blackmail note is delivered, it's an impossible ask. Maxwell tries to fire me, the senator wants me to negotiate with KJ, and Pete and John threaten me again instead of hearing what the senator is offering. None of it makes any sense."

Richam chewed that over a bit, before shaking his head in

consternation. "And now there is a connection between Pete and John and Delilah Friday? It seems like everybody is on the same side, sort of making any sort of blackmail a moot point."

"Sadly, the only link between them is not much more than gossip, two guys who look like the Boy Scouts having drinks with Miss Friday. But, hey, it's about the only lead I have right now, so we might as well keep our eyes open. Why don't you go into the tavern and lobby and see if she's in there?"

Richam sighed in exasperation, but he was curious, too, about this woman who seemed to have set the tongues of half the population of the coast of Maine a'wagging. "Okay," he said. He opened the door, stood up, and froze. "I believe that Miss Delilah Friday is coming out right now."

Langdon swiveled his head around to the back entrance, and sure enough, here she came with a valet in tow, pulling her huge suitcase behind him with a carry bag wrapped around his shoulder. She was pecking away at her phone with an annoyed look on her face. "That's her."

Delilah Friday wasted no time pulling the car out and exiting the hotel lot once the valet had stowed her bag in the trunk. Richam was caught unaware, and had to cut across traffic to keep her disappearing Mercedes in sight. Luckily, Langdon spotted her getting on 295 North, and they were able to slide in a few cars behind her and discreetly follow.

"She isn't bad looking," Richam commented wryly.

"I almost feel bad refuting her story that I slept with her," Langdon rejoined.

"Where do you think she'll lead us?"

"I don't know, but she sure enough seems to be twisted up in this whole mess in some way."

"Looks like she checked out of the Bernard."

"She's going the wrong way if she's returning home to Virginia."

The Mercedes veered off onto the Topsham exit, and then into the

Topsham Fair Mall. It pulled into a corner of the parking lot next to a GMC Yukon Denali. Delilah Friday got out of her car and climbed into the back seat of the Denali.

"Circle around," Langdon said, sliding down in his seat and averting his face. They parked across the way where they'd have a view, but not too close. "That's the vehicle the Boy Scouts drive. Why don't you have a walk past, and make sure it's them." He pulled his phone out and displayed the fuzzy picture of Pete and John to Richam.

"Great picture," Richam said with a wry smirk. "And you think those two are the cold-blooded assassins of those Russian gangsters?"

"Be careful," Langdon said. "Don't let them see you."

Richam had to circle around as if leaving the Hannaford's to cross over in front of the Denali. He wondered if it would be a red flag that he wasn't carrying shopping bags, or if he was already on the Boy Scouts' radar as an associate of Langdon, or if it was possible to note his anxiety as he tried to casually saunter past. The man in the driver's seat was staring at him as he risked a look, and he did his best to hold it, and then nonchalantly kept walking. To avoid suspicion, he continued on across the road and through the parking lot of Arby's, before carefully wending his way back to his own car.

"Well?" Langdon asked.

Richam wiped his brow with his hand. "It could be them."

"*Could* be?"

"You show me a fuzzy picture of two guys and want a positive identification at night through the windshield of an SUV parked in the shadows?" Richam vented his anxiety. "I can't be sure, but it certainly could be."

Across the lot, Delilah Friday climbed out of the Denali and back into her Mercedes. The lights of both vehicles came on as they roared back into life.

"We staying with Friday?" Richam asked.

Langdon breathed deeply. "No. Let's follow the Boy Scouts."

At the entrance to the mall, Friday took a right towards Brunswick, and they stayed with the Denali as it went left, and then merged onto 295 North. Ten minutes later, they took the Bowdoinham exit. Once off the highway they needed to hang back further to avoid giving themselves away.

Langdon knew it was unlikely the two men hadn't noticed themselves being tailed, as they were professionals, but he refrained from saying anything to Richam. What else could they do? When the Denali turned into a driveway, they continued on past, turned around, and with the lights off, coasted back by again, just in time to see the vehicle lights go off down by a house with several lights on, about a quarter-mile off the road.

"Take the next left," Langdon said

"Do you think they saw us?" Richam asked.

"Can't say for sure, but why would they bring us here if they saw us?"

"Could be a trap."

Langdon nodded. "Turn the car around and pull over on that side."

Richam did as directed. "What are you thinking?"

"I'm thinking that that farmhouse is less than a half-mile through the woods right there," Langdon said, gesturing to the trees on the side of the road. "I'm going to approach the house from this side, where they won't be expecting me to come from if it is a trap, and see what's going on."

"You're going to do what?"

"I'm going to sneak up to the house and see what I can find out."

"The hell you are! Do you have any idea how stupid that is?"

"It's not like I have much choice, now, do I?" Langdon spread his hands wide. "I'm wanted by the police for murder. My wife thinks I cheated on her. Somebody ran my goddamn dog over." He opened the door. "And I don't have a clue what's going on, but I'm pretty sure the answers to all my questions are in that house."

"Getting yourself killed isn't going to help," Richam said.

"I hope to avoid that as well," Langdon said dryly.

"What about me?"

"You stay with the car. I'll text you if something changes."

"You still got the phone you called me on earlier?"

"Yeah, it's Danny T.'s."

"Do you have a gun?"

"Nah. It's back in the Jeep."

"Aha, I thought the Glock might have been yours."

Langdon started to correct him, realized it was an attempt at levity, and instead gave a strained smile. "Give me two hours and then call Bart to bring in the cavalry."

Luckily, the sky was clear and there was most of a moon helping illuminate the way. Still, Langdon seemed to be at war with the trees, whose branches scratched his face and poked into his body, whose roots reared up to make him stumble. It took him a half-hour to navigate his way to the house. He approached it from the unlit side away from the drive, and then crawled down closer to a lit window. The window was cracked slightly, but he could hear nothing, and finally raised himself to his knees and risked a look inside. It appeared to be the dining room, a solid oak table surrounded by eight sturdy chairs. Only one of them was occupied. KJ sat in it with her hands tied behind her back and a gag in her mouth.

A shadowy figure emerged from the darkness and approached the front door, Langdon pressing himself into the ground and breathing as shallowly as he could without panting. Once the phantom went inside, Langdon crawled down to the next window and peeked in. It was the kitchen. John Smith sat at the counter atop a stool. The man named Pete stood in the doorway. Langdon was able to hear them through the open window.

"Nothing," Pete said. "There's no sign of a car on the road and nobody in the fields." He tossed a pair of bulky goggles on the kitchen island. Langdon guessed they were some kind of night vision optics.

"Maybe it was just coincidence, but I don't believe in coincidences. Somebody was following us," John replied. "I don't think we should do the lady here, just in case whoever may have been following us calls the police."

"How and where do you want to do it, then?"

"We have to make her disappear. I know a spot where we can bury the body and nobody will ever find her, but we best clear out of here."

Langdon felt around with his hands and found a rock the size of a baseball. He'd been a pretty good player in high school, but that was a ways back. There was a balcony over the front porch, up on the second floor, and he could see the glint of a glass doorway. He stood out of view of the kitchen window, wound up, and threw the rock through the middle of the door. The glass shattered, and Langdon heard an exclamation from inside. He didn't take time to ensure the two men went upstairs to investigate, but instead, cut into the screen with his jackknife and pulled it out. He pushed the window up as far as he could, and then as quietly as possible, he pulled himself up to the window.

He could hear the Boy Scouts running up the stairs, and he tumbled through the window, hoping their own noise would drown out the clatter he made. KJ was staring at him with wide eyes, and he held his finger up to his lips, an unnecessary motion he realized, as she was gagged. Her hands were bound by a black zip-tie, which proved surprisingly tough to saw through, stealing precious seconds. Langdon could hear John and Pete yelling upstairs for whoever to come out, and he could imagine the scene as they covered each other going from door to door. With a violent wrench, he snapped the heavy-duty plastic binding her wrists.

KJ immediately pulled the gag from her mouth. "My legs are tied, as well," she gasped, retching.

Her legs were bound with nylon rope and Langdon was able to make short work of that just as they heard a curse from upstairs. He imagined that meant they'd found the rock, and were now realizing the diversion. He was not wrong, as the sound of footsteps came clattering down the stairs.

"Out the window," Langdon said, half-helping, half-shoving KJ through the opening. He dove out behind her, landing on her just as she started to rise, both of them tumbling to the ground again. "Stay close," he whispered, rising and running half bent over for the woods.

They had just reached the edge when four shots cracked out one after the other, so close together, it almost sounded like one, and a small birch in front of them exploded in a shower of white bark. Langdon dove to his right and KJ ran over the back of him as they spilled into the protective cover of the forest.

"Come on," Langdon said, rising and pulling her after him.

His thoughts were on the night vision goggles. They ran heedlessly forward, branches tearing at their faces and bodies, rocks and logs and holes causing them to stumble and fall. Voices were calling for them to stop, and gunfire lit up the darkness, but then the road was there. Langdon spotted Richam's car about 100 yards back behind them, but the lead pursuer saw them at the same time, just as the vehicle shot into motion. As they lunged into the car, the back windshield burst into kingdom come, and then they were hurtling away to safety.

Chapter 23

Friday

Langdon woke with a start. He was naked and intertwined with a beautiful woman. It was his wife. Where was he? Then the events of the night before began to reassemble themselves as if the pieces of Richam's shattered back window slo-moed backwards to become whole again. On two wheels, tires screeching, Richam had driven them around the corner and out of the line of fire.

Once they'd ascertained nobody had been shot, they had ridden in silence, only interrupted by Richam asking where to go, and Langdon directing them to Starling's. He knew he should've grilled KJ to find out more, but they were all in shock at how close they had come to death, still plucking pieces of glass out of their hair as Richam sped down the highway, taking them as far and as fast as he could away from the two stone-cold killers.

Richam had dropped Langdon and KJ at Starling's, collected his wife, who was quite drunk on wine, and then had continued on to Bart's camp in Phippsburg. There was little doubt that the Boy Scouts could track any license plate down, and Richam and Jewell were not interested in meeting up with them on this night, or any time soon.

Starling lived in a ranch on Boody Street, a quiet dead-end within walking distance to Bowdoin College. Sitting in the small living area were Missouri, Chabal, Jack, Tug, and Starling. Langdon had received, and given, a hug to Missouri, as she looked askance at his scratched and bloody face, arms, and legs. In words as succinct as possible, he told those gathered what had happened.

Missouri and Jack had been dispatched to collect dog, and then to go to Bart's house for the night. Langdon knew they would be safe with the surly policeman. Starling had then shown KJ to a bedroom for the night, giving Langdon and Chabal the second guest room, as it were, before bringing blankets and pillows out for Tug to sleep on the couch, as there were only three bedrooms.

As the silence had descended upon the house, Chabal had whispered that she knew Langdon had not cheated on her and that the girl Friday was a lying sack of shit. They had updated each other on the day's happenings, as one by one, items of clothing were discarded, each piece symbolizing the weight of the wearisome events of the previous eighteen hours. Then, it was only the two of them, their every care erased, leaving only their immediate physical world, as they made gentle love that helped straighten their tilted universe.

Langdon looked at the window, and even with the curtains pulled, realized it was still dark outside. A glow from the side table led his eyes to the time: 5:00 a.m. He eased his limbs from their entanglement with his wife's and set about the task of collecting his clothes from the floor. Once he was dressed, he cracked the door and slid through.

He risked a light in the kitchen, trying not to disturb Tug sleeping on the couch, as he searched for coffee, realizing what a total mess his clothes were. There was no way he'd fit into Star's clothes, but Chabal had to go home later this morning to oversee the police investigation at the house, so perhaps she could get him some things to wear once they'd left.

He found the coffee and the pot, and as it began to percolate, KJ came out of her room and sat at the table. The table was an antique that Starling had found at a garage sale. One of his favorite pastimes was hunting for valuable junk to be bought cheaply. Langdon only knew this because he had had to come over one day after work to help wrestle the heavy, early 18th century table inside. Once the coffee had brewed, he poured two cups and sat down across from KJ.

"I guess I owe you a thank you for saving my life," KJ said.

"I'm surprised you're still here," he said.

"You know I'm not the running type," she replied with a faint smile.

"Funny you should say that. Last time I saw you, I was chasing you, and you were definitely running."

"Touché. Did the senator hire you to investigate me?"

"I think so, but I'm not sure," Langdon replied. He liked the way she made eye contact when she spoke, and even having just escaped being executed, she seemed at ease as she sipped her coffee with the man hired by her possible executioners to find her.

"What do you mean you're not sure?"

"I was approached by a man who put me in a room with the senator and her husband. It appeared she hired me, but I'm beginning to wonder if that was just because she thought I'd fail."

"Why would she do that?"

Langdon noticed that her clothes might be in more disrepair than his. "What is your part in all of this?" he finally asked.

"Was." KJ sighed. "To sleep with the senator," she finally said.

"Why?"

"To get pictures to blackmail her to push the President back into the Paris Climate Accord, or so I thought. I mean, I knew that wasn't going to happen, but I was hoping to achieve something good for the earth."

"You knew there was no chance of getting back into the Paris Accord?"

"Do you watch football, Mr. Langdon?"

"Sure."

"Sometimes, when you try to score a touchdown, you get twenty yards, or ten yards, enough for a first down. You advance."

"So, never mind the ultimate goal, you would have settled for a gain of any sort, the more substantial, the better?" Langdon liked a woman who made a football analogy. He decided that she couldn't be all that bad.

"Yes, but now I'm afraid I was being used for another purpose." KJ's eyes turned steely, suggesting an anger and strength lurking below her easy-going nature. "You know the two guys you just saved me from? Glasses and Eyebrows?"

Langdon laughed, and then choked back another chuckle, remembering those still asleep, especially Tug, who was no more than ten feet away on the couch. "We were calling them the Boy Scouts, but now we know their real names, John Smith and Peter Yeager."

"You know more than me, then," KJ replied. "They gave me some phony names when they came out to South Dakota and enlisted me to blackmail the senator. They said they were from some secret faction of the Earth Liberation Front, but I should've known better. Truth was, I did know better, but I was bored and poor and sick of being bored and poor. And I missed Maine. So I came along."

"You think they were lying?"

"I've had my suspicions, nothing concrete, but they aren't your typical environmental activists. They're more like mercenaries of some sort than tree-huggers. I thought I might be able to twist the game my way once the deed was done, but they certainly weren't keeping me in the blackmail loop once I'd slept with the senator, and then they came to the house last night and tied me up and talked about killing me right in front of my face."

"On two previous occasions, they threatened me to bugger off the case." Langdon concurred. "I even told them I had an offer from the senator, but they didn't seem interested."

"So, if they don't work for Earth First, who do they work for? And what do they want?"

"Let me ask you something," Langdon said, rising and pouring himself more coffee. He raised the pot in her direction, but replaced it when she shook her head no. "The day I chased you out to the Greenlander Motel, what caused you to run?"

"Glasses called me, told me to get out and that you were onto me."

"Was he watching you? The motel? How did he know?"

KJ thought for a moment. "He didn't say, but I'm pretty sure he wasn't watching me, because he said he was in Bath. He told me to give it fifteen minutes, and then they would pick me up on Route 1 South right behind the motel."

"The deal was that I would call Maxwell Mercer, the senator's husband, when I located you. Half an hour after I did, you slid out the door and escaped."

"You think that Glasses and Eyebrows work for the senator? That doesn't make much sense, now, does it?"

"I was thinking that, but then we discovered that they are both employed by Goldenrod."

KJ's next words proved she needed no description of Goldenrod. "You mean they are *mercenaries?*"

"More or less, but private mercenaries, not official mercenaries." Langdon couldn't help adding, "I guess that makes them even spookier."

"A couple of guys like that would have no trouble bugging the Mercers' phone. Hell, their cars, and their whole house—right down to briefcases and the senator's pocketbook—must have some sort of listening device planted."

This is what Langdon had been thinking as well, but it wasn't until that moment that he realized that it most likely also pertained to him and his own home. It was probably best that he'd thrown his phone in the river, had his Jeep impounded by the police, and deserted his house.

A rustling indicated Tug's awakening. The young Burundian showed no sign of sleep, his step light and his eyes bright. Langdon wondered how long he'd been lying there listening. Tug poured himself a cup of coffee and sat down.

"I am sorry, ma'am, I did not get a chance to meet you last night," Tug said.

"I am the blackmailer, Kamrin Jorgenson," she said ironically, stretching out her hand.

He took the hand and shook it firmly up and down twice. "I am Tug, the immigrant framed for murder," he responded equally ironically, adding, "and possibly one of the most reviled men in the United States."

"You've been cleared," Langdon admonished.

"The public listens to and believes what it wants to, Mr. Langdon. The entire country read the reports of my arrest with malice in their hearts, while few noticed that I was actually innocent, and of those, most did not care."

Langdon opened his mouth to argue that it was untrue, but then closed it again, realizing the authenticity of the words. "Perhaps when we get to the bottom of this, the story will come out and vindicate you fully," he said instead, albeit weakly.

"I am a journalist by trade, Mr. Langdon. People will read the headline, perhaps the first paragraph, some will skim the story, but few will pick up buried deep within that the fellow from Burundi did nothing wrong. That is the reality in which I live."

"On the other hand," KJ interjected, "in a few months' time, you will be forgotten."

"That is the best I can hope for, Miss Jorgenson, to be forgotten," Tug agreed. "And I thank Mr. Langdon, and his friends, for their efforts to free me from jail and prevent me from being deported. It gives me hope in the good nature of man."

"I was just telling KJ about your discovery that John Smith and Pete Yeager are mercenaries working for Goldenrod," Langdon said, changing the subject.

"We didn't get a chance to tell you last night, but Missouri linked Goldenrod to MacLeod Brandt, the arms manufacturer," Tug said.

"Linked?"

"Goldenrod is a subsidiary company of MacLeod Brandt. I believe that is the correct definition."

"Good morning," Chabal said, coming out of the bedroom.

"What's good about it?" Starling asked, having opened his door at that moment.

"Are you always so grumpy first thing in the morning?" Langdon asked him.

Starling shuffled over and took the near-empty coffee pot. "Only when I wake up to no coffee, because it has been drunk by three fugitives." He poured the last bit into a cup and handed it to Chabal and went about making more. "Usually I wake and quietly read the newspaper. Today, I awake to find a man wanted by ICE, another wanted by the police, and a third person being hunted by mercenaries. On top of that, I probably have to go open the bookstore and run it by myself all day?"

"We can close it for a family emergency," Langdon replied.

"Or for Labor Day weekend," Chabal said.

"And what? Stay here and wait to see who gets here first? I'm betting on the mercenaries, but it could be tight with ICE and the police. Nah, I'm better off going to work than staying around here."

"Is 4 by Four picking you up at 8:30 to meet up with Lieutenant Moss?" Langdon asked his wife.

"Yes. What should I do after they leave?"

"Why don't you come back here?"

"Make sure you're not followed," KJ said.

Chabal gave KJ a look that made it clear she did not need her advice.

~ ~ ~ ~ ~

The 1966 Ford F100 Ranger Styleside rumbled up Route 1 at a steady fifty miles an hour. Starling had bought this antique at a junkyard ten years earlier and spent almost the next decade restoring it to the near-mint condition it was in now, right down to the "Twin I-Beam" emblem on the front fender. Star had not wanted to let Langdon take the turquoise pick-up truck so dear to his heart, but Langdon had promised to treat it kindly. When Langdon tried to leave KJ behind, he had not been very persuasive, and she now sat shotgun—not that they had a weapon of any kind, unless you counted Langdon's pocket knife—as they trundled north to Bath.

They had both shorn their hair, an attempt at disguise that Chabal insisted on, and Star had only been too happy to supply the clippers. KJ wore a pair of jeans and a white-collared shirt, also from Star, which, with the addition of Chabal's sunglasses, did indeed change her look substantially. They'd stopped at the Goodwill out at Cook's Corner, and KJ had gone in to shop for Langdon, which is why he wore overalls over a white tank-top with a red MAGA hat pulled down over his face.

There was a christening of the latest destroyer at the Bath Iron Works, and Senator Mercer was one of the speakers, the guest of honor spot reserved for the mother of the boy who the ship was named after, a soldier in Iraq who, years earlier, saved many lives by covering a grenade with his own body. Langdon knew better than to show up in a crowd of people with his poor disguise, as he was too well known. But, he was betting that Senator Mercer would go home afterwards, just a bit over a mile down the street, before continuing on with whatever else her day held.

The driveway was shaped like a cursive Y, the access from the street so close to the house on the right that KJ could have touched the wall out of her window. Fifty yards back, the drive split to left and right, with two cars on the right side, and the left side leading to the garage. Langdon doubted anybody was there, but parked on the right, and went and knocked on the door. When there was no answer, he and KJ circled around to the back. There was a screened-in patio, locked, but easy enough to pry open with his jackknife. They sat down to wait, the Kennebec River flowing past about thirty feet from them, the very same river that the newly-christened destroyer would soon be making its way down on its way to the Atlantic Ocean.

"I could use a scotch," Langdon said.

"I could use a Wild Turkey," KJ replied.

Behind them was a wicker bar, with various bottles on a shelf.

"Do you think there's ice? I could always go neat, but I like a few cubes to take the edge off the bite." Langdon stood, and walked around the bar. There was, of course, a glass door half-fridge under the counter, but also next to it of equal size was a stainless steel icemaker. He found two glasses, plunked three cubes in each, and filled them almost to the rim. The scotch was an eighteen-year-old Macallan, and, surprisingly enough, among the bar's limited selection was also Wild Turkey. They clinked glasses and drank.

"How is Jimmy 4 by Four?" KJ stared fixedly at the river.

"You mean since you kicked him in the face twenty years ago?"

"I liked him. I didn't mean to hurt him."

"You broke his jaw," Langdon said sarcastically.

"Yeah, I read about that," she admitted. "But I meant emotionally. Does he talk about me?"

Langdon took a huge gulp of the brown liquor in his hand. Women would never cease to confuse him. "No."

"Fair enough."

"Do you think about him?"

"Yeah, for some reason I can't get that man out of my head. We had one afternoon, and I was just using him and all of that, but he's the one I remember."

Langdon pondered that as they sat in silence. "You know, I believe that it's quite possible that you had a profound affect on his life, as well."

"No need to be sarcastic," she said.

"I'm not," Langdon replied. "Really. He was a changed man after you left. Started working out. Dressing snappy. Stopped smoking so much dope. And I don't think he's been in a relationship with a woman for longer than ten weeks. I hadn't thought about it before, but you might be the one that got away."

"Did he ever talk about me?"

"You already asked me that, but no, and we wouldn't have given him much chance if he had." Langdon and the others had given Jimmy such a rash about being clocked by a woman after the incident, that he probably wouldn't have dared open his mouth, even if it hadn't been wired shut. Could it be that the incident had turned Jimmy into the womanizer that he was today? "What is it that you've been up to for the last twenty years?"

"After the whole DownEast Power affair, my Flower First party pretty much disintegrated under the police scrutiny. I barely slipped out of the state and made my way out west."

"Still saving the earth, I take it?" Langdon asked.

"Yeah, I was out in California for a awhile, but when the government named environmental activists the number one domestic terror threat, things started to go downhill. I was part of the group that was going to bomb the Nimbus Dam, but when that fell apart, and my boyfriend at the time, Eric, got arrested, I moved on to South Dakota. It's getting harder and harder every day. I supposed that's why I grasped at this opportunity even though I knew it was too good to be true."

Life sure was strange, Langdon was thinking as he finished his drink, how sometimes things come full circle. It was then they both heard a car pull into the driveway. The christening must be over.

It wasn't long before the command to freeze and raise their hands came, a contradictory type of statement Langdon thought, but he did his best to accommodate the order. Of course, they had been waiting for Dwayne, the senator's bodyguard, to do this very thing. This was a gamble, coming to visit the senator, for the police wanted him, and her proper course of action would be to simply call and have him taken away. Not to mention that KJ, sitting next to him, had slept with the senator and then blackmailed her. Arresting the both of them would certainly create an awkward scenario, now, wouldn't it?

"Put the gun away, Dwayne," Senator Mercer said. She walked

around to the front of them, pulling a chair so that it faced them, and sat down. Maxwell Mercer did the same on the other side.

"Nice hat," the senator said dryly.

Langdon blushed and pulled the MAGA cap from his head.

"Nice haircut," she said. "What are you doing here?"

"You hired me to negotiate terms with Kamrin Jorgenson," Langdon replied.

"Hello, Margaret," KJ said.

"Hello, Kamrin," the senator replied.

Maxwell was nervously picking up red pistachios and popping them into his mouth one by one. "What are you doing here? We don't have time for this. Margaret has a speaking engagement, and I have to go clean out *Swing Vote* for the winter."

"I thought it perhaps best if we all sat down together and made sure we were on the same page." Langdon could feel the menacing presence of Dwayne behind him, and wondered if the man was there for more than protection, perhaps also engaging in enforcement?

"I think everything's all set," Senator Mercer said. "The second blackmail note was much closer aligned with my own beliefs, and I'm in the process of holding up my end of the bargain. I am sure that once I have done this, Kamrin will be only too happy to hand over everything she holds?"

"Second blackmail note?" Maxwell blurted out.

The senator looked at her husband. "I am sorry Max, you know that I am unable to share everything with you."

"But I wasn't aware of a second note," he said weakly, a bewildered look overtaking his normal smile. "What were the demands?"

"As I said, I can't share them with you, but as I also said, I am sure that Kamrin will be happy with the results." The senator looked knowingly at KJ.

"I know nothing of a second blackmail note," KJ said in a low voice.

The senator's face blanched for just a split-second. "What are you playing at, my dear?" she asked.

"There was no second blackmail note," Maxwell said.

"On the contrary, there *was* a second blackmail note, delivered to me several days ago." Senator Mercer rose and poured two fingers of brown liquor into a glass.

"Dwayne, do you think it would be okay if I got a refill?" Langdon asked, raising his glass. His intention was not for the man to serve him, but merely not shoot him, but the senator nodded, and the bodyguard refilled both his and KJ's glasses. Maxwell chose to light his pipe, his fingers shaking slightly as he packed the bowl with tobacco.

"I did not send a second note," KJ said once they'd settled again.

"If not you, then who?" the senator asked.

"KJ—Kamrin—was approached in South Dakota by two men a few months back. They claimed to be from the Earth Liberation Front, and engaged her services in blackmailing you to protect the environment." Langdon decided to clarify a few points for all in the room. "What did the second blackmail note ask for?"

The senator shook her head. "I can't tell you that."

"These same two men tried to kill her last night," Langdon said.

The senator had noted the scratched and bruised faces of both of them. She refrained from asking further, though, realizing the less she knew, the better.

"The two men who…" Maxwell started, stopped, and then spoke again. "They tried to kill her last night?"

The senator cast a warning look at him. "Max."

"It turns out these men are not from the Earth Liberation Front at all, but work for a company called Goldenrod," Langdon said.

"Goldenrod?"

"How do you know that?" Maxwell asked.

Langdon looked at Mr. and Mrs. Mercer, and wondered that perhaps there were many secrets kept between them, ranging from politics to partners. Too many. He made a mental note to follow up on Max's confusing reaction. "So, I ask you again, Senator Mercer, what was in the second blackmail note?"

Senator Mercer looked at her husband. He was indeed acting stranger than normal. She made a note to pursue what he was hiding at a later time. She looked at Dwayne, who stood behind Langdon and KJ with his hand on his holstered pistol. There was still much to be established and untangled before reaching any final solution. Her eyes flitted to Langdon. He seemed to be such a buffoon, but Maxwell had insisted she hire the man, and he had proven his worth, perhaps too well. For the first time she looked Kamrin in the eye, and her heart beat amplified in her chest and her throat tightened. The woman was beautiful. As well as gentle, considerate, and intelligent, the senator remembered, before locking her emotions behind closed doors.

"Are you in possession of the proof of our affair?" The senator directed the question at KJ.

Danny T.'s phone buzzed in Langdon's pocket. He pulled it out and saw the call was from Chabal. He considered ignoring it, but he'd barely mended the fences with his wife and love, and thought it best to not jeopardize her trust again. "Dwayne, I am going to answer my phone," he said carefully. He pulled the phone out. "Hey babe, I'm in the middle of something. Can I call you back?"

The reply came screaming through the airwaves. "They took Missouri!"

Chapter 24

Still Friday

"Here they come," John said, nudging Pete awake.

It was just about 10:00 in the morning, the sun up in the east with a few lazy clouds drifting past. After Langdon and Kamrin had escaped the night before, John and Pete staked out Langdon's home, and were rewarded when Missouri and Jack had shown up. After just a few minutes they'd reappeared with the dog, and John and Pete decided to follow, hoping they would return to wherever Langdon was hiding out, but instead, they had gone to the house of the cop they called Bart. Once midnight rolled around, the two men left to catch a bit of shuteye, and then returned at 5:00 this morning to keep an eye out for them.

Missouri and Jack stopped and went into the Coffee Dog Bookstore, and Pete went in to keep watch on them. The man, Starling, was working behind the counter. Missouri chatted at the counter with him for a few minutes, while Jack disappeared into the back room. After a bit, they came out carrying a folder full of papers and got back into the car, turning left on Maine Street, left on Mill Street, and then they almost lost them on Pleasant Street as they went through the drive-thru at Dunkin' Donuts. John had pulled off into a car wash, but got stuck behind an exiting vehicle in no apparent hurry, and had to burst through a red light as they turned left onto Church Road, but luckily, neither Missouri nor

Jack seemed aware of the obviousness of the car trailing them.

"Who lives here?" John asked as they watched the two enter a house on Boody Street.

Pete was busy tapping away on an iPad and had his answer in just seconds. "Jonathan Starling. The guy who works in the bookstore."

"What do you think?"

"I say if Langdon and Kamrin are here, we kill them."

"And the others? The girl and the boy we followed here?"

Pete was silent. His instinct was to kill them, too, but he knew the body count was climbing. It was one thing to knock off Russian gangsters, especially once it was established that they were the Old Port Killers, but to leave a local business owner and his children dead might blow the lid off the entire operation.

John Smith took his glasses and cleaned them with the end of his tie, more an exercise of thoughtfulness than need. "I imagine that Langdon would do just about anything to save his daughter."

"We take the girl?"

"If we can do it without killing anybody."

"Should we call M?"

As if on cue, the phone buzzed and John picked it up, checking the number, and then answered. "Smith here."

"What the hell are you two doing?" The voice was angry.

"We've tracked down Langdon's daughter and stepson to a house in Brunswick. We're not sure if Langdon and Jorgenson are in there or not." John thought he should give the good news first to defray the verbal lashing that seemed imminent.

"Well, he's not. He is currently at Senator Mercer's house with Kamrin Jorgenson. I can only imagine what they are talking about."

Smith looked at his watch. It would take almost half an hour to get there, and by then, chances were they'd be gone. "Have you contacted the police?"

"I am afraid that the damage may be done. We need to ensure that he has no further communication with the senator."

"Do you want us to… take care of him?"

"No. The senator would certainly be curious if he turns up dead, and we can't have her poking around, not until the upcoming vote, at least."

"We were just discussing the idea of kidnapping Langdon's daughter."

"To what purpose?"

"He turns himself into the police and keeps his mouth shut and we let her go unharmed in a week's time."

"Where will you keep her?"

"The farmhouse is blown. We'll need to get a new place, but that's not really a concern."

"Bring her here."

John put the phone down and looked over at Pete. "Okay. We take the girl. We don't kill anybody." Pete looked at him balefully. "What?" John added. "You have any better ideas?"

~ ~ ~ ~ ~

At 12:20 John pulled the Yukon Denali into the driveway of the house on Boody Street and went and knocked on the door. At the exact moment that Jack opened the door, Pete was coming through the back door, having picked the lock. John said something about a survey, and then jammed a stun gun—the Vipertek VTS-989, designed to look like an innocuous flashlight—just below Jack's ribcage and dropped him like a sack of potatoes. Pete had been just a step behind in incapacitating Tug in the same way, the two young men twitching on the ground like dogs dreaming of chasing rabbits.

Dog came off the bed, stumbling due to his bad leg, and came careening at John with teeth bared. John was just able to lash out with a kick and send the canine spilling sideways, his injuries slowing him down. Before dog could regain his footing, John pressed the stun gun into the animal's ribcage. He was right next to the bathroom, and so he grabbed the dog's leg and pulled him in, shutting the door.

Missouri had taken the split-second opportunity to crash a small wooden sculpture she'd plucked from a side table into Pete's ear, knocking him sideways. Pete raised his hand to his torn ear and cursed angrily. Missouri was conflicted, not sure whether she should flee and leave Jack and Tug behind, as well as dog, or continue the fight. Those few seconds of hesitation sealed her fate. John advanced on her with the compact stun gun held casually in his hand, waiting for the opportunity to use it. Missouri backed into a corner, holding the wooden man by his head menacingly in front of her.

As John took a step forward, she flickered her eyes away from Pete, who stepped in and punched her in the forehead, this being a more satisfying retaliation than using a stun gun. He followed up with a jab into her midsection, and as she bent over, he brought his knee up into her face. Missouri crumpled to the ground, bits of a tooth flecking her lip, gasping for air that refused to fill her lungs.

Pete zip-tied her hands, his knee firmly in her back. He grabbed her by the hair and pulled her head back, while John readied the needle with a fast-acting sedative that he plunged into her carotid artery. Once Missouri had gone limp, they applied the zip ties to Jack and Tug, and then John went back to the Yukon and returned with a triple-wall, corrugated cardboard box, constructed to support the weight of the average human body—human corpse, that is. It was six feet long, three feet wide, and two feet deep. He poked holes in one end for air, as he didn't want her to become a corpse. They zip-tied her hands over her chest and her ankles together, and then lifted her into the box, which they then secured with packing tape.

John turned his attention to Tug and Jack, who were stirring. He stuffed a rag into each of their mouths, and crouched down between them, balancing easily on the balls of his feet. "You tell Langdon to turn himself in and keep his mouth shut if he wants to see his little girl again. He has," John looked at his watch, "twenty-four hours.

At 1:00 tomorrow, I will begin delivering a finger an hour. Do you understand?"

Jack nodded his head.

The two men grabbed either end of the box, eased themselves out the door, and then slid the box into the back of the Yukon.

~ ~ ~ ~ ~

Langdon put the phone in his pocket. "Are John Smith and Pete Yeager working for you?" he asked the senator. His voice had lowered an octave, emerging as if from some crypt buried deep beneath the surface.

"All I know about those two men is what you have just told me," she replied.

"I need to go now. If I find out you are lying to me, I will be back."

"What's happened?" Max asked. "Who was that on the phone?"

"They have my daughter. They put her in a box and took her away."

"John and Pete? Took your daughter? Why?"

"They want me to drop the case, turn myself in to the police and keep my mouth shut."

"What case? There is no case. I have agreed to the demands set forth in the second note," the senator said.

"Who is actually blackmailing you, Senator?" Langdon rose and walked out through the screen door with KJ following along behind.

"Tell me what happened," KJ said once they turned the truck around and started back down the driveway.

Langdon took Danny's phone from his pocket and called his brother, Lord.

~ ~ ~ ~ ~

Lord Langdon put his phone away and went to find his twin brother. The two of them had hired onto a construction job, basically grunt labor that held no real ties for them, but paid the bills. They'd only been in New Orleans a few months now, most recently having spent a few years in Austin, Texas. They were finishing a job tearing down a four-story apartment building, a job that Hurricane Katrina had started some years ago. Lord was a dapper man, even on a construction site, his shirt and pants were carefully ironed, his face smoothly shaven each and every morning, and his hair styled with a part to the side and shaved high and tight on the sides.

"Nick, we have to go," Lord said, coming up behind his brother who was wheeling a load of bricks to a dump truck. Nick's powerful arms glistened in the sun, his T-shirt ragged and ripped, three days growth of beard sprouting on his face, and his hair hanging down to his shoulders under the hard hat.

"Go?" Nick set the wheelbarrow down and turned to face his brother.

"Langdon just called me." Much like everybody else, the two other Langdon boys, younger by six years, called their elder brother by his and their own last name.

"Called you? Now? What's up?"

"They took Missouri."

"Took Missouri?" Nick asked, tossing his hat aside and falling into step with Lord.

"A couple Boy Scouts, he said. Mercenaries who work for Goldenrod. Told him that they were going to start sending her fingers to him if he didn't do what they asked."

Nick's pace picked up speed. "We stopping by the apartment first?" he asked.

"Suppose we might need guns," Lord replied. Together, they had amassed quite a gun collection, and they loved going to the shooting range.

The foreman yelled at them, and when they didn't acknowledge him, came running over, arriving just as they reached their bikes. He was demanding to know what they thought they were doing as they kicked their Harley Road Kings to life. The deep rumble drowned out his insistent demands. While Lord's bike was a subtle black, Nick's was a harlequin green pattern. The two bikes swooped out of the lot like lionesses going out to hunt, except much louder. The expensive motorcycles should have been the first clue to the foreman that these two brothers weren't planning on staying long at a job paying them twelve bucks an hour.

Six years older and shouldering the responsibility of their absent father, Langdon had been much more than a brother to the twins, the only father they'd ever known, really. He was their mentor, brother, friend, father, and protector all rolled into one. He had helped with their schoolwork, straightened out bullies, attended parent-teacher events, and taught them how to excel at sports. They had spent the last twenty-five years traveling around the country experiencing life. Lord had tried out marriage for two years, but it hadn't really taken, and he'd caught up with his brother in Roswell. They owned little but the shirts on their backs, the Harleys, a collection of guns, and over a million apiece in stocks. They liked to eat, drink, love, fight, carouse, and to suck the marrow out of the bones of life.

"How long to Brunswick, you figure?" Nick asked as they left the apartment.

"Google says twenty-five hours," Lord replied. "Langdon said the mercenaries are going to start sending fingers in twenty-four."

As soon as they hit I-10 North, they opened up their throttles, the lionesses roaring in anticipation of the hunt.

Chapter 25

Still Friday

Langdon could feel his anger descending on him like the night sky, blowing in like an impending storm, rising up from the earth like the dead promising vengeance. First they threatened his wife. Then, they hit his dog with a car. Now, they had taken his daughter. The Viking blood coursing through his veins had mostly lain dormant his whole life, but it had, on occasion, been known to rear its ugly head. This anger scared him but was something that he had no control over.

"I'm sorry," Jack said for the tenth time. There were two burn marks just below his ribcage that looked like the fang marks of some deadly snake. "I never should have opened the door."

"It wouldn't have mattered. The second man was already in the house," Tug said.

Chabal had arrived from the ransacking of their home by the police to find the two young men tied on the floor and dog locked in the bathroom. She was scared for her son, realizing how close a brush with death he'd just experienced, and terrified for Missouri who'd been taken away by this evil spawn. But her fears and concerns were slowly being replaced by anger, for somebody was playing games with her family, with the people she loved, and this was just not acceptable. After calling Langdon, she'd summoned the others as well, and over the past hour, the house on Boody Street had begun to fill up.

Langdon and KJ had been the first to arrive, he quizzing Jack and Tug about every detail they could remember. Starling closed the bookstore and came home, getting a ride from Bart who left work "feeling poorly." Jimmy, Richam, and Jewell were not far behind. Once they'd assembled, Langdon took charge, again going over the recent events.

"Let me get this straight," Bart said. "You were initially hired by Senator Mercer to track down a blackmailer and negotiate a settlement?"

"At first, I was only supposed to find her, and then later I was asked to negotiate a settlement," Langdon replied.

"And that blackmailer turned out to be the woman sitting next to you, whatever the hell she calls herself now?" Bart pointed a finger the size of a large carrot at KJ.

"Kamrin was approached by our two Boy Scouts, John and Pete, out in South Dakota. They told her they were from Earth First and she could help tremendously in reshaping our country's environmental policy." Langdon stood and began pacing around the small confines of Starling's crowded home. "We think now that that was just a hustle to engage her services. We have since learned that these two men do not work for Earth First, but rather, are mercenaries for Goldenrod."

"Can you clarify who Goldenrod is again for me?" Richam asked.

"Goldenrod was founded right before the 9/11 attacks," Jack said, reading from his laptop screen. "Initially, they were known as Marshland. They are a private military firm whose business boomed as the war on terror expanded. They were contracted by the United States Government for a wide array of services in Iraq and Afghanistan. After they were involved in a massacre in Baghdad in which twenty-three private citizens were killed, they moved their facilities to Nebraska and rebranded as Goldenrod."

"Why Goldenrod?" Jimmy asked. "Sounds like some James Bond thing."

"State flower of Nebraska," Jack replied.

"They are a subsidiary company to MacLeod Brandt," Tug said.

Realization struck Richam. "And Marisa Wilkes, the CEO of MacLeod Brandt, flew into Brunswick on Wednesday."

"Coincidence? I think not," Bart said.

"And what is your take on this?" Chabal posed the question to KJ. "I mean, we all remember you from before. Are you saying that you are no longer part of this?"

KJ looked around the room of people, her eyes pausing on Jimmy for a moment. "I have always fought for the environment. No matter what you believe, the well-being of the earth is my primary concern. Would I blackmail the senator if I thought it would help climate change? You bet your bottom dollar, I would. And I thought I was. But in reality, I was never in possession of the blackmail pictures. That was Glasses and Eyebrows, the two you call the Boy Scouts. Apparently, there was a second blackmail note delivered to the senator that I know nothing of. And then last night, Glasses and Eyebrows tried to kill me."

"The two Boy Scouts?" Chabal asked.

"Yes," Langdon said. "The men we now know as John Smith and Peter Yeager. They both work for Goldenrod."

"Who has acquired their services, do you suppose?" Bart asked.

"That is the million-dollar question," Langdon replied. "But KJ and I have some suspicions in that regard."

"And?"

"Last night when they had me tied up and were wondering what to do with me, they discussed calling somebody they referred to only as M," KJ said. "It was not to determine whether or not to kill me, but rather, how to dispose of my body."

"And then today," Langdon continued, "when we confronted Senator Mercer, we both noticed that her husband was acting strangely."

"Maxwell Mercer," Jewell said.

"M," Chabal said.

"Or Margaret Mercer?" Starling asked.

"She seemed very surprised by the whole thing," Langdon said.

"While he was acting extremely strangely," KJ said.

"And that reminded me of a conversation I had last week with him in the bookstore," Langdon said. "He was talking about being tired of the limelight, wanted his wife to not run for reelection, perhaps take a job as a lobbyist."

"What are you saying?" Chabal asked.

"That Maxwell Mercer set the whole thing up to drive his wife out of politics." Even as Langdon said it, he could hear the hollowness to the accusation.

"You think he hired a couple of mercenaries to blackmail his own wife?"

"It's quite possible."

"That he was blackmailing his wife just to get her to drop out of politics?"

"He asked me if I knew the name of a single lobbyist, and I had no clue. He also said she could make a million dollars a year, and that many former congressmen take jobs as lobbyists."

"But she didn't want to?"

"That was the impression I got."

"Who is Maxwell Mercer?" Richam asked.

"Jack and Tug did some digging into his background. He is a real mover and shaker in D.C. He's been involved in almost every facet of politics you can imagine, except elected office. His most recent gig was at a political think tank and consulting firm with strong right-wing ties."

"The blackmail note addressed the Paris Climate Accord, did it not?" Jewell asked.

"That was from me," KJ said. "Glasses and Eyebrows had me put it together and delivered it for me."

"But, this morning, the senator alluded to another request from the blackmailer. This one, according to her, was something she was inclined to comply with," Langdon said.

"I did not write a second note," KJ said.

"And you think it might have suggested that she not run in 2020 if she wants to keep her sexual inclinations private?" Jimmy asked.

Langdon shrugged. "Maybe. I don't know. Maxwell seemed pretty shocked to hear there was a second note."

"And how does the killing of the Russians fit into your plan? We still believe that it was the Boy Scouts who did that, don't we?" 4 by Four asked.

"I don't know. Perhaps the Boy Scouts have their own agenda. Or maybe their own Boy Scouts, who knows? But I mean to find out."

"And somehow they're tied to the Old Port Killer as well," 4 by Four said. "The Russians kill the coeds and frame Tug, and then they are, in turn, killed by the Boy Scouts, if that is our line of thinking. Too much to all be just coincidence, don't you think?"

"Let's not forget that bitch Delilah Friday," Jewell said. "She's tied into this whole thing as well."

"*Cui bono*," Starling said.

"What's that supposed to mean?" Bart asked.

"It is Latin for 'who stands to benefit' from this crime," Starling said.

"I don't think that John, Pete, or Delilah are anything more than flunkies of some sort," Langdon said. "Who is really pulling the strings? We have Maxwell and Margaret Mercer, seemingly at odds with each other."

"I think there is still a piece missing," Starling said.

"Enough about what has happened so far," Bart grunted. "What are we doing moving forward?"

"How about you go check out the house in Bowdoinham? See if you can dig up anything that might lead us to the Boy Scouts," Langdon said.

"I'll go along for the ride," Starling said. "Unless you're bringing your buddy, Lieutenant Moss, along?"

"Great," Langdon curtailed any sharp retort from Bart. "Richam and Jewell? Maybe you can ask around town, find out if they've been seen with someone else or snooping around, what kind of questions they've been asking, you know the drill. Start with Danny T. and Rosie, and then check your place and Goldilocks. Jack, do you have some high quality pictures of Pete and John?"

Jack reached into a folder and distributed pictures to everybody present. "I also have a picture of Delilah Friday," he said.

"Where'd you get that?" Langdon asked. "Did you find her on the internet, too?"

"It was on the counter of the bookstore when we stopped by this morning to make copies of the Boy Scouts' pictures, so I threw it in the copier as well, thinking it might come in handy."

"Good thinking. If you get a chance, run her name through the computer and see what you can dig up on her." Langdon stood and moved toward the door. "One last thing," he said. "We should assume that our houses and vehicles are bugged. Probably our phones as well. Maybe even our clothes. Goldenrod operatives are the real deal."

"What about me?" 4 by Four asked.

"You stay here with KJ, Jack, and Tug. They're going to do some further digging on Maxwell Mercer, Senator Mercer, Goldenrod, the Boy Scouts, and Delilah Friday, and see if anything turns up. They might have use of your legal knowledge."

"I'm tired of hiding out," KJ said.

"You're also wanted by the police," Langdon replied. "And who knows who else?"

"So are you," she retorted.

"But they have my daughter," Langdon replied.

4 by Four started to argue and then stopped. He rather liked the idea of being left with KJ.

"We have until tomorrow morning to get her back before all hell breaks loose," Langdon said grimly.

"They gave you a deadline of 1:00 tomorrow afternoon, didn't they?" Jewell asked.

"Yeah, but the twins will be here in the morning. I called them earlier."

"Lord and Nicky?" Richam asked.

"Holy shit," Starling said.

~ ~ ~ ~ ~

"She's going to be alright," Chabal said. There was a flat blackness to Langdon's eyes that concerned her.

"Shouldn't I just be turning myself in?" Langdon stared woodenly at the road. They did not have far to go, and once the process was started, it would be awful hard to stop or even slow down.

Chabal had to pick her words carefully. She did not want to point out that the two Boy Scouts were stone-cold killers and there was little to no guarantee that they would set Missouri free when they were done with her. "We have until 1:00 tomorrow to see what we can untangle. If we haven't made any progress by then, well, you might consider it."

"They start sending fingers at 1:00," Langdon said. His thoughts were fixated on Missouri's fingers when she had been two years old, tiny little stems that had come from Langdon. Fingers whose nails he couldn't bear to clip because he didn't know where the discerning line between flesh and nail was, and he was terrified that he'd nip off an end in the process. "At noon, I turn myself in if we haven't found her."

"The charges against you will never stick," Chabal said, changing the subject. "You have Bart and Rosie and an entire diner as your alibi that morning."

"Time of death makes it possible for me to have killed the Russians and then driven up to pick up Bart and go to breakfast," Langdon said absently. His mind was still on two-year-old fingertips.

Chabal hadn't been aware of that. No alibi and the murder weapon in his possession? Plus, his involvement in trying to clear Tug from the murders actually committed by the Russians provided possible motive. She could see the prosecution painting a picture of Langdon confronting the Russians at the Blue Cat Café and the meeting turning violent, so he shot and killed them, hid the weapon under his seat, and then drove up to Brunswick to create an alibi.

They pulled into Nate's Marina. Langdon was fairly certain that this was the home berth of the Mercer's vessel. Earlier this morning, Maxwell had claimed he needed to clean up *Swing Vote* for the winter, and that the senator had a speaking engagement. That suited Langdon fine, because he wanted a chance to grill Maxwell without his wife there. A variety of boats were already out of the water, all in various states of winterization, Labor Day weekend being the unofficial end of boating season in Maine. Some merely awaited trucks to haul them to their winter storage spots, while some had been shrink wrapped, a few had canvas coverings, and others, such as *Swing Vote*, were not yet covered up.

Maxwell Mercer was pressure-washing the sailboat. He was methodically working the powerful stream of water back and forth over the hull. He'd changed into a Hawaiian shirt decorated with pineapples, and he wore cargo shorts and sandals. Langdon had not realized how spindly his arms and legs were until this very moment.

"Mr. Mercer?" Langdon called out, as he got closer. "I need to speak with you."

Maxwell stopped the spray and turned to face them as they approached. The wand was pointed at them, threatening as if it were a gun. "I don't have anything to say to you."

"I think that you do," Langdon replied, walking up to within a foot of the man, causing him to take a half-step back.

"This has nothing to do with me," Maxwell said.

"I think you're lying." Langdon was done playing. The life of his daughter was at stake, and time was of the essence. "What are you hiding?" He grabbed Maxwell around the neck with one hand and shoved him back against *Swing Vote*. The wand dropped from his hand, shooting a spurt of water up into the air when it struck the ground.

"What do you want?" Maxwell looked like he was on the verge of tears.

"What is your connection to Peter Yeager and John Smith?"

"I don't know who you're talking about."

Chabal stepped up next to Langdon and extended her 9mm Beretta APX Compact so that the barrel came to rest against Maxwell's forehead. "We don't have time for your bullshit."

"Okay, okay," Maxwell said. His face was pasty-white, matching his bushy mustache in color. "Can you remove the gun from my head?"

Chabal stepped back and put the Beretta back in her purse, and Langdon let go of his grip on the man's neck.

"I just wanted life to be normal," Maxwell said.

"This morning my daughter was knocked unconscious and stuffed into a box and taken away," Langdon replied. "The two men who I have asked you about were the ones who did it. Is that the 'normal' you're talking about?"

"How do you know it was them?" Maxwell was rubbing his neck where Langdon had grasped his throat. "And why would they do that?"

Chabal pulled the Beretta back out of her purse and waved it at the man. "Answer the goddamn question, Mr. Mercer."

"I hired them to blackmail my wife," Maxwell said in a barely audible tone.

"Why?"

"I want our life back. I want *my* life back. We can't go anywhere without somebody attacking us for her vote on health care or some other thing."

"How does blackmailing your wife have anything to do with getting your life back?" Langdon asked.

"I've tried to convince Marge to retire and become a lobbyist. It would mean more money, more free time, and more anonymity, but she would have none of it. She likes being a United States Senator too much to step down, to not run again in 2020."

"So, you thought threatening to expose her as a lesbian would be the shove necessary to push her into stepping out of the spotlight?" Chabal asked incredulously. She continued pointing the pistol at him as if she were considering shooting him on general principle.

"They thought it best if we sent a note in regards to her climate change position, you know, so that she wouldn't suspect that the whole thing was just to get her not to run for reelection."

"Why did you hire me?" Langdon asked.

"Marge wanted to get outside help to squash the whole thing, and when she wouldn't take no for an answer, I suggested your name," Maxwell admitted.

"Because you thought I wouldn't find anything?" Langdon pressed.

"Yes."

"How did you find them?"

"Pete and John?"

"Yes."

Maxwell bit his lip and looked over at where two men were pulling a boat from the water. A few people were sitting at the picnic tables over by the small restaurant, but nobody seemed to notice the confrontation taking place in the corner of the yard.

Langdon slapped the man, causing him to stumble. "How did you find them?"

"Michael put me in contact with them," Maxwell said. His eyes rolled around in his head like they'd come disconnected and he was breathing raggedly.

"Michael Glover?"

Maxwell nodded.

"Did you know they worked for Goldenrod?"

"No," Maxwell said, shaking his head emphatically. "I was over at Michael's house one evening, had one drink too many and spilled my marital woes. He wasn't at all surprised that my wife is gay nor that I wanted her to forgo another election campaign. He just listened to what I had to say and then told me he might be able to help, that he knew a couple of fellows. One thing led to another," Maxwell spread his hands wide, "and it just got crazier and crazier."

Langdon put his hand on the man's shoulder and pressed him back against the hull of the boat again. "Are you saying that the whole idea was Michael Glover's?"

"No, it was my idea, it just got away from me," Maxwell muttered, but his eyes suddenly squinted.

"You wanted Senator Mercer to retire, but whose idea was it that you blackmail her?"

Maxwell started to speak and then stopped. He rolled his tongue over his lips and then bit them in thought. "It was Michael. Bloody hell. All this time I thought it was my idea, my plan, but I was just being used as a patsy, wasn't I? It was Michael that suggested we hire you. And that's why John stopped returning my calls. What have I done?"

Chapter 26

Still Friday

Missouri Langdon prowled the room hungry for a thought, an inspiration, or a creative angle on how to escape her current predicament. She had regained consciousness in darkness, a few rays of light dotting her face. She had been unable to move and, at first, was terrified she was dead, in a coma, or paralyzed, but after a bit, realized she was just trussed tight like a Christmas hog. She must have been in a car, but she didn't know for how long, only that soon after she regained her wits the vehicle had stopped, and the box she was in that now lay on the floor next to her had been picked up and lugged inside. The box had been cut open, the ties on her wrists and ankles severed, and then the two men had left, locking the door behind them before she had been able to so much as stir a finger.

The room had six sides to it, all approximately eight feet long, and the ceiling was higher than two of her. The sole door was in one wall, while the rest had no windows or any sort of openings at all. The door was steel and did not budge in the slightest. The floor was concrete, as were the walls. There was a single bed along one wall, and a toilet and sink on the opposite side of the room. There was no partition for privacy. The illumination in the room came from ten lights recessed into the ceiling, suggesting that it was not made of concrete, and might be her only possible means of escape. The bed was bolted into the floor and had proved immovable.

The room was certainly an improvement on the box, but she was still feeling the claustrophobic effects of captivity. Missouri Langdon had not liked tight spaces since an incident in Peru when she was eighteen. She'd decided to take a gap year before going to college, and had spent six months in Cusco working in an orphanage, teaching the children English. One day, after she'd just worked up the nerve to buy a Guinea Pig on a stick from a street vendor, she'd walked around a corner onto a dark street, and that was all it took. A cab pulled up next to her, and before she could wave it away, a bag was placed over her head, and then she was tumbled into the trunk.

She had no idea how long she was actually in the trunk for, but she could barely breathe with the burlap bag over her head, until she was finally able to twist it off, only to discover the rancid air of the trunk was not much better. The car only drove a short distance before stopping and parking for what seemed to be an unbearable amount of time, then starting up again and driving further. Finally, it stopped again, and she could hear voices arguing, or rather, haggling, over her price. Then the trunk was pulled open and she was jerked free and to her feet. She found herself being inspected by two Latino gangsters in suits, one who pinched her lip with his fingers, and then fondled her breast, before making an offer that was acceptable to her captors. As he was paying, she ran, taking them by surprise, more by her speed than her action, and she'd actually gotten clean away.

She had been too scared to report it to the police, who were quite possibly corrupt and involved in the shady business of human trafficking. She had not told her father. She considered herself a coward for not trying to expose this awful business, but a few weeks later when she returned to the United States, she had effectively turned her back on doing the right thing, and this caused her a great deal of anxiety. Missouri Langdon had tucked this terrifying incident away in a corner of her heart and thrown away the key, but her fear of tight spaces was its way of trying to escape. The past few years living in New York City, she had one prerequisite of apartments and that was plenty of windows, which was not always an easy accommodation in the city, especially on her budget.

The ache in her jaw was balanced by the shooting pains emanating from her broken tooth, but these discomforts paled in the face of her growing anger. She had seen her brother, Jack, the man called Tug, and her dog all twitching in agony on the ground and hoped they were all right. The last time she'd been confined and escaped, she had not done the right thing. This time, she would not hide, and if she ran, it would only be to return with reinforcements.

Why had she been taken? Missouri wondered. When she had been young, her constant question to her parents was 'how do you know?' Why the sky was blue, the earth was round, or why a Popsicle was sweet—the question was almost beside the point. This had evolved into asking for further proof of the answers given, demanding 'show me' to any casual explanation, needing confirmation with her own eyes of its logic. This drive for the why, the rationale, and the logic had driven her through high school in Brunswick, college in Gettysburg, and now into grad school at Columbia. Her thoughts traced a frantic path between seeking a way out of this mess and understanding what the purpose of her kidnapping was.

The door suddenly opened, and Pete Yeager stepped in with one of those unnerving shocking devices held in front of him, backing her up to the far wall. Another man came through the doorway behind him, this one wearing a Barack Obama mask. She found this slightly comical, as the man possessed the figure of Donald Trump, and she found herself smirking at the irony.

~ ~ ~ ~ ~

Langdon knocked on the door, three long and two short knocks, even though Bart had rolled his eyes at a secret knock. All things considered and due to recent events, the group had agreed it was not a bad idea. The curtain covering the glass was shuffled aside, and then

Jack pulled the door open. Langdon stepped aside and grabbed Maxwell's elbow and propelled him into Starling's house, as Chabal followed him through the door, her hand fondling the butt of her Beretta in her purse.

"Maxwell, this is my stepson, Jack. Your boy John Smith almost killed him this morning." Langdon pulled the door closed and locked it. "That's Jimmy 4 by Four over there with the woman you hired to blackmail your wife, Kamrin Jorgenson. The young man on the computer is Tug. Russian gangsters framed him for the Old Port Killings, and then those same hoodlums were killed by your two mercenaries, John and Pete. Do you have any idea why they did that?"

"I'm sorry," Maxwell said. "I have no idea."

"What's he doing here?" 4 by Four asked.

"He's agreed to help us find Missouri," Langdon replied. "To atone for his sins."

"How's he propose doing that?" KJ asked.

"You're the one that slept with his wife," Langdon said. "I thought you might have some ideas."

"Let's play nice," 4 by Four said.

"Do you have any ideas on where she might be?" Jack asked.

"Go ahead and tell them," Langdon said, looking at Maxwell.

Before the man could speak, there came three long knocks followed by two short. Chabal pulled her Beretta out as Langdon went to the door, peeked through, and let in Richam, Jewell, and Danny T.

"Come in," Langdon said. "Maxwell Mercer was just about to tell us that Michael Glover is the man behind Pete and John, but I guess me saying it steals his thunder."

"Who is Michael Glover?" KJ asked.

"He is a retired former attorney for the Goldenrod Corporation," Tug said. "Mr. Langdon asked me and Jack to look into him. He retired two years ago as the lead lawyer for Goldenrod, and he also sits on the board of MacLeod Brandt."

"Michael Glover. Goldenrod. MacLeod Brandt." Langdon stood impatiently. "We have the players, but what is the motive?"

"The budget vote," Jack said. "There is a huge vote on the budget coming up, and the most contentious issue is that it's the largest defense budget in our history."

"Which, if passed, would mean a great deal of money for MacLeod Brandt," Jewell said slowly.

"We're talking billions," Richam added.

"And the tie between MacLeod Brandt, Goldenrod, the mercenaries John and Pete, and Senator Mercer is Michael Glover," Chabal said.

"Fuck." Langdon shook his head. "You mean to tell me the villain has been hiding in plain sight all this time? For Chrissake, he's the one who first came to me. What is he playing at?"

"Obviously, he's not retired," Chabal said.

"What's that mean?"

"Glover is on the board of MacLeod Brandt, which happens to be the parent company of Goldenrod, which he used to be the head attorney for, and now he ends up in Brunswick, Maine?" Chabal asked in reply.

"And he bamboozles me into hiring two men who happen to be Goldenrod mercenaries to blackmail my wife," Maxwell added, not even aware he was talking, the pieces beginning to fall into place in an ugly picture of how badly he'd been used.

"Suppose you were an idiot, and suppose you were a member of Congress; but I repeat myself," Chabal said.

"That's Mark Twain, right?" Jewell asked.

"I am an idiot," Maxwell said.

"Fucking right, you are," Bart said.

"Let's focus, people," Langdon said. "What else do we know about Michael Glover?"

"He's intimately acquainted with the bitch that told Chabal she was sleeping with Langdon," Jewell broke in.

"What's that?" Langdon asked. "Because of her connection with the Boy Scouts?"

"We went and picked up Danny T. this morning and then went showing those pictures that Jack gave us around town," Richam said.

"We had zero hits on the Boy Scouts," Jewell added.

"But several men remembered seeing Delilah Friday," Richam said.

"She's a hard one to forget," Chabal concurred.

"And then I showed the picture to Kelsey Jacobs," Danny T. said excitedly. "She does house cleaning. Has a bunch of clients out to Mere Point, she does. She immediately recognized the girl Friday, said she'd seen her a couple of times at the Glover residence. As a matter of fact, she walked in on them one day, not that they even saw her, but she said she knocked and when there was no answer, she used her key to open the door. Said that sometimes Glover was there when she cleaned, but not always. She thought he was kind of creepy, like he liked to watch her and what not."

"Danny T., get to the point," Langdon said.

"Well, she walked in on them, he must have forgotten it was cleaning day, and he was sitting right in his living room eating red pistachios, and she was down on her knees between his legs bobbing for apples, if you know what I mean."

The room silently contemplated this new clue, the men slightly jealous, the women slightly more justified in their hatred of that bitch, who now appeared to be not just a home wrecker, but connected to the evil puppeteer pulling all of the strings.

"It certainly sounds like Glover is the one behind all of this," Langdon said. "He hoodwinks Maxwell into thinking he's blackmailing his own wife, is the former attorney for Goldenrod, which is the employer of John and Pete, and has Delilah Friday yanking my chain to distract me from the blackmail case."

"So, he must know where Missouri is," Chabal said.

"Maybe he even has her," Jack said.

"I could find out." All heads swiveled to stare at Maxwell Mercer.

"What?" Langdon asked.

"I could find out whether or not Glover has your daughter," Maxwell said.

"How?"

Chapter 27

Saturday

Maxwell Mercer took a deep breath and pulled into the driveway leading to the Michael Glover's Mere Point estate. Partway down the driveway was a man he'd never seen before, sitting in a chair next to a tree, with an ominous-looking weapon that must have been some sort of assault rifle held casually in his hands. The man jerked his chin towards the house when Maxwell slowed down, indicating he should continue on.

Maxwell had called Glover the previous afternoon after coming up with a reason to need to visit. He'd pretended to be panicked at not being able to get in touch with John Smith, and that his wife had told him a second blackmail note had arrived. Glover had suggested that he come over in the morning to have a face to face with John Smith. It could not have worked out better, unless, of course, they planned to kill him.

He was sweating, even though the morning was cool. There was the distinct possibility that he was keeping an appointment with his own death, and that Glover had decided that Maxwell Mercer had become a loose end that needed tying up. He didn't think the man would be brazen enough to kill the husband of a sitting senator, but a little voice in a corner of his mind kept suggesting that the man seemed to have no compunction about killing, nor fear of being exposed or caught, given all he'd learned about Glover the previous day. If it were true, the man had ordered the killing of several young women, three Russian gangsters, the blackmail of a United States Senator, and the kidnapping of a young woman.

Another man with black sunglasses and the same sort of rifle as the driveway guard stood by the doorway to the house. Maxwell got out and approached the door, the stench of his own nervousness rancid in his nostrils.

The man, dressed in green camouflage, stepped into his path. "I've got to pat you down, Mr. Mercer."

Maxwell lifted his arms like he'd seen people do in the movies, and the man set down his rifle and frisked him, a little too thoroughly for comfort.

The door opened before he could ring the bell. Michael Glover stood there with a wide smile plastered between his fleshy cheeks. "Maxwell, good to see you."

"What is this all about?" Maxwell asked, nodding his head to indicate the soldier of fortune with the sinister weapon, who had turned his back and was again facing the driveway.

"Just a precaution," Glover said, pulling him in and shutting the door. "A man I helped prosecute years ago recently got out of prison and this coincided with another threat to my life, so I thought, better safe than sorry. Right?"

"I suppose you're right," Maxwell responded.

"Of course I'm right."

Maxwell refrained from asking why he'd been patted down if the concern was a known quantity just released from prison. He suspected the search had been for a wire and not a weapon, which would mean either way that Glover was suspicious of his motives. "Is Smith here?"

"He's in the living room," Glover replied. "Why don't you tell me what's going on?"

"How about the three of us talk about it?" Maxwell suggested.

"After you," Glover said, extending his hand to the opening at the end of the entryway.

John Smith was sitting on the couch across from the fireplace in a position from which he could see the door. He was popping red pistachios into his mouth and looking at his phone. "Mister Mercer," he said.

"Mr. Smith," Maxwell replied.

"I understand you have concerns about how I'm handling the blackmail of your wife?"

"You haven't been returning my calls," Maxwell said. His eyes were searching the room for anything that might suggest that Missouri Langdon had been there, but he had a fairly good notion where the girl would be if she were on the premises.

"I was forced to get a new phone," Smith said, tilting the new device forward. "And I have been quite busy."

"I want to drop the entire thing," Maxwell blurted out.

"Why?"

"It was wrong to do it in the first place," Maxwell said.

"It's a little late in the game for cold feet." Smith stood up and walked over to where Maxwell and Glover stood. He slipped his phone into his pocket, his jacket flapping open to flaunt the shoulder holster and pistol. "You hired me and my partner to do a job, Mr. Mercer, and we intend to complete it."

"Marge said she got a second blackmail note?" Maxwell asked. "One that had nothing to do with the Paris Climate Accord?"

"What did you hire us to do, Mr. Mercer?"

"To blackmail my wife," Maxwell said, the words brutal and ugly as they came out of his mouth.

"You hired us to convince your wife to not run for reelection in 2020," Smith said. "That is what we are doing."

"How?"

"By whatever means necessary. It would be best if you did not know the specifics."

Maxwell tried to keep his eyes neutral, but his insides screamed at the beast he'd unleashed on his wife. Even though he now realized that he was being played by Glover, he couldn't escape the fact that it was he who had invited this evil into his home.

"Are you okay, Max?" Glover put his hand comfortingly on Maxwell's shoulder.

"I'm fine," he muttered, feigning discomfort with a hand over his stomach. "Do you think I could use your bathroom?"

"You know where it is."

Maxwell stepped back into the entryway, just out of sight of the two men, and went left instead of right. The original Cape Cod style house had had two additions built onto it when Glover bought it a few years earlier. On either side of the house he'd built structures resembling lighthouses. The one on the right was an immense bathroom, quite lavish, and meant to impress guests. The lighthouse on the left was the only part of the house Maxwell had not been shown when he'd originally gotten the tour, but he had wondered about the heavy steel door. If Missouri Langdon were here, this is where she would be.

He walked through the kitchen and through the door on the far end. There was a small room there with two armchairs and a table that led out onto a patio with a barbecue grill. Sitting in a wooden chair next to the steel door of the lighthouse room was Pete Yeager.

"I'm sorry," Maxwell blustered. "Is this the bathroom?"

Yeager looked at him with a sardonic twist to his expression. He had a toothpick in his mouth, rolling it around his tongue, his hand sliding inside his jacket. "You got the wrong side of the house, Mr. Mercer. Bathroom is on the other side."

Maxwell turned and banged his shoulder on the doorway, and then hurried through the kitchen and on through the entranceway, the study, and into the bathroom. He immediately locked the door behind him, took a huge breath, and splashed cold water across his face, before doing what he'd come here to do. Once this was accomplished, he exited the room, hoping that he'd be allowed to leave.

~ ~ ~ ~ ~

"They got at least two guys outside," Maxwell told the group. "Plus, Smith and Yeager inside."

"Is my daughter there?" Langdon asked.

"I didn't see her, but Yeager was sitting outside a room as if he were guarding something," Maxwell said.

"She must be there," Bart said. "Why else would they have so much firepower?"

Starling's home had been rearranged into a large conference room, the combined kitchen, living room, and dining area cleared with seats ringing the space. Danny T. had left to go to work, and because he wanted no part of it, but the rest of the gang was all present. Langdon sat by the front entrance with Chabal directly to his left, and then Jewell and Richam. Across from him were Jack and Tug, both of them sitting on the sofa against the wall with their faces pressed into their computer screens. On his right were Bart, Starling, Jimmy, and KJ.

Maxwell answered a few more questions, but then excused himself from the impending action, opening the door just as a distant rumble closed in on the house on Boody Street, and two Harley Road Kings rocked the quiet neighborhood with their vibrations. The hogs rolled onto the small front yard, idling with a dull roar, before shutting down. Two soot-covered men dressed in leather stepped stiffly from their seats and immediately removed the long cases attached to either side of the bikes and walked up to the open door where Maxwell Mercer stood with his mouth agape.

The first rider took his leather helmet and goggles off, shaking out thick, shoulder-length hair, and flashed a white smile against the grime of his face. "Good morning. We're going door to door this morning encouraging folks to read their Bible. The answers that it gives to important questions often surprise people. For example: Deuteronomy 20:1. 'When you go out to war against your enemies and see horses, chariots, and an army larger than yours, do not be afraid of them, for the *Lord*, your God, who brought you out of the land of Egypt, is with you'." He turned and gestured to the man behind him as Maxwell Mercer felt terror sidle up to his body.

Langdon pushed him aside and stepped onto the front walk. "Nicky!" He hugged his brother and then clasped the hand of his second sibling. "Lord!"

"We're not too late?" Lord asked.

"Not at all," Langdon replied. "We were just about to plan a rescue mission, but come inside—we should get out of view."

Chapter 28

Jewell and Richam were the first to leave. They had parked around the corner in the Junior High School parking lot. It being the Saturday before school started for the fall, the lot was empty, save their car sitting conspicuously in the corner. They took Pleasant Hill Road and then cut down to Flying Point Road before turning onto Lower Flying Point, truly nothing more than a well-developed jetty protruding into Maquoit Bay.

Jewell drove while Richam gave directions from the GPS, which led them almost to the end before directing them that their destination was on the right. Stan Shea came into the Wretched Lobster every Tuesday and Thursday and had exactly two beers. Their conversation usually centered on Stan's fishing boat and him trying to convince Richam to come out fishing with him.

Jewell grabbed her purse from the back, checking to make sure that the ancient 1970 Smith & Wesson was in there. She had refused the offer of a more efficient weapon from Lord and Nick, who seemed to have brought an entire arsenal with them from Louisiana. Richam had accepted the suggestion that the Blaser R93 Tactical sniper rifle might be appropriate and easy to smuggle aboard the boat at a length of just forty-four inches.

Stan opened the door and yelled a hearty greeting as Richam was pulling the duffel bag containing the rifle from the backseat.

Greetings were made, small talk ensued, and finally he led them around the house and down to the dock. Richam risked a glance across the way at Mere Point, and imagined that with binoculars he could probably see Michael Glover's house hidden in the trees over there. It had taken a lie about wanting to impress Jewell on their special anniversary, a promise to come fishing soon, and the offer of free beer for a month to allow them to leave Stan behind.

Stan gave a twenty-minute instruction course as Jewell fidgeted and Richam fought his impatience. He knew boats, even if he didn't own one. Finally, Stan stepped aside, and they slipped the rope and puttered into Maquoit Bay. The morning sun had barely warmed the chill from the air, but they knew that things were about to heat up. What they were doing was terrifying, and under different circumstances, neither one of them would be in a boat in the bay waiting for the sound of gunfire before heading towards, and not away, from that violence. Once past Williams Island, they dropped anchor behind tiny Sister Island and proceeded to wait.

They had known Missouri Langdon since the day she was born.

~ ~ ~ ~ ~

Chabal and KJ climbed on the back of the Harleys with their arms wrapped around Lord and Nick Langdon. They had to cut across to Bart's house, find the key under the pot, and retrieve his Cadillac from the garage. They had thought it best not to try and sneak up on the enemy on the rumbling hogs. Lord handed KJ a Beretta very similar to the one Chabal carried, telling her she might as well take it now. He put the two rifles in the trunk, a Steyr SSG 69 for himself, and a Barrett M95 for Lord. It would not do to be pulled over with these weapons in plain sight.

Nick got behind the wheel and Lord rode shotgun, while the two women climbed into the back. It was a twelve-minute ride back down Mere Point, and Nick spent the time quizzing Chabal about how her kids were doing. Just as they entered the private development of Mere Point, there was a road that branched to the right and they took this. It was less than a half-mile long before coming to a dead end.

Lord pulled the Caddy to the side in a small copse of trees and they got out without a word. They knew what needed to be done. There was no use in idle talk, and each seemed lost in his thoughts. They looked in the direction of Glover's house, hidden from view by a grove of eastern white pine trees. They had studied the Maps images intently, knowing that the terrain might be different, not knowing how long ago the pictures had been taken, the one unchanging fact that the house was about 300 yards from where they now stood.

Langdon had argued about either Chabal or KJ going, a battle that he would have lost even if they weren't the only ones small enough for the task at hand. Lord checked his watch and nodded at each of them that it was time. Nick led the way, walking crouched over at first, and then dropping to a crawl, and finally a slither. Chabal was second, KJ third, and Lord brought up the rear.

When the house came into sight, Lord moved to the left while the others continued to work their way around the back of the building. Lord crawled his way to within fifty yards of the house, from which he had a clear view of the man at the door. Lord had rubbed dirt over the M95, and he made sure that the bright September sun did not glint off the glass of the scope. He could not see anybody else, and after a bit, attached the bi-pod and centered in on the man by the door.

Nick slithered and slid through every bit of available cover until they'd reached the far side of the house. He had seen no other mercenaries, but that didn't mean they weren't out there somewhere. Still, his primary job was preventing the guard partway down the driveway from reaching the house, and to give covering fire to Chabal and KJ. He did not set his rifle up on a tripod, not being sure in which direction the enemy would come. In spirit, Nick Langdon was not that much different than a child playing cops and robbers. He had no fear of failure, it being little more than a game, but a game that had to be won. If necessary, he would take a bullet so that his niece could live, not that this was even a conscious thought, but rather, an indisputable fact.

Chabal had no such ice in her veins. Her breathing was ragged, and she was afraid that she might have a heart attack. *What the fuck am I doing?* She wondered for the umpteenth time, but she knew full well that there was no choice. She had watched Missouri go from a baby to a toddler to a child to a young adult, and finally, to a woman. She had parented her for most of that time, and felt that she made no small difference in her life. Chabal realized suddenly that the fear she felt was for Missouri, and not for herself, and that she actually liked the adrenalin and excitement rippling through her body at that moment.

Kamrin Jorgenson did not know Missouri Langdon. The little bit she'd spent with the group preparing this rescue had given her an inkling that they were all good people. There was something about that hipster lawyer, Jimmy with the funny last name, that set her blood to racing, but she had decided at an early age that her actions would never be dictated by a man. She had come back to Maine in order to help the environment, and in turn, she had been used for another purpose, and this she could not abide. Her principles, after all, were all that she had.

~ ~ ~ ~ ~

Langdon climbed into the 1966 Ford F100 Ranger Styleside truck that was Starling's pride and joy. Jack and Tug had already piled into the front seat next to him. Their rifles were in back, wrapped in a blanket. He backed the truck out of the driveway and went towards Maine Street, turning right, and then finally curving to the left on the Mere Point Road, checking his mirror to make sure that Bart's cruiser with Starling and 4 by Four was keeping up.

He supposed that he could just turn himself in. It was ten minutes before noon. If he surrendered and kept his mouth shut, his daughter would be released unharmed. There was still time. That is, if he could trust the likes of Michael Glover. John Smith and Pete Yeager were professional mercenaries and had most likely planned for any sort of exigency. No, he, Langdon, had to walk into the lion's den and face down the evil that was threatening his daughter.

Images of Missouri tumbled through his head as he drove. She'd been so tiny, yet so grownup, the day she graduated from daycare with a mini-gown draped around her, as she danced and sang with the others. The Girl Scout trip to the Boston Aquarium when she'd tried to jump into the pool to swim with the fish. In fifth grade, Missouri had written a petition against the principal of her school for favoring the boys over the girls. For her efforts, she'd earned detention—that is, until Chabal stormed into his office and gave him a piece of her mind. Langdon was not quite sure when she'd grown into an adult, but a full-grown and mature woman she was.

At the entrance to the private section of Mere Point, Langdon pulled over by the mailboxes, and Jack and Tug jumped out. They were armed with only their cell phones, had strict instructions to call the police when gunfire broke out, and to hide if any escaping villains came speeding their way. They were the last and first line of warning. If anybody that looked to be coming to the Glover house came by, they were to text out a group warning. Langdon knew the difficulty they would all have discerning between residents and the enemy in the heat of battle, and cautioned them to be careful.

He continued on in the truck with the cruiser following. Once the shit hit the fan, Bart was going to block the driveway with the police vehicle, and he, 4 by Four, and Starling would take up position behind it with their weapons. It was unlikely that anybody would make it past them, and this is what Langdon counted on, for he certainly did not want to put Jack, or Tug for that matter, in any more danger than was absolutely necessary. If it was up to him, he'd have left Jack at the house, but the boy was actually a man of thirty-two, and this was not an option, so he'd compromised.

Langdon paused at the mouth of the driveway, took a deep breath, and continued on. Halfway down, exactly as Maxwell Mercer had said, a man in camouflage stepped out from behind a tree with a black assault rifle. He looked to be a carbon copy of John Smith and Peter Yeager with his clipped flat-top, smoothly shaven face, and eyes that stared a thousand yards and nowhere at all. Langdon rolled down the window with the hand crank. The entire plan was delicately balanced upon being allowed to continue on to the house. The easiest way out of this mess would be to kill Langdon on sight, but Langdon was gambling that Glover would want to gloat a bit before doing so.

"Goff Langdon to see Michael Glover," he said.

The mercenary spoke into the lapel of his collar, listened, and then nodded for him to continue down the drive. At the house, a second man met him as he climbed out of the truck, and pushed him against the hood and frisked him. Langdon was the only one of the group unarmed, for he knew he'd be searched. Lord had offered him a small derringer that could be strapped to his ankle, but he'd turned it down, and in fact, the agent now made him remove his shoes.

The door opened and Michael Glover stood there with a wide smile. "Mr. Langdon, to what do I owe the pleasure?"

"Hello Mr. Glover. I've been having a difficult time contacting Senator Mercer."

"Do you think that might be because you're wanted by the police and she is avoiding communicating with a man on the lam?"

Every piece of Langdon wanted to wrap his hands around the man's neck and shake it, but he had to ascertain that Missouri was indeed there and obtain her freedom before doing so. "Do you think that I might come in?"

"I'm not so sure that would be a good idea." The smile was gone from the man's fleshy jowls.

Langdon sighed. He was down to his last card. "Mr. Glover, I know that you have my daughter. I would like to offer an exchange. Me for her."

The friendliness in Glover's eyes followed the smile in dissipating. "Why do you think I have your daughter, Mr. Langdon?"

With a grunt of exasperation, Langdon elbowed past the man into the entryway of the house and walked back towards the living room area he'd first come into just a week earlier. The plan required him to be in the house. John Smith sat in an armchair smiling in an evil, yet charming, sort of way. "Mr. Smith," Langdon said. "If you have hurt my daughter in any way, I will tear you limb from limb."

"Right," Smith said.

"The deal was that you would let her go," Langdon said.

"If you turned yourself into the police, I believe, is what the deal was," Glover said, passing by Langdon and sitting down on the sofa. He patted the cushion next to him. "Sit, Mr. Langdon."

Langdon sat down, noticing that Smith had pulled a Glock from his shoulder holster and laid it on his lap. "I thought it better to go to the source."

Glover laughed, a sound indicating that he believed he was again in control of the situation. "You have been more of a thorn in my side than I ever imagined when I first suggested to Maxwell that he and his wife hire you. Do tell, what have you actually figured out?"

"I know that you were the former attorney for Goldenrod and that you sit on the board of MacLeod Brandt," Langdon said. His job was to distract. "And I know that John over there works for Goldenrod, as well as his pal, Peter." Langdon looked around the room, ignoring the pistol in Smith's hand. He leaned forward and grabbed a handful of red pistachios from the bowl on the low table in front of him. "Do you have any scotch, Mr. Glover?"

"I suppose if I am not providing a last meal that I should at least provide a final drink," Glover said. "Delilah," he called. Delilah Friday's head appeared in the doorway within seconds. "Bring us the bottle of eighteen-year-old Glenlivet and four glasses. Do you prefer ice, Mr. Langdon?"

"Hello, Del," Langdon said. "You know how I like my scotch. Cold, exactly the opposite of my women."

She stared at him with hard eyes and then disappeared to fetch the brown liquor.

Glover chuckled. "Quite a fine piece of ass, wouldn't you say, Mr. Langdon?"

"She is certainly built like a brick shithouse," Langdon concurred. "Shit being the operative word in that sentence. Do you know if she ever found her sister?"

Glover was still laughing when Friday returned with a rolling cart that housed the booze, glasses, and an ice bucket. She poured two glasses neat for Smith and Glover, and then with three cubes for her and Langdon, waiting for Glover to nod before sitting down on the second sofa.

"You were saying, Mr. Langdon?"

"It seems that you had John, here, hire Russian gangsters to rape and murder college students, and then to place the blame on a young immigrant from Burundi. When I managed to make the connection between the murders, the frame of that immigrant, Tug, and the Russians, you sent your Boy Scouts to kill the Russians. Am I right so far?"

"I don't suppose you'd consider working for me, would you?" Glover asked.

"But what I don't understand is why?" Langdon took a small sip of the Glenlivet.

"Maine votes sixty percent Democratic, Mr. Langdon," Glover said. "What does that mean? That means they support immigrants and oppose the defense budget. Do you understand?"

"You're saying that you were trying to win the hearts and minds of the population of Maine by leading us to oppose immigration and favor an enormous defense budget? And, I would assume, Brandt

MacLeod would benefit enormously from this?"

"We hoped to start an anti-immigration movement. For a few years we've been working on Lewiston, but this opportunity tied in nicely with our plans," Glover said.

"Say it however you want. You are trying to get a huge defense budget passed, and Senator Mercer's vote is crucial," Langdon said.

"Senator Mercer rides that narrow line between supporting the defense budget and opposing it. If she believes that her constituents fear the rising tide of terrorists invading our country, well then, it will be an easy vote for her to cast."

Langdon nodded, took another slug of scotch, shook the glass, and set it down. "So, when I made the connection between the Russians and the murders, I played right into your hands? Now, not only do we fear the immigration crisis, but the Russian interference as well?"

"That was a contingency for which we hadn't actually planned, but your persistence surprised us, and it certainly played into what we were doing." Glover stood and walked over to the fireplace.

"And your girl Friday was brought in to distract me?" Langdon asked.

"You were stirring the pot too much," Glover agreed.

"So, tell me, Del, are you a whore or do you fuck your boss for free?"

"Who is the whore, Goff?" Delilah Friday glared at him. "Me? Or the married man who was slobbering after me like a basset hound wanting a table scrap?"

"You are a pretty woman, no doubt about it," Langdon said. "But entirely lacking in substance. Big tits will only get you so far in life, and then you have to get on your knees and do what you have to do."

"So I can be married and living in the fucking suburbs working in a bookstore like your plain wife? I'd stick a gun in my mouth first," Delilah spat.

"Either way, you end up with something in your mouth," Langdon said.

"No need to get nasty, Mr. Langdon. Miss Friday is an employee with a variety of tasks," Glover said, raising his hand to calm an angry Delilah Friday.

"And the blackmail note from Kamrin Jorgenson?" Langdon asked. "She was a patsy to take the fall, and then you had John send a second note with your real demand, which was to support the impending vote on the defense budget, and to award Brandt MacLeod a contract worth billions?"

"You have certainly fit the pieces of the puzzle together very well, Mr. Langdon."

"What if I blow the whistle?" Langdon finished his drink. It was almost time.

"You would never take the chance of your beautiful daughter being harmed, Mr. Langdon. But that is beside the point, because you will never walk out of this room alive."

John Smith stood up and pointed the Glock at Langdon waiting for the command.

"But, what if I had stopped you?" Langdon asked, desperate to gain a few more seconds, wondering what the holdup was.

Glover laughed. "Do you think that Brandt MacLeod has put all their chips into the vote of Senator Mercer of Maine? I am but one of the new breed of lobbyists, Mr. Langdon. Private lobbyists. Men and women not bound by laws, restrictions, or the timetables of D.C. offices. We have infiltrated the home states, the neighborhoods of every moderate, and middle-of-the-aisle congressman. We are like moles, working our way seamlessly into the fabric of the homes of key politicians, and rising up when called upon." He walked to the window, noticing a boat puttering towards his dock. "Shoot him, Mr. Smith."

At that moment, the air erupted in a crescendo of gunfire from outside.

Chapter 29

Still Saturday

As Langdon had gotten out of the car what seemed like a lifetime earlier, Chabal took her cue and led the way forward with KJ right behind her. There was just a short open space to scuttle across and then they were flat in the northern bayberry bushes that led all the way to the side of the house, or in this case, a small lighthouse rising into the sky. These shrubs were only about two feet high, but provided enough cover if they did the elbow-forward crawl made famous by that little green army man. Growing up with four brothers, Chabal had often played countless hours of army games with these plastic soldiers, her personal favorite being the flamethrower dude.

It had taken them fifteen minutes to reach the side of the lighthouse—there were some sort of rose bushes scattered among the bayberry, and those prickly stems had to be carefully avoided, plus the group didn't want to be seen from above. Nick had whispered to them that he thought he'd seen movement in one of the windows circling the top of the lighthouse, and that it made perfect sense for them to have a lookout up there, what with its 360 degree view of the grounds.

Chabal looked back at KJ and nodded. With a deep breath, she stood up and pushed open the small bathroom window that Maxwell Mercer had left cracked. She felt KJ grab her bent knee to boost her, and then something cracked into the shingles inches from her head. Slivers of wood burst forth and embedded themselves in her face.

Immediately there was a burst of fire from behind them, and then with scarcely a gap in time, the crashing sounds of guns washed over the scenic coastal Maine manor. She squeezed through the aperture and tumbled to the floor, hoping the noise outside was muffling her arrival. She quickly turned and grasped KJ's shoulders, the other woman wrestling her way up and through the window, until with a firm jerk, she pulled Kamrin into the relative safety of the lion's lair.

~ ~ ~ ~ ~

Nick Langdon watched the two women slither their way forward through the bayberry. It wasn't that he was opposed to the feminist movement, but something in him was deeply averse to putting women in danger. There was no doubt in his mind that the opposite sex was every bit as smart as their male counterparts, and most likely, more resilient and tougher. Yet there was something about it—it was a man's duty to protect the fairer sex and that made this most difficult for him. He also knew better than to argue with a woman who had made up her mind, and he knew Chabal well enough to keep his mouth shut, and this Kamrin Jorgenson seemed every bit as unyielding.

A shadow flickered across the top of his vision and he glanced up, but was too late to see anything or anybody. It didn't matter, for he knew there was somebody there now, and he could prepare for it. He wasn't able to stand up and still remain under cover, so he rolled to his back with his neck tilted back, the SSG 69 alongside his head so that he could raise and fire as need be. He'd now been up for thirty straight hours, and twenty of that had been hauling ass north on his Harley. The sun was warm, a few rays trickling through the bushes to reach his face, and he fought the sleepy feeling invading his body.

As it was, when the side window of the top of the lighthouse was suddenly thrust open and a man leaned out to shoot downwards, Nick was ready, and he slid the SSG 69 smoothly into position and fired a burst, the bullets cutting the man to ribbons, but not before he was able to get off a shot. As the man slumped across the windowsill, slowly toppled over it, and then fell to the ground, Nick rolled back onto his stomach. He was gratified to see KJ being pulled through the opening and disappearing into the bathroom. The question as to whether or not Missouri was being held inside had been answered, as soldiers in towers shooting at trespassers was extreme for even the private citizens of Maine. Nick Langdon had no regret over killing the man.

Lord Langdon had the M95 set on the bi-pod with his sights set on the soldier of fortune guarding the front door. He was waiting for the text from Nick that the women were safely in the house and then he was going to take him out. He planned on shooting low and disabling the man, but was fully aware that once gunfire began, anything could happen. He had some misgivings about ambushing a man with no warning, but his family's lives were at stake, and he reassured himself that he had no other options.

A sudden barrage of fire from the other side of the house startled him just momentarily, but this tiny fraction of a second was all it took for his shot to miss the mark of the trained assassin diving for cover. It was a clean miss, and Lord cursed, but the next shot was not, as a bullet spat out and hit Lord in the forearm, just missing his head. He immediately rolled, trying to judge where the bullet had come from; he guessed it had been from the lighthouse that towered up the side of the house. He didn't stop moving until he was twenty yards to his left, having a better view of the top floor of the lighthouse, the front door, and had covering fire of the driveway for the merc that was positioned there, but most likely moving this way.

It sounded like Nick had moved and was engaged in gunfire with an assailant. Lord waited until he saw a shadow flicker in the top window and sent a burst of lead into the top of the lighthouse. The glass shattered and a man stood there with a rifle at his shoulder, returning fire, the bullets cutting branches, kicking up dirt, and raining down around Lord. He steadied and put a bullet in the middle of the man's head. That was much more satisfying than mowing down an unaware target. He heard the sound of a revving engine and spinning tires coming down the driveway.

~ ~ ~ ~ ~

Bart was crouched down behind the cruiser with his service pistol, the Colt M1911, held over the hood of the car. As far as Bart knew, he had no living blood family, except for maybe a father who didn't know he even existed. On the last day of his deployment to the Brunswick Naval Air Station some fifty-plus years earlier, Bart's father had met his mother in a bar and had a one-night stand, and then continued on with the rest of his life, never knowing he'd left behind a son. Some twenty years ago, Bart's mother had died, and a small circle of friends that he was outwardly gruff towards, but inwardly he was fiercely protective of, had adopted him.

He looked over at 4 by Four and Starling peering around the back of the car, awkwardly holding the pistols given to them by the Langdon twins. He wasn't sure that either one even knew how to pull the trigger, much less hit the broad side of a barn. When the shooting started, his mind was already made up. Bart stepped to the driver's door and told the other two to take cover on either side of the driveway and to make sure to stay hidden while preventing anyone from escaping. He then settled his bulk into the seat, cut the wheel, and gunned the vehicle down the driveway.

An agent in camouflage was scurrying down the side of the driveway towards the house as Bart came rattling around a curve, his pale face turned momentarily towards the approaching vehicle. Bart drove straight at the man, who tilted his assault rifle and sent a spray of bullets into the engine before diving out of the way. The car slammed into a pine tree, and Bart, surprisingly agile, stepped out of the car, the good old American pistol in his hand. The mercenary on the ground twisted to bring his rifle out from underneath him and Bart shot him three times in the chest and then once in the head, knowing the man was probably wearing body armor. With just a quick pause to make sure the man was dead, Bart turned and strode down the driveway towards the house.

There was sporadic fire piercing the air as Bart came walking around a corner to within thirty yards of the house, his Colt hanging at his side, his legs eating up distance with each step. Bart's eyes swept the terrain and came to rest on a man in camouflage, clearly visible to Bart, but hidden from the crossfire of Nick and Lord Langdon who had now concentrated their fire on this last gunman.

"Police! Freeze!" Bart yelled.

The man spun around and came to his feet, bringing his rifle to bear, and Bart was a tad slow in firing, but Nick and Lord were not. The soldier of fortune toppled to the ground, gasping for air.

~ ~ ~ ~ ~

As the gunfire erupted outside, Langdon was staring at John Smith, who was holding a Glock leveled at his head. The pistol did not waver, nor did the man take his eyes from Langdon, proving he was a consummate professional.

"Delilah, go tell Yeager to bring the girl out here," Glover commanded.

"Do you want me to shoot him, Glover?" Smith asked.

"Not yet, it sounds like we might need a little insurance."

A moment later, Yeager came into the entrance of the room with his hand grasping the crook of Missouri's arm and a pistol pointed at her head. Delilah Friday sidled past them and went to the rear French doors, thought better of it, and went to stand next to Glover.

"Let me go, you piece of shit," Missouri said, yanking on her arm.

"Calm down, honey, it would be a shame to splatter such a pretty face all over the wall," Yeager snarled at her. He dragged her into the middle of the room. "Besides, I've got plans for you before I kill you."

"Everybody just relax," Langdon said. His elation at seeing Missouri was crossing over into fear.

"I should kill him," Smith said. "We'll still have the girl."

Glover looked over at Missouri, and then Langdon. "Who is out there?" he asked.

"Beats me," Langdon replied. "Maybe your boys saw some rabbits?"

"I have a speedboat tied to the dock," Glover said to Smith. "Think we can make it there and get away?"

"Don't worry, the boys outside are professionals. They'll take care of it," Smith replied. "Unless the dumb asshole called the police."

"Did you bring in the police, Mr. Langdon?" Glover asked.

Langdon stared back. What was the right answer? His fear began to boil into a rage as he realized these men meant to kill his daughter. There was no way they could let her go after what she'd seen.

Into this exchange, a slight lull in the gunshots caused them all to cock their heads, and then loud and clear came the order, "Police! Freeze!"

"Okay, let's go then," Glover said, walking towards the rear door with his hand guiding Delilah Friday along in front of him. "Bring the girl out first, then me and Del, and finally Smith with Langdon."

Chabal stepped into the doorway of the living room from the hallway to the bathroom and shot Pete Yeager in the collarbone. The bullet, traveling 900 miles an hour, slammed him to the ground, showering Missouri with blood.

John Smith turned his gun towards Chabal and snapped a shot that missed as she dove to the side.

KJ pivoted around the doorway on her knee and pulled the trigger, the shots smashing a lamp next to Smith, who turned his Glock towards her and fired. The bullet went wide as KJ rolled onto her side and behind an armchair.

Before Smith could fire again, Langdon tackled him over the back of the sofa, the two of them slamming into the wall. He was hoping this would have loosened the man's grip on his pistol, but he clung grimly to it, and turned the weapon towards Langdon's body. Langdon was just barely able to knock it down, the bullet driving into the hardwood floor at their feet. Smith gnashed his teeth in frustration and drove his thumb at Langdon's eye, the nail catching his cheek as Langdon turned his head, leaving a ragged gash. Smith spun away and swung his Glock up to shoot, and Chabal shot him in the leg.

"Look out."

KJ stepped in front of Chabal with her pistol aimed at Yeager on the floor who had managed to bring his own gun to bear on her. The two pulled the triggers at the same time, her bullet hitting him in the face. Yeager's three bullets struck her in the chest so closely together in time and space that they appeared as one, and KJ fell flat over on her back.

Smith grunted, and turned his gun on Chabal, as Langdon came to his feet with a fire poker in a home-run swing and cracked him on the side of the head. His ear splattered like a too-ripe tomato thrown against a brick wall, and he screamed in pain, the blow knocking him to his knees. Somehow, he retained his grip on the pistol and raised it to shoot Chabal, steadying his aim for just a moment to ensure accuracy, and Langdon swung the poker back through, the hooked end embedding itself in the Boy Scout's eye, the popping sound of the exploding eyeball extremely grisly even in the midst of the helter-skelter violence swirling through the normally serene coastal neighborhood.

Missouri stood still in shock, blood covering her face and body.

Yeager was quite dead on the floor.

Chabal dropped to her knees next to KJ.

Langdon kicked the gun away from the writhing figure of John Smith on the floor.

"I never meant to hurt anybody," KJ whispered. Chabal leaned closer. "I just wanted to save the earth."

"It's going to be okay," Chabal said. But she knew better, at least for KJ, because blood was billowing from her chest like a freshwater spring.

Glover and Friday were gone.

~ ~ ~ ~ ~

Glover propelled Delilah in front of him, more as a shield than to save her from the carnage in the house. *Everything has gone to shit*, he thought as he scurried towards the dock. But everything could be salvaged as long as he escaped. Men of his wealth did not go to jail. Men of his power might face a little bad publicity, but that would soon die down, and at the worst, a slap on the wrist would follow. He could always strongly deny the facts as long as he was not captured by the police at the scene of the crime. Unhappily, he could hear the wails of sirens coming down the peninsula now.

They stumbled onto the dock. It was now only a matter of slipping the rope, firing the engine, and roaring across the bay and down the coast to Yarmouth where Glover had a car stashed. He was so caught up in escaping that he didn't notice the fishing boat tied up to the opposite side of the dock.

"Stop," Richam said, stepping onto the wooden wharf, leveling the sniper rifle at them.

Glover ignored him and bent to pull the loop free of the piling. Richam slammed him in the head with the butt of the rifle, his body slumping halfway in and halfway out of the speedboat.

"I'm not part of this," Delilah Friday said, raising her arms over her head.

"Sure you are, bitch," Jewell replied. She stepped forward and crashed the barrel of the Smith & Wesson into her perfect nose. "Try flirting your way out of this with a broken schnoz."

Chapter 30

A few weeks later

Langdon pulled his Jeep into the narrow driveway leading back to Senator Mercer's house in Bath. Dog sat next to him, fully recovered from his injuries and quite ready for the next adventure. The top was still off of the Jeep, even though this morning had delivered a temperature under forty degrees, warning of the impending winter.

He rang the bell and Dwayne answered, the bodyguard proving no match for dog, who shot past him into the interior of the house. Langdon followed the man to the screened patio overlooking the Kennebec River in the rear of the house. Senator Margaret Mercer and her husband, Maxwell, sat together on the wicker sofa overlooking the river. Dog had immediately jumped up between them and was now trying to get on her lap, not quite understanding that he was far too large.

Langdon sat down kitty-corner to them without saying anything.

"Good morning, Mr. Langdon," Senator Mercer said. "Would you like a Bloody Mary?" She and her husband both had half-full glasses in front of them.

"Coffee if you have it," Langdon replied, and then thought, what the hell? "With a shot of whiskey." It was not yet 9:00 a.m.

Maxwell got up and disappeared into the house, reappearing with a coffee cup, steaming slightly, and raised a bottle of Wild Turkey with a questioning look. Langdon nodded, and he poured a generous dollop into the cup. It would be a suitable homage to KJ.

"How is your daughter faring?" the senator asked.

"She insisted on returning to New York and school." Langdon shrugged. "At least she agreed to see a therapist once a week to work through it all."

"And your wife?"

"She shot two men," Langdon said. "I imagine that will be hard to get over, but she is a tough cookie. At least she didn't kill either of them."

"I am sorry about Kamrin," the senator said.

"She saved Chabal's life, and probably mine and Missouri's as well. We will never forget her. It was too bad that she was used in the way she was." Langdon looked pointedly at Maxwell.

"I never wanted anybody to get hurt," Maxwell said stiffly.

"They did, though, didn't they?" Langdon said.

"I just wanted to leave the limelight behind."

"Some people have a conversation with their spouses about their career choices," Langdon said. "But, I have to say, hiring an environmentalist activist to seduce and sleep with your wife and then blackmail her using soldiers of fortune as backup is a good second option."

Maxwell said nothing. Really, what could he say? Dog jumped up and went to the screen door and Langdon rose to let him out. He'd spotted a bird down by the river and went tearing after it.

"Did it work?" Langdon asked.

"Did what work?" Senator Mercer turned from watching dog cavorting by the riverside and focused her piercing eyes on his face.

"Will you be running for reelection next year?"

"I will have to see," she replied.

"Voters do seem to have short memories," Langdon said.

"Did Glover really say that every moderate Congressman has a private lobbyist assigned to them in order to influence their vote?" Senator Mercer asked.

Langdon didn't reply.

"I suppose I will have to have background checks run on everybody I know," Senator Mercer said. "It used to be much easier being in politics."

"I hear Smith is cutting a plea deal in exchange for serving up Glover on a silver platter?" Langdon asked.

"The powers that be at Goldenrod have disavowed any connection with Smith or Yeager. They claim the two went rogue and were acting on their own," Senator Mercer said.

"That will tie up the courts for years to come," Langdon replied.

Senator Mercer nodded. "The woman Friday is also cooperating with authorities."

"What about the 'sister's husband'? Paul Springer?" Langdon asked.

"He claims he was just an actor hired to play a part and didn't know anything about the rest of it."

"I saw that you voted in favor of the defense budget," Langdon said. "Probably could have used some of that money for health care, don't you think?"

"Sometimes you have to give up something to get something," the senator said.

"You will see to it that Tug is not deported?" Langdon asked.

"Yes."

Life, indeed, was a set of compromises, but there were certain things that shouldn't be compromised, Langdon thought. He noticed dog cocking his head upriver, and he looked in that direction to see a huge ship easing its way down the Kennebec. The latest Arleigh Burke class destroyer was heading out to sea to take up its assignment defending the United States of America against its enemies.

Langdon had seen the news like everybody else, that BIW had just gotten another contract to build five more DDG 51 destroyers to house hypersonic weapons, the latest technological advance.

Langdon finished his coffee and Wild Turkey, thinking of KJ as he set the cup back down. He stood up and walked out the rear door, and whistled for dog, and the two of them walked around the side of the house. He had brought his bill for the senator, but left it in his pocket. He didn't want the money. He and dog climbed into the Jeep and pulled back onto the open road, dog with his feet up on the dash, the wind cleansing them both. Langdon didn't want to be late for opening the store, as there were books to be sold.

About the Author:

Matt Cost aka Matthew Langdon Cost

Over the years, Cost has owned a video store, a mystery bookstore, and a gym. He has also taught history and coached just about every sport imaginable. During those years—since age eight, actually—his true passion has been writing.

I Am Cuba: Fidel Castro and the Cuban Revolution (Encircle Publications, March, 2020) was his first traditionally published novel. *Mainely Power*, the first of the Mainely Mysteries featuring private detective Goff Langdon, was published by Encircle in September, 2020, followed by book two, *Mainely Fear*, in December, 2020, and book three, *Mainely Money*, in March of 2021. Also forthcoming from Encircle Publications are his Clay Wolfe series: *Wolfe Trap*, *Mind Trap*, and *Mouse Trap*; as well as his new historical fiction novel, *Love in a Time of Hate*.

Cost now lives in Brunswick, Maine, with his wife, Harper. There are four grown children: Brittany, Pearson, Miranda, and Ryan. A chocolate Lab and a basset hound round out the mix. He now spends his days at the computer, writing.

Questions for Discussion

How would you describe the protagonist?

Does Langdon have a compelling voice?

What characters did you identify with? Or like?

What plot twists were unexpected?

What emotions did the antagonist evoke in you?

How do you feel about the romance in the novel?

Do you believe that the events of this book could/do happen?

For additional questions related to this novel, contact the author:

Matt Cost
matthew-cost@comcast.net
www.mattcost.net

If you enjoyed reading this book,
please consider writing your honest review
and sharing it with other readers.

Many of our Authors are happy to participate in
Book Club and Reader Group discussions.
For more information, contact us at info@encirclepub.com.

Thank you,
Encircle Publications

For news about more exciting new fiction, join us at:

Facebook: www.facebook.com/encirclepub

Twitter: twitter.com/encirclepub

Instagram: www.instagram.com/encirclepublications

Sign up for Encircle Publications newsletter and specials:
eepurl.com/cs8taP

CPSIA information can be obtained
at www.ICGtesting.com
Printed in the USA
BVHW050615240722
642291BV00001B/19